JBC
13.95
7/16

MW01028585

Tears
Of a
Hustler
4
You've Been Warned

A Novel By

Silk White

Good2Go Publishing

Hatchie River Regional Library
63 Executive Dr.
Jackson, TN 38305

Copyright © 2012 Silk White

All rights reserved, therefore no part of this book may be used or reproduced in any manner whatsoever without written permission expert in case of brief quotations embodied in critical articles or reviews. For more information, contact publisher.

This novel is a work of fiction. All of the characters,organizations, establishments, and events portrayed in this novel are either product of the author's imagination or are fiction.

Published by:
GOOD2GO PUBLISHING
7311 W. Glass Lane
Laveen, AZ 85339
www.good2gopublishing.com
Cover design: Davida Baldwin
Typesetter: Rukyyah
Editor: Keshia Buckhana
ISBN: 978-0985673475

Acknowledgement

To everyone reading this right now... Thank you for stepping inside the bookstore, stopping by the library, or downloading a copy of Tears of a Hustler 4. I hope you enjoy this read from top to bottom... My goal is to get better and better with each story. I want to thank everyone for their love and support. It is definitely appreciated... Now without further ado ladies and gentleman, Tears of a Hustler 4... ENJOY!!!

Chapter 1
The Intro

"Fuck that, I need to speak to the boss myself," Carlos yelled into his cell phone before ending the call. It had been over two weeks now that he'd been trying to get in touch with his connect and each time Carlos was given a middle man to speak to and take care of and cover his order. But that wasn't what upset Carlos. What upset Carlos was the fact that his connect had upped the prices on him out of the blue without giving him an explanation or a valid reason for the increase. Carlos was sick and tired of playing all of these phone games. He was from the old school and he liked speaking to people face to face. That was the way business was supposed to be handled; face to face.

Carlos cruised through a rich gated community searching for his connects house. He had seen the place once, but he had never been inside. Carlos wasn't a kingpin or nothing, but he wasn't a slouch either. His money was always correct. He was a good guy and he just wanted a valid explanation on why the prices had increased. He also wanted to know if the price increase was for everyone or just him.

A lot of other hustlers feared Carlos connect, but not Carlos. He could care less about all of the stories he had heard. To him they were nothing more than myths and fairytales that were told to keep people scared, nervous, and on the edge.

Carlos was missing out on a lot of money cause of this new price increase and he planned on letting his connect know just how he felt. He knew just popping up at his connects house was a risky, bold, and brave move, but Carlos didn't care. He needed answers and somebody was going to tell him something. He was a good customer and if he had to, he planned on threatening his connect to take his business elsewhere if his demand wasn't met.

"Damn," Carlos mumbled when he finally pulled up on the mansion that favored Tony Montana's mansion in the movie Scarface. Carlos pulled up on the property and saw several Muslim security guards walking around with dark colored suits, ear pieces in their ears, and mean looking scowls on their faces. Just from the looks of things, Carlos could tell that each and every Muslim security guard was strapped, locked and loaded. He knew they wouldn't hesitate to shoot at will and on site. The further and further Carlos pulled into the property, the more he was beginning to think just popping up out of the blue unannounced was a bad and stupid idea.

It was too late for Carlos to turn back now. He had already crossed the point of no return. "Here we go," Carlos said taking a deep breath when he noticed two Muslims heading over towards his vehicle. Carlos slowly stepped out the vehicle and met the Muslims head on.

"How can we help you?" the taller one out of the two Muslims asked looking the Spanish man up and down.

"I need to speak to the boss," Carlos demanded. "I've been calling and calling and all motherfuckers been doing is giving me the run around and I'm sick and tired of that shit."

"The boss is busy," the Muslim told Carlos. "The best I can do for you is to relay a message or..."

"Fuck a message!" Carlos snapped. He was sick and tired of playing games with these cocksuckers. "I need to see the boss and I ain't going nowhere until I'm seen." "I don't give a fuck," he said not budging. Carlos had come this far so he figured he might as well go all the way. Carlos watched as the Muslim man spoke in a hush voice into his sleeve. After a brief conversation with whoever was on the other end of his earpiece, the Muslim informed Carlos to hold out his arm so he could be frisked upon entrance.

Carlos held his arms out as the Muslim security guard roughly and thoroughly hand frisked him. He removed Carlos' .38 from his waistband. Once the Muslim guard was done with him, the shorter Muslim guard pulled out a hand held metal detector scanner and scanned Carlos thoroughly from head to toe. Once security was sure that Carlos was unarmed, he was finally allowed to enter the mansion. Carlos stepped foot inside the mansion and couldn't believe his eyes. He couldn't believe that one person could achieve so much and own a house like this. "Damn this shit is bigger than a museum," he said to himself. After walking for what seemed like a mile, security finally led Carlos to a big oak door.

"The boss will be with you shortly," the taller Muslim said as him and his partner walked off. Guarding the big oak door stood two big gigantic Muslim men who stared a hole through Carlos while not hiding their dislike for the stranger.

As Carlos waited to be seen, he noticed that the security in the mansion was crazy. He had never seen this many security guards in one place in his whole life.

Carlos sighed loudly looking down at his watch. "Excuse me but do you know how much longer the wait is going to be?" he asked politely. The two Muslim guards remained silent and continued to stare a hole through Carlos. They were waiting for him to give them a reason to put hands on him. They were just looking for a reason to break a few bones and they were definitely looking for a reason to impress the boss.

"Fake ass Muslims," Carlos mumbled under his breath as he pulled out a pack of Newports.

"No smoking in here!" one of the Muslim's voice boomed. "Don't make me have to talk to you again," the guard warned with his hands turning into a fist.

Carlos exhaled loudly while shaking his head from side to side. If he was strapped, Carlos would have shot both of the fake tough guys that stood before him without even thinking twice and he wouldn't have loss an ounce of sleep over it either.

Thirty minutes later the wooden oak door opened and a body was tossed out of the room. The body crashed down to the floor right in front of Carlos' feet. Carlos looked down and saw the half dead man lying stretched out by his feet. The collar of his shirt was ripped and the man's face was covered in blood. Carlos could tell that the man had been beaten with some type of pipe or foreign object.

"Don't you ever pop up over here unannounced again motherfucker!" Malcolm huffed while cleaning his bloody hands off with a handkerchief.

Instantly Carlos began to get nervous and a little scared as he watched the two security guards each grab one of the half dead man's ankles and drag him away. The man's body left a red nasty bloody trail.

"Who the fuck are you?" Malcolm asked while looking the Spanish man up and down.

"Ummm…Carlos" he said suddenly remembering his name.

"What the fuck do you want?"

"Ummm, I'm here to see the boss," Carlos said realizing that just popping up unannounced might not have been a good idea after all.

Malcolm laughed while looking down at Carlos. "The boss doesn't have any appointments lined up today," he said.

"I know but I really need to holla at the boss." "It's important," Carlos said. "Just let her know that Carlos is out here," he said like his name held weight.

"Oh Carlos," Malcolm said fronting like he had heard the man's name before. "Right this way. Why didn't you say your name was Carlos," Malcolm said escorting Carlos in the office with a smirk on his face.

Carlos stepped foot in the office and immediately spotted Pauleena sitting in a comfortable expensive looking chair with her freshly pedicured toes kicked up on her desk. Pauleena wore her hair in a loose ponytail, up top she wore a tight fitting black wife beater, and a pair of black Good2Go leggings covered her bottom half.

"God Damn," Pauleena cursed loudly at the seventy inch flat screen T.V. that rested on the wall. On the T.V., The Terminator was beating the shit out of his opponent that stood in front of him. It was one of the biggest fights of the year and a lot of people had a lot of money riding on this fight.

Carlos cleared his throat loudly trying to get Pauleena's attention. Pauleena looked over at Carlos and then over at Malcolm. "Who the fuck is this clown?" she asked Malcolm as if Carlos was invisible and not sitting right there in the room with them.

"Said his name is Carlos," Malcolm smirked.

"Never heard of him," Pauleena replied turning her attention back to the flat screen. A frown rested on her face. Pauleena had bet a million dollars on The Terminator's opponent and to have to have to watch The Terminator beat the man like a child made her very, very upset. If it was one thing that Pauleena hated, it was to lose money.

"Excuse me, but I got some serious shit that I need to talk to you about," Carlos said in his tough guy voice.

"Can't you see that I'm watching the fight?" Pauleena said never taking her eyes off of the flat screen.

"Fuck that!" Carlos snapped. "That shit can wait!"

Pauleena turned and faced Carlos with a smirk on her face. "How can I help you?" She asked with a smirk on her face. She admired Carlos' courage and figured she might as well hear the man out.

"What's up with you raising your prices?" Carlos asked. "I'm a good customer and I'm not really trying to pay these high ass out of town prices; for all that I can go cop from another supplier with more reasonable numbers."

"I didn't just raise the price on you," Pauleena told him. "I raised them on everyone so I don't understand what the problem is...Everybody else has been paying the increase with no problem. You the only one complaining!"

"Well I ain't everybody else!" Carlos went on, "and like I said if you don't' lower your prices..."

"OOOOH!!" Malcolm's voice boomed. Immediately Pauleena's head turned back towards the flat screen. She cursed loudly as she watched the replay of The Terminator knocking his opponent out cold and out of the ring with a sharp right counter uppercut to the chin.

"A million dollars down the fucking drain!" Pauleena cursed as she stood to her feet. "Remind me to pay our friend The Terminator a little visit," she said out loud to Malcolm as she walked over and removed a golf club from the rack. Pauleena then headed over towards Carlos.

"Now what's this stupid shit you over here talking about?" Pauleena asked invading Carlos personal space.

"He said he doesn't like how you raised the prices on him," Malcolm instructed. "And that you better lower the prices or else," he laughed. Violence and seeing people get hurt turned Malcolm on.

"You interrupted me from watching the fight to tell me that?" Pauleena asked holding the golf club with a two handed grip. "You popped up at my house to tell me that?"

"Nah...Nah...," Carlos stuttered. "I just wanted to explain to you that..."

In a quick motion Pauleena swung the gulf club with all her might. The gulf club made a whistling sound as it cut through the air and connected with Carlos' face causing the chair that he sat in to tip over as blood flew all over the place. "Don't...you...ever...in ya mutherfucking life...pop up at my motherfucking house...talking some stupid shit...like I give a fuck about...what you think!" Pauleena spat as she beat Carlos' face in with the golf club like it was a piñata. When she got done beating Carlos' face in, the golf club was bent up and it looked deformed.

"Damn!!! You could of at least saved me some," Malcolm said looking down at Carlos' dead body.

Pauleena poured herself a strong drink. "Get this piece of shit out of here and then get dressed. I feel like going out tonight. I'm tired of being cooped up in this house. It's time to let the city see my face again," she said with specs of blood on her face. "The Queen Is Back!"

Tears of a Hustler 4

You've Been Warned

Chapter 2
"The Spades"

Dice lay in his bunk in his cell staring up at the ceiling. O.B.C.C. on Rikers Island had been his home for the past six months. The only thing he had to look forward to was that he would be released in two months. Dice didn't really talk too much and usually stayed to himself most of the time to avoid getting into any unnecessary trouble. As Dice lay on his bunk, he looked at the picture of his new born son that he had yet to see in person. Him and his baby mother Tonya had been together since high school, but the two's relationship began going downhill when Tonya began hanging out with a well known pimp that went by the name of "Champagne". Champagne was well known in New York City for having the baddest and sexiest bitches in the whole city. He was also known for his violent and don't take no shit attitude. When Dice heard about Tonya hanging around the well known pimp while she was pregnant, he ended their relationship. While Dice had been locked up, he had heard rumors about how Champagne now had Tonya out on the strip selling her pussy and mouth for him along with the rest of his hoes. Hearing those stories made Dice sick to his stomach. Ever since Tonya began dealing with the pimp she slowly but surely began to erase Dice out of her life completely. The letters stopped first and then the visits. Then finally she stopped answering his phone calls. During these hard times Dice stayed positive and did his best not to take his anger out on anyone else. In two months he would be a free man again and he would be able to live a normal life again. The first thing he planned on doing when he got out was to go and see his son.

Dice's cell popped open and immediately he knew that it was lunch time. He stepped out his cell and hopped in the chow line.

"How you feeling today?" An older man named Lewis asked standing behind Dice in the line.

"I can't complain," Dice replied looking around checking out his surroundings. Dice looked over at the back tables and around twenty men, all brothers wearing all black sitting at the combined tables eating amongst themselves. For the past four months Dice noticed the group of men stayed to themselves and didn't really interact with any of the other inmates. "What's up with those guys back there?" Dice asked nosily.

"Who, the Spades?" Lewis asked looking back at the group of men that sat in the back. "They a bunch of loose cannons trying to start up a movement that's sure to get them all killed!"

"A movement?" Dice repeated "What kind of movement?" he asked curiously.

"They claim they gone be the next Black Panther party, but much bigger and better," Lewis said fanning his hand. "They say they going to clean up the streets when they get out."

Dice smiled. The more Lewis told him about The Spades, the more interested he became and the more he wanted to know. "How do they plan on cleaning up the streets?"

Lewis shrugged as him and Dice grabbed their food trays and sat down at an empty table. "What they need to be worrying about is, how and who gonna clean up all the blood they going to shed going on a suicide mission like that." Lewis laughed.

"What's so funny?"

"Jail is crazy," Lewis said. "Niggas in jail always got all these plans on how they going to do this and do that," he chuckled. "But as soon as they get out they jump right back into the shit that got them locked up in the first place. Shit is crazy!"

"True," Dice agreed as he looked back over at The Spades. He heard what Lewis said, but these group of men looked serious and all about their business. As Dice looked on, The Spades seemed to be in a deep conversation. Whatever they were over there talking about, it must have been serious.

"You see the one that's talking right now?" Lewis said nodding towards The Spades. "That's the leader and his name is Wolf. They guy sitting over to his left is his right hand man and his name is Live Wire and he definitely lives up to his name."

"Where did they get the name The Spades from?"

"I have no idea," Lewis replied. "I don't know what they up to, but it definitely looks like something about to go down."

****

Wolf and Live Wire sat back and watched a young knuckle head sell dope to a few customers. Wolf and The Spades had already approached the young man that called himself Zoe and told him to stop slanging that poison in the jail, but of course Zoe continued to get his hustle on. Since the Bloods were backing Zoe up, he felt like he was untouchable and ignored The Spades warning.

"I'm about to go clap that nigga," Live Wire said looking for any reason to put in some work. He was in charge of security and the muscle in the organization. Live Wire was a violent and vicious man who lived for action.

"If we catch him make another sale, it's on. Until then, we chill," Wolf said. He was the leader, the creator, and the brains behind The Spades. The whole purpose of The Spades was to clean up the community and get rid of all drug dealers and anybody who was trying to destroy the community. Wolf knew he had a lot of work ahead of him and he also knew the task wouldn't be easy, but he was definitely up for the challenge.

Wolf and Live Wire watched as Zoe slid inside another inmate's cell to make a sale.

Immediately Wolf, Live Wire, and two other Spades members stood to their feet and headed up to the cell that Zoe had slid inside. Just as they reached the cell Zoe was on his way out.

Zoe sucked his teeth. "What you niggas want now?" He asked as if The Spades were becoming an annoyance. "I'm not in the mood to hear no speech or lecture right now," he said trying to squeeze through the four men.

Wolf quickly stepped in Zoe's path. "Do I look like the type of nigga that likes to repeat himself?"

"Come on with all this Malcolm X shit," Zoe huffed. "You can't stop niggas from getting high. If niggas wanna get high...." Wolf snuffed Zoe while he was in the middle of his sentence. Before Wolf got a chance to hit him again, Live Wire and the other two Spades members were already on Zoe like a pack of wolves. They were kicking and stomping Zoe's face into the dirty concrete floor.

Dice and Lewis watched from their seats as The Spades beat Zoe half to death. A smile appeared on Dice's face. He knew exactly what Zoe was doing in the jail and he was happy to see The Spades step to him. As Dice continued to watch the action, he saw the man they called Live Wire spit a razor out of his mouth and slice Zoe across his face. Seconds later Dice saw the homeys (Bloods) approach The Spades. A few words were exchanged before fist started flying and a big brawl erupted. Minutes later a gang of C.O.'s ran up in the housing unit wearing riot gear and separated the two crews. Once the police regained order, all the inmates were forced to lock in until further notice.

Chapter 3
"I Don't Know"

Dice and the entire housing unit had been on lock down for seven long days before they were finally allowed to come back out of their cells.

"These fucking animals make me sick," Lewis huffed giving Dice a fist bump. "Locked down for a whole week for nothing!"

"It could always be worse," Dice pointed out. He on the other hand didn't think that they were on lock down for nothing. He understood the reason and purpose behind the brawl and respected what The Spades were out trying to do. "I was thinking about joining The Spades," he said throwing it out there to get Lewis' opinion about his decision. Not that it mattered, but he just wanted to hear what he had to say.

"You joking right?" Lewis asked seriously, "Please tell me that you are joking!"

"Nah, I'm dead serious."

"Didn't you see what happened last week?" Lewis said excitedly, "You're gonna get yourself killed!"

Dice smiled. He liked what The Spades were about, but he still wanted and needed to know a little more about the organization before making a final decision. "I'm curious," Dice admitted.

"Boy if you join The Spades, all you gone be doing is digging an early grave for yourself," Lewis told him. "Wolf and Live Wire ain't nothing but bad news!"

Dice stood to his feet. "I'll be back in a second," he said heading over towards where The Spades sat. As Dice walked up on the table, he was met by two rough look Spades members.

"Wassup?" One of The Spades members asked looking Dice up and down.

"I need to holla at Wolf for a second," Dice said confidently. He was a little nervous on the inside, but the only way he would get the answers to the questions that he had was to ask.

"He said he wanna holla at you for a second Wolf," the Spades member yelled over his shoulder.

"Let him through," Wolf said. He had seen Dice throughout the housing unit, but the two never said one word to the other. "State ya name."

"My name is Dice and I was interested in joining The Spades," Dice said. "But I would like to know a little bit more about this movement first."

"Yo shorty get the fuck up outta here," Live Wire huffed shaking his head from side to side. "This movement ain't for church niggas like you! Beat ya feet before I get upset!"

"I wasn't talking to you," Dice said turning to face Live Wire.

"What?" Live Wire shot to his feet and moved in Dice's direction until Wolf stopped him with a hand to his chest.

"Chill out," Wolf said giving Live Wire a pat on the back. "Come take a walk with me," Wolf said as him and Dice spinned off away from the crowd. "Sorry about that," Wolf said. "Sometimes Live Wire can be a little over board."

"I ain't worrying about him," Dice said humbly. "So can you tell me a little bit about what The Spades are about and what they represent?"

Wolf smiled. "The Spades is basically an organization that's out to help and give back to the community. Making the community a better place is our goal."

"Kind of like The Black Panther Party; right?"

"Ummm...Something like that," Wolf smiled. "The Black Panther Party was a self defense movement out to defend themselves from the racist cops who were out back in the day doing whatever they wanted." He paused. "The Spades aren't about self defense. The Spades are about cleaning up the community and opening up businesses so our people can be able to work and not have to rob and steal or sell drugs to eat. I'm going to open up a chain of black businesses and hire only black people." He went on. "That way the younger kids can see their dads or role models working and follow in their footsteps instead of them looking up to the drug dealers and hustlers. I don't want the younger kids thinking it's okay or cool to slang poison to their own people. Do you see where I'm going with this?"

Dice nodded. "But how do you plan on cleaning up the streets?" he asked curiously.

"Simple," Wolf said. "We going to get rid of all of the drug dealers, pimps, stick up kids, crooked cops, and whoever else is doing harm to the community."

"You said get rid of them...get rid of them how?" Dice asked.

"Easy! We're going to kill them. We're going to kill them all," Wolf said seriously while taking a second to take in Dice's reaction. "The Spades are sixty members strong so far, but by next year I'm estimating thousands of Spades members," he smirked. "Each and every one of us know that more than likely we're going to be killed or sent to jail for a very long time."

"Then why risk it?"

"Because in order to make history you got to do some historic shit," Wolf said with a smile. "Only brothers that are serious about the cause and the movement are allowed to join. Each and every member is willing and ready to die right now for the cause." He paused. "The children are our future. If we don't make shit right for the children, shit ain't never going to change...look around," Wolf said. "All of these jails are filled with Black and Spanish men...we have to break this cycle and it starts by getting the drugs out of the community...of course this isn't something that can be done over night, but we need to get started as soon as possible."

"When do you go home?"

"In three days," Wolf smiled. "Both me and Live Wire."

"Word?"

Wolf nodded. "The Spades have a lot of work to do and we don't have any time to waste."

"I want to join," Dice said. He had a serious, nervous, and excited look on his face. Even though he knew it was a chance that he'd more than likely get murdered or put in jail for a long period of time. "I want to become a member."

"How old are you?" Wolf asked.

"Twenty-two," Dice answered proudly.

"You got your whole life ahead of you," Wolf began. "Why would you want to risk it to join The Spades?"

"Like you said, the children are our future and we have to make things right for them," Dice said. "I just had a son myself and I always hear a lot of parents say that they will do anything for their kids or do anything so their kids can have and live the best life." He paused. "Me joining The Spades will be the first step towards me making the future a better place for my son as well as for all of the rest of the children out there."

"You ever killed anyone before?" Wolf asked.

"No."

"Shot anyone before?"

"No."

"You do know you are going to have to get your hands dirty; right?" Wolf asked with a raised brow...He needed to know that he could trust and depend on Dice to pull the trigger when the time came.

"Yes I know I'm going to have to get my hands dirty," Dice said coolly. "And no I've never shot or killed a man, but I will if I have to."

Wolf smiled. He liked Dice and saw the hunger and fire in his eyes. Wolf didn't know Dice that well, but he had always been a good judge of character and what he saw in Dice was loyalty, passion, drive, and a lot of heart. The two men's conversation was interrupted by a C.O. announcing that it was time to lock in for the night.

"Yo sleep on it tonight," Wolf said giving Dice a fist bump. "In the morning if you still want to become a Spade, me and Live Wire will talk it over and make our decision."

"Say no more," Dice said with a smile as he went to his cell and locked in. Dice sat in his cell and thought about everything that Wolf had explained to him. He had to admit that yes the job was risky, but the cause and purpose of the entire operation was what had lured Dice towards The Spades in the first place. A light knock on Dice's cell grabbed his attention and when he looked up, outside of his cell stood Wolf.

"Here, read this tonight," Wolf said while slipping a book under Dice's cell door.

Dice picked up the book and read the title out loud.

"Spirit of a Panther, The Story of Huey P. Neuton."

"Read that so you can get a little glimpse of what lies ahead," Wolf said with a smile and then walked off.

The next day Dice came out of his cell and walked straight over towards The Spades' table. After thinking long and hard all night he had finally reached a decision. "I want to join The Spades," Dice announced. He knew his decision would change his life forever, but inside he felt like he had made the right decision and also a wise decision.

"Give me and my man Live Wire a moment to discuss whether or not we feel that you joining our organization would be a good move or not," Wolf said as he watched Dice step off to the side giving The Spades room and space to come up with their decision. As Dice stood off to the side his mind started to think about his son and who was taking care of him. If Tonya was out on the strip all day and night then where was Lil Dice and more importantly who was watching him? Dice did his best to try and think positive while being in such a negative situation. "Less than sixty days to go," he kept telling himself. Dice did his best to not think about Tonya and that whole situation because the more he thought about it, the angrier he became. After a fifteen minute discussion, Wolf called Dice back over to their table.

"You're in," Wolf said with a smile as he gave Dice a firm hand shake.

"Thank you," Dice said while smiling like a kid in a candy store.

"Now that you are in, you better not let me down," Wolf told him.

"Time to show and prove," Live Wire added. "I don't like you... Not one bit and if I see any signs of weakness, you are outta here!"

"When you come home?" Wolf asked as he scribbled a number down on a small piece of paper.

"Two months," Dice answered.

"When you get out, make sure you call this number." Wolf handed Dice the piece of paper. "By the time you get out, The Spades name definitely will be buzzing all around the five boroughs," Wolf said with a smile.

Chapter 4
"The Beginning"

Wolf pulled up in front of a church in his brown Hooptie. "This the right church?" He asked while glancing over at Live Wire who was sitting in the passenger seat.

"Yeah, this the right church," Live Wire said as the two slid out the Hooptie. Wolf had been a free man for three days. After seventy-two hours of strategizing and coming up with a blue print, The Spades were finally ready to get shit popping. Two cars filled with Spades members pulled up directly behind the Hooptie. Wolf and Live Wire entered the church with a duffle bag while the rest of The Spades waited outside.

Wolf and Live Wire walked inside the church and saw a man sitting in an office at a desk with a pair of reading glasses on his face looking down at what looked like some important paperwork. Wolf walked up to the open door and knocked lightly.

The man stepped out the office with a smile on his face. "Wolf?" He asked with his hand extended. Wolf nodded as the two shared a firm handshake.

"I'm Pastor Anderson," the pastor said introducing himself. "Nice to finally meet you brothers," he smiled. "I heard about what The Spades are all about and I'm glad that finally someone is willing to step up and gain back control of our community."

"It's only right," Wolf replied.

"Follow me," Pastor Anderson said leading Wolf and Live Wire down to the basement. "Well here it is," Pastor Anderson said cutting on the lights. "Now y'all can use the basement as your headquarters as long as y'all throw me something every month and keep the police away from here."

"You got yourself a deal," Wolf told him. Pastor Anderson left the two men to handle their business. Ten minutes later Live Wire escorted the rest of The Spades down into the basement.

"Our first target is a guy that goes by the name Frank," Wolf announced as he handed each member a hand gun from out the duffle bag that rested down by his feet. "Everyone gets a warning first," Wolf said as him and The Spades exited the church's basement.

****

"Yo y'all niggas line the fuck up!" Frank barked peeking his head out the window of the abandoned building. Outside behind the building was a long line of dope fiends who waited to get served. The line was so long that the fiends started to get antsy and began pushing and trying to skip the line. Frank shook his head as he watched two dope fiends get into a fist fight over who was next in line to be served.

Frank turned to his young worker named Tye. "Yo hurry up and serve these ugly motherfuckers and get em up outta here," Frank ordered as he scrolled through his iPhone. He was trying to decide who would be the lucky woman that he would sleep with tonight.

Wolf parked his Hooptie on the side of the abandoned building that was being used as a dope house and killed the engine. Across the street sat two cars full of Spades members waiting and itching to begin the process of cleaning up the streets one block at a time.

"Damn," Live Wire said looking at the long line of dope fiends who waited and craved their daily fix. "That's a lot of money down in that alley."

Wolf didn't reply. Instead he hopped out the driver's seat and headed towards the front door of the dope house with Live Wire close on his heels.

"Hey so skipping the line," an ugly dope fiend yelled out.

Live Wire swiftly turned and stole on the fiend knocking him out cold. The fiend collapsed face first into the ground with his body hitting the ground like he fell out of a second floor window. Wolf reached the front door of the abandoned building and pushed a fiend out of his way as him and Live Wire stepped inside.

"How many?" Tye asked looking at both Wolf and Live Wire.

"I'm here to see Frank," Wolf said looking past the worker that stood in front of him. Behind Tye Wolf saw Frank talking in a low tone on his cell phone.

"Frank busy right now," Tye huffed. "Now how many you want?" Tye's head violently snapped back from the stiff jab that Wolf landed causing blood to spray from his nose. Live Wire followed up by grabbing an empty Heineken bottle off the floor and shattering it over Tye's head.

When Frank saw what was going on, he quickly ended his call and pulled his .380 from his waist and aimed it at Wolf's chest. "What's popping," he yelled!

"Me and my man need to have a word with you," Wolf said showing no fear even though he had a gun pointed at his chest. "We don't want no trouble." Wolf began. "Me and my friend here are here to inform you that you can't sell drugs out of this building anymore."

"Y'all gone have to kill me for this building," Frank said holding his gun sideways.

"Me and my man Live Wire here represent The Spades and we are an organization out to clean up the streets and our community. We are asking that you please stop slanging this poison to your own people in our community."

Frank looked at Wolf like he was crazy. "Fuuuuck you, your people, and this raggedy ass community!"

A smirk danced on Wolf's lips. "You've been warned," he said as him and Live Wire turned and exited the dope house.

Wolf and Live Wire made it back to the Hooptie and popped the trunk. Wolf nodded at the two cars full of Spades members as he pulled a canister of gasoline out of the trunk.

"Stupid hard headed niggas always want to be tough," Live Wire said cocking back his P89. Him and Wolf then made their way back over to the dope house. As Wolf crossed the street, he watched his Spades members run up in the dope house. Seconds later the sound of loud gun fire could be heard followed by the long line of fiends scrambling to get out of harm's way. Wolf and Live Wire entered the dope house and saw Tye laid out in a pool of his own blood with a bullet hole in his head. Next to Tye laid Frank with his hands holding his stomach trying to stop the blood from pouring from his stomach. Several bullet holes decorated the walls along with specs of blood.

"Please don't kill me man; I'm sorry!" Frank cried. "I need an ambulance! I can't feel my…"

Wolf ignored Frank and poured gasoline all over his body and face interrupting Frank's plea for his life. Wolf stepped over Frank's body and splashed gasoline all over the house.

"Jackpot," Live Wire said returning from the back carrying two bags. One was full of money and the other was filled with several bundles of dope. Wolf took the bag full of dope and walked over to the bathroom. He dumped the drugs down into the toilet and flushed it. The Spades plan was to get all the drugs off the streets and take the drug money that they took from the hustlers and put it back in the community.

Live Wire stomped Frank's face into the floor when he heard him mumbling something that he couldn't understand. "Shut the fuck up!" Live Wire yelled. Once The Spades had everything they needed, they all exited the house in a hurry. As Wolf was on his way out the door, he struck a match and tossed it over his shoulder. He heard the flames erupt behind him as he made his exit.

Wolf and Live Wire hopped back in the Hooptie and headed to The Spades new head quarters.

"I love this shit!" Live Wire said excitedly. Putting in work is what Live Wire lived for. He lived to inflict pain on people and see on their faces while he was doing it. He

lived for action and he definitely lived by his name...
"Who's next?"

"Some cat named Rico," Wolf said keeping his eyes
on the road. "Heard he's the manager at some club
downtown. Word is he sells tons of E pills and coke out of
the club."

"When we taking that clown down?" Live Wire
asked as they pulled up in front of the church to drop off the
money they had just lifted from Frank.

Wolf looked at Live Wire with a smile and said
"tonight."

Chapter 5
"The Night Life"

"**D**amn," Rico huffed after sniffing a line of coke off of his desk. He stood in this office upstairs in the club looking down at the packed dance floor filled with club goers. Rico smiled just thinking about which one of the beautiful women in the club that he would take home tonight. Women, drugs, and money controlled Rico's entire life. He lived for those three things and he had unlimited access to all three.

Rico headed downstairs with the rest of the party goers. He badly needed a drink and felt like mingling with a few sexy women. Everyone knew Rico. He was a well known asshole and could care less what people thought about him. His motto was they could call him whatever they wanted as long as they didn't call him broke.

Outside Wolf, Live Wire, and four other Spades walked up to the club's entrance and paid the bouncer a hundred dollars to skip the long line and head straight inside the club.

"I don't have a clue what this Rico clown looks like," Wolf announced. "But from what I hear, he's supposed to be some fake ladies man type of nigga so we might have to split up and holla at a few chicks and see if one of them can point him out to us."

The Spades stepped foot inside the club and was immediately attacked by the heat and loud bass bumping from the speakers. Rick Ross new single had the club rocking. Wolf looked over and saw Live Wire smiling from ear to ear. This was the first time Wolf, Live Wire, and the rest of The Spades had been inside of a club in a while since most of them were freshly released from prison.

"Stay focused," Wolf yelled in Live Wire's ear over the loud music. Live Wire replied with a head nod and a wink. All of the half naked women prancing around dancing like strippers had Live Wire's mind somewhere else. He was all for The Spades movement, but since he had been home he had been so busy putting in work with The Spades that he hadn't had a chance to spend on time with a woman.

"You and two Spades take that side of the club and me and the other two Spades will take the other side," Wolf said as the six men split up in search of Rico.

Wolf pushed and squeezed his way through the crowd in search of Rico. Ever since he had been going to clubs, the bathroom was the spot where people went to get high and most of the time a dealer always hung around the bathroom or either inside the bathroom to catch the customers. After a seven minute struggle trying to get to the other side of the club, Wolf finally reached the men's bathroom. Wolf and The Spades busted up inside the bathroom and saw three men all laughing while doing white lines on the counter of the sink.

"I'm looking to cop some blow," Wolf said to the three men who stood by the sink getting high right out in the open in plain view.

"What you need," a man with long corn rows said popping up out of nowhere. He stood over in the cut with a suspicious I'm up to something look on his face.

"What you got?" Wolf asked.

"Y'all not cops; right," the man with the corn rows asked with a raised brow while taking in Wolf's and the other three men that stood with him's appearance. Each man that stood before him wore all black.

"Do we look like motherfucking cops?" Wolf huffed. "Matter fact, where's Rico? I hate dealing with you new jacks!"

"My bad," corn rows apologized. "I work for Rico. I got some twenties of coke and some triple stack E pills," he told Wolf.

"Aight let me get twenty pills and five, twenties of coke," Wolf said. "And that coke better not had been tapped danced on."

"Trust me, we got the best coke in the city," corn rows boasted. "Everyone knows Pauleena got the best product out right now."

Once Wolf saw the man with the corn rows reach down into his pocket, he quickly stole on him. He watched as the man's head violently bounced off the wall. While Wolf continued to fuck corn rows up, the rest of The Spades made everyone else who wasn't a Spades leave the bathroom.

"Please take anything you want," corn rows yelled while balled up in a corner.

"Everything you got on you; I want it!" Wolf said as he smacked the shit out of corn rows one last time. Corn rows dug into his pocket and handed Wolf a big stack of twenty dollar bills. He reached down in his other pocket and handed Wolf a Ziploc bag full of E pills. Wolf stuffed the bills down in his pocket, then walked over to one of the stalls and flushed the drugs down the toilet.

"Back when I was hustling, bitch ass niggas like this wasn't even allowed to hustle," one of The Spades members said looking down at the man with the corn rows balled up in the corner like a bitch.

Wolf reached down in his 40 below boot and removed a small .22. "Get ya punk ass up!" Wolf growled while snatching the man with the corn rows up to his feet. "Take me to Rico," he said jamming the .22 in the man's ribs as all five men exited the bathroom.

****

Live Wire walked up to the bar and ordered a Vodka and Orange Juice.

"Wolf said no one is to drink or use drugs," one of The Spades reminded Live Wire.

Live Wire sipped his drink slowly. It had been nearly two years since he had a drink. "Shut the fuck up!" he huffed. "And don't speak unless you're spoken to," he told the soldier. The nerve of the young punk. Live Wire thought about snuffing the man for not minding his own business.

Live Wire led the pack through the club. They were supposed to be looking for Rico, but all Live Wire was looking at was ass. It was so many beautiful women in the club that he found it hard to focus on the mission at hand. Meek Mills song "I'm a Boss" bumped through the speakers and turned the club into a frenzy. Live Wire squeezed through the club and stopped in front of a thick red bone chick with a short hair cut. The red bone wore a white spandex fitting shirt that was cut low in the front exposing the majority of her breast. Down low she wore a white pair of Good2Go leggings.

"Damn ma, you wearing the shit outta them leggings," Live Wire said in the red bone's ear. As he smoothly slide his free hand around her waist and then down to her ass.

"I bet you say that to all the girls," red bone said with a smile as her body began moving to the beat.

"Only to the bad ones," Live Wire said matching red bone's rhythm as his hips glided smoothly back and forth to the beat. Live Wire pulled out his cell phone and handed it to red bone. "Throw your number up in there."

Red bone stored her number in Live Wire's phone then handed it back to him. "By the way, the name's Rosey aka Thunder Clap," she said with a seductive sexy smile.

"Thunder Clap," Live Wire repeated taking a sip from his drink. "Is that right," he said while dropping his eyes down to Rosey's super fat ass. The spandex Rosey was wearing made her ass look even bigger. Luke's song "Doo-Doo Brown" bumped through the speakers and brought the freak out of everyone in the club. Rosey quickly spun around and gave Live Wire a little demonstration of the thunder clap. Live Wire sat and watched Rosey's ass jiggle and bounce like it had a mind of its own. Rosey then pushed her ass back into Live Wire who was grinding on her ass with his genitals practically resting in the crack of her ass. Rosey glanced over her shoulder and gave him a look that dared him to keep up with her. While Live Wire and Rosey got their freak on, on the dance floor; the other Spades were asking each and every women they saw if they knew where they could find Rico at.

After dancing for three songs straight, Live Wire and Rosey walked over to the bar and got drunk and flirted with each other.   While they were in mid conversation, Rosey sucked her teeth.

"What's wrong?"   Live Wire asked with his arm around Rosey's waist.

"Here comes some trouble making asshole that I used to mess with," Rosey said with a disguised look on her face. Prince and his five man entourage strolled through the club like they owned the place.   Prince worked for Pauleena and he was here to drop off more drugs to Rico.   Prince was a big time trouble maker and he was as violent as they come. Every other week his name was involved in all kind of shit from murders to robbery, to kidnapping, and several different shoot outs.   Prince went up to Rico's office looking for him but he wasn't up there.   Knowing Rico, Prince figured he was on the dance floor somewhere.   As Prince strolled through the club, he spotted Rosey draped all over some fake looking tough guy.   As Prince walked pass, he made sure he bumped shoulders with Rosey's new friend on purpose.

Prince bumped into Live Wire causing him to spill his drink on his shirt.   "Damn lil nigga," Prince huffed.   "When you see the God coming through, get the fuck out the way!"

Live Wire turned and snuffed Prince without thinking twice.   Prince took the blow well as he snuffed Live Wire back.   The two men went blow for blow as both crews collided.   Fist and bottles flew from each and every direction. During the scuffle Live Wire slipped a street razor from his pocket and cut Prince's face sending blood flying everywhere.   Before things got too out of hand, several bouncers quickly jumped in between the two crews and separated them.   Prince and two members from his entourage stomped a Spades member who lay on the sticky club floor unconscious from a champagne bottle to the head.   Prince tried to stomp the man's face through the floor.   They were stomping the Spades member so bad that the D.J. had to stop the music and cut the lights on.

****

Corn rows led Wolf and the other Spades straight to Rico. Rico sat up in a V.I.P. section with two sexy ladies who invaded his personal space. Corn rows got Wolf and The Spades past the big bouncer and into the V.I.P. section.

"Rico, these gentlemen would like to have a word with you," corn rows said in a nervous tone.

"I'm all out until Prince gets here," Rico said not even bothering to look up from his two lady friends.

Wolf handed corn rows off to The Spades member next to him. Then he walked up on Rico. "Get lost," Wolf growled roughly pushing one of Rico's women out of her seat and down on the floor. Once he had Rico's full attention, Wolf spoke with seriousness in his voice. "My name is Wolf and I represent The Spades," he yelled over the music. "I'm here to ask that you stop selling drugs to our people. This is your warning. The Spades are for the people and about the people. If you continue to sell drugs to my people, you will be handled accordingly… You have officially been warned!"

"What's your name again?" Rico asked removing his sunglasses. Just by the look on his face, Wolf could tell that Rico hadn't heard a word he said. Wolf's hand quickly shot out and back slapped Rico across his face. His other hand aimed the .22 at Rico's chest. "Take me upstairs to your office," Wolf said in Rico's ear while he jammed the .22 in his ribs.

"Do you have any idea who I work for?" Rico asked slowly leading Wolf and The Spades out of the V.I.P. section and over towards the steps that led to Rico's office. As Rico walked Wolf over towards the stairs, he saw Prince and his five man entourage entering the club. Thoughts of calling out to him and his crew crossed Rico's mind, but Prince and his team were too far away and the music was far too loud for his voice to be heard.

"Wait right here for me until I come back down," Wolf said over his shoulder to The Spades as him and Rico made their way up the steps. Once inside the office Wolf shut the door behind them. "Where's the stash?"

"Oh so that's what this is all about?" Rico chuckled. A .22 bullet pierced through his thigh and replaced the grin that was on his face with a look of pain and agony.

"aarrghhh!" Rico howled out in pain as he leaned up against the wall for support.

"The stash," Wolf repeated in a cold tone with the .22 pointed at Rico's face.

"Alright, alright!" Rico pleaded with his hands up in surrender. He hopped over to the other side of the room and removed an expensive looking picture from the wall revealing a combination safe inside the wall.

"Open that shit slowly," Wolf instructed easing up on Rico from behind. Once the safe was open, Wolf carefully watched Rico stuff all the bills into a garbage bag. Once the bag was full, Rico tied the strings of the bag together and sat the bag down in front of Wolf.

"When my boss finds out about this...." A bullet to the head silenced Rico forever. Wolf watched Rico's body crumble down to the floor. He grabbed the garbage bag off the floor, then turned and made his exit. When Wolf stepped out the office, he saw that the lights in the club was on and the music was off. All of the party goers nosily stood around looking to see what was going on. Several phone cameras were also in the air trying to capture anything ignorant so they could put it on YouTube or World Star.

When Wolf made it back downstairs, The Spades quickly surrounded him and escorted him out the club keeping Wolf out of harm's way. Wolf held the garbage bag in one hand while his other hand rested in his pocket with his finger wrapped loosely around the trigger. At any sign of trouble, Wolf was going to shoot first and ask questions never. Outside Wolf saw Live Wire and a couple of The Spades arguing with another group of men. Several police officers stood close by making sure that all the two crews did was argued.

"Yo, we out!" Wolf yelled getting Live Wire's attention. The Spades hopped back inside the cars they came in and pulled off one by one and one after another.

Chapter 6
"Home Sweet Home"

Dice stepped foot out of the prison's gates with a huge smile on his face. He was happy to finally be released and be a free man. The first thing Dice did was call the number that wolf had given him. A man with an angry voice answered on the third ring and gave Dice the address to the church and told him to show up first thing tomorrow morning. While Dice was in jail, he had heard about all the noise The Spades were making out on the streets. He couldn't wait to play his part and contribute to the movement. After calling the number that Wolf gave him, Dice called Tonya. The phone rang a few times then went to the answering machine. Dice cursed Tonya out in his head as he wondered what she could have been at this time of night that she couldn't answer the phone. He didn't have time for the games. Dice walked over to the curb and flagged down a cab and headed straight for Tonya's address. For the entire cab ride Dice sat in the back seat staring blankly out the window. He was shocked and surprised at how much things had changed since he had been gone. Dice knew he had a rough road ahead of him, but he accepted the challenge with open arms. If it was one thing about Dice, he wasn't afraid of hard work and he didn't want anything handed to him. He would rather work for his. The cab pulled up in the front of Tonya' apartment and Dice paid the cab driver. He slid out the back seat and walked up to the front door. He gave it a stern knock. After five minutes of knocking without getting a response Dice turned and left. He was pissed off! He was pissed because Tonya wasn't home and he didn't know where his son was at this time of night. He was also pissed because he had paid a cab to travel all the way across town and Tonya wasn't even home. Dice flagged down another cab and hopped in the back seat. There was only one other place that Tonya could have been at this time of night.

****

"Hey handsome!" Tonya smiled leaning half way in a stranger's car through the passenger window. "You trying to have some fun tonight," she asked licking her lips seductively. Tonya didn't really like her job, but she knew that if she didn't reach her quota that Champagne would be pissed and when he was pissed, his foot always winded up in someone's ass. Tonya was in love with Champagne and did everything in her power to keep him happy at all times. She could care less how many hoes Champagne had. He was her man and the rest of his hoes were just here to help her and Champagne make enough money so the two could move to paradise. At least that's what Tonya believed. Champagne had promised her that as soon as he had enough money to retire, him and her would move to paradise and never return back to New York City. Everyone called Tonya stupid, but to her everyone was just jealous of her and Champagne's relationship.

"How much for that mouth?" The John asked admiring Tonya's full thick glossed lips.

"Sixty dollars and I promise you it will be more than worth it," Tonya said throwing it on thick. She didn't care what she had to say. All she cared about was the end result and that was getting paid. After more seconds of negotiating, Tonya hopped in the front seat and the John drove a few blocks down and parked on a dead end street/alley. The John placed the car in park and then pulled out his dick and began jerking it in front of Tonya. "You want some vanilla ice-cream?" the John asked

"Vanilla is my favorite," Tonya said excitedly as he opened a condom and tossed it in her mouth. She went down on the John and when she came back up, the condom was rested perfectly on the John's dick.

"That's what I'm talking about," the John groaned as he grabbed the back of Tonya's head and pushed her head down into his lap. Ten minutes later the John dropped Tonya off right where he had picked her up at. Tonya hopped out the car and applied more gloss to her lips as she searched for the next customer.

"So this what it's come down to, huh?" Tonya spun around in the direction that the voice came from and saw Dice standing there with a pissed off look on his face.

"When you get out?" Tonya asked slipping a cigarette in between her lips. Dice was the last face she had expected to see.

"Where's my son?" Dice asked and the look on his face told Tonya that he was disgusted with her.

"He's with my mother," Tonya replied quickly blowing smoke out through her nose.

"Call your mother and tell her that I'm coming to get my son."

"You bugging," Tonya huffed. "I ain't letting my son go with you and be around all of your bitches."

Dice looked at Tonya like she was crazy. "How you don't want him around my bitches, when you a prostitute," Dice huffed. "It's ok for him to be around prostitutes all day, but not who I'm dealing with? Come on, you bugging right now."

"Hmmp!" Tonya huffed. "I've seen some of your bitches and trust me, he'll be better off around some prostitutes," she said in a matter of fact tone. The truth of the matter was, Tonya was just doing everything in her power to make Dice's life a living hell for no reason. Lil Dice was all that Tonya had to connect her to Dice and she knew if she let Dice get his son, he wasn't going to bring him back and Tonya didn't have time for no bullshit.

"Listen," Dice said. "All I want to do is see my son. That's all I care about. I could care less what you out her doing."

"Okay, I'll think about it," Tonya said nonchalantly. She knew she was getting on Dice's nerves and she loved every minute of it.

"You'll think about it," Dice repeated. He was doing his best not to snap and rip Tonya's head off, but she knew just what buttons to push.

"You got some money on you right now?" Tonya asked.

"Yeah... Why; wassup?"

"My time is money so if you wanna continue talking to me, you gone have to pay," Tonya smirked holding her hand out.

"Yo, stop playing with me!" Dice snapped. He wrapped his hands around Tonya's neck and forced her back up to the wall. On his first day out of jail the last thing Dice needed was for the police to roll up on him and catch him with his hands wrapped around Tonya's throat. "Word to my mother, if you don't let me see my son I'm going to hurt you!" he growled with his hands still wrapped around Tonya's neck.

"We have a problem over here?" Dice heard a voice call out from behind him. Dice turned around and saw a tall slim man in an all black expensive looking suit. By his side stood two beautiful women. Immediately Dice figured the man that stood before him to be Champagne.

"Yeah actually we do have a problem," Dice replied. "A big problem!"

"I'm listening," Champagne said coolly with him and Dice never losing eye contact.

"All I want is to see my son," Dice said. "Tell Tonya to let me see my son and I'll be on my way."

"Lil Dice is my son now!" Champagne said. "I own his mother and all of her possessions," he said with a smirk. "But for the right price we might be able to work out something."

Dice went to charge the low down, trifling pimp, but stopped in midstride when the two women who stood by Champagne's side both quickly removed guns from their purses and aimed them at him.

"Better pump your motherfucking brakes," one of Champagne's hoes said. Her tone showed no respect.

"Bitch get over here!" Champagne snapped his fingers. Tonya jumped like someone put fire to her ass quickly making her way to Champagne's side.

"Yes Daddy," Tonya sang hoping she wasn't in trouble.

"What the fuck is you out here doing talking to this broke ass nigga?" Champagne asked.

"Daddy I tried to get him to leave, but he kept on following me. I was about....."

Champagne's hand shot out in a flash and back slapped Tonya across her face like she was a piece of trash. "You supposed to be out here getting this money, honey." He paused. "If the nigga ain't got a buck, then he must be a duck and shit outta luck," Champagne said in a fast pitch smooth tone. "A nigga with no cash gone always finish last!"

"I know Daddy and I'm sorry! It won't happen again," Tonya said like an obedient puppy with her head hung low.

"Sorry my ass, bitch," Champagne said looking at Tonya like she was crazy. "When we get home you going into the pit!"

"Are you serious?" Dice said not believing his eyes. He had heard the stories in jail about how Champagne had his hoes on smash and in check, but to see it live and in living color was a totally different story. "You gone break up our family for this clown?" This just didn't make sense to Dice. "The nigga say a few rhymes and now he's your Daddy? Can't you see that he don't give a shit about you or our son?"

"Listen, I'mma tell you this one time and one time only," Champagne said in a smooth tone. "Stay the fuck away from my hoes," he said as he and all of his hoes hopped in an Escalade that was parked on the street. A sexy blonde hair driver sat behind the wheel watching Dice's every move until Champagne and his hoes were safely inside. Dice stood there and watched as the Escalade pulled off. Inside he wanted to cry, but on the outside he had to remain strong. Dice didn't care what he had to do, he was going to get his son back even if it was the last thing he did.

****

The next day Dice stepped foot in the church's basement and saw what looked to be around six hundred Spades members wearing all black with serious looks on their faces. In the past few weeks, Wolf had opened up a pizza shop and a seafood restaurant. He only hired African American workers and mostly the ones who had felonies and had the mentality that no one would ever hire them. Wolf donated money to Pastor Anderson and the church and he also put each and every Spades member on the pay roll. He made sure each and every member got paid every two weeks just to keep everyone happy and to keep things peaceful.

"Okay, let's get down to business," Wolf said getting everyone's attention before he began. "Officer Antonio," he said. Just the mention of the cops name caused an uproar of chatter to breakout in the basement. Office Antonio had gunned down two innocent black teenagers in the past two years and got nothing more than a slap on the wrist. Office Antonio's nonchalant attitude helped bump his name up on The Spades list. The Spades weren't just going to sit around and watch anybody come in the community and gun down their people. More needed to be done. Jessie Jackson and other activist speaking on the victims behalf was cool, but in Wolf's eyes he felt way more needed to get done. "He's next on The Spades hit list," Wolf announced. "Myself along with ten other Spades members of my choosing will go and take care of this today," Wolf said. "As for the rest of you; I need y'all out there getting rid of these mid level dealers.... We will clean these streets.... One block at a time," Wolf said with a smile as he watched all The Spades exit out the basement to go handle their business.

Once Wolf was done with his announcement, Dice walked up to Wolf. "What's up," he smiled. "I'm ready to get in where I fit in."

"Welcome home," Wolf said giving Dice some dap. "How's everything?"

"I have a little situation that I might need your assistance on," Dice told him. The Champagne situation was still heavy on his mind.

"I'm listening," Wolf said giving Dice his full attention. Just by looking at the man, he could tell that something was wrong.

"My son's mother is involved with some nasty pimp and I need him out of the picture so I can see my son," Dice explained.

"I'll take care of it for you," Wolf replied. "Before the night is over, just give me the pimp's information."

"I got you!"

"As a matter of fact, I want you to come with me on this officer Antonio job," Wolf told him. "Go see Live Wire and he's going to give you a gun and some just coming home money." He nodded over towards Live Wire. Thirty minutes later Wolf and his ten man team hopped in two all black vans and headed straight for Officer Antonio's house.

****

The two black vans pulled up in Officer Antonio's driveway and Spades members hopped out like the police. A husky three hundred pound Spades member brought his leg back and came forward with his size fourteen shoe and kicked the front door open. BOOM! Dice watched as The Spades bum rushed the house. He held his .38 in a two handed grip as he entered the house through the front door. Throughout the house he heard a lot of noise, a few screams, and glass breaking.

Wolf and Live Wire were the last to enter the house, making sure they closed the door behind them. Wolf stepped foot in the living room and saw one of The Spades dragging Officer Antonio's wife and teenage daughter down the steps by their hair.

"Tie their hands up," Wolf ordered as he watched the two women get their wrist duct taped behind their backs as they struggled to break free.

The wife and daughter looked terrified; mainly because their living room was filled with a bunch of mean faced black men. "What do you people want?" the wife blurted out.

Wolf walked up to Officer Antonio's wife and smacked the shit out of her. "Where's your husband at?"

"He's at work. Why, what's all this about?" The wife asked scared to death. She knew that the black community was mad and upset about what her husband had done, but she never expected for them to take it this far.

"This is about putting an end to your racist ass husband's foolish ways," Wolf told her.

"My husband is a good man," the wife said sticking up for her husband like she was supposed to.

Wolf handed the wife the cordless phone. "Call your husband and tell him to come home immediately because something horrible has happened to his daughter."

"Something horrible has happened to his daughter," the wife repeated with a confused look on her face. Live Wire quickly walked up to Officer Antonio's teenage daughter and placed his .357 to her head and pulled the trigger.

The wife let out a loud scream when she heard the loud blast followed by her daughters warm blood splashing across her face.

"Shut all that screaming up," Live Wire growled pressing the hot barrel of his .357 to the back of the wife's head. Wolf slowly walked up to the wife and held out the cordless phone "Call your husband!"

****

"Spread your fucking legs," Officer Antonio yelled as he roughly frisked a young African American teenager. He was cruising down the street and pulled over and hopped out on the young man just because his pants were sagging off his ass.

"Where are the drugs?"

"What drugs?" the teenager asked nervously. He was a good kid and this was his first time being harassed by the NYPD.

Officer Antonio sighed loudly. "Now you wanna play games," he said as he hand cuffed the teenager's hands behind his back. "I'm going to ask you one more time. Where's the shit?"

"I swear to God, I don't have nothing on me. I'm clean."

Officer Antonio shoved his Taser in the teenager's ribs. "Stop resisting," he yelled as he continued to tase the young man repeatedly. The only thing that got Officer Antonio to lay up off the kid was his ringing cell phone. "Yeah," he answered when he saw his wife's face flashing across the screen on his cell phone.

"Baby something is wrong with Beverly," his wife yelled into the receiver. "Drop whatever you doing and come home now," his wife said hanging up in her husband's ear.

His wife wasn't the type to raise her voice so when Officer Antonio heard his wife yelling, he knew that whatever was going on had to be serious. He quickly uncuffed the teenager, hopped back in his squad car, and pulled off leaving the young man laid out on the concrete.

****

"Fuck taking this cracker so long," Live Wire huffed as he walked over and grabbed a hand full of the wife's hair forcing her to look at him. "Bitch if your husband ain't here in the next ten minutes, I'm going to blow your motherfucking brains out!"

"Please," the wife pleaded. :"We have money," she blurted out. "$30,000.00 and it's upstairs in our bedroom closet."

Live Wire nodded towards another Spades member signaling for him to go up the stairs and grab that cash.

"We got company," Dice announced peeking through the blinds.

"Officer Antonio?" Wolf asked.

Dice nodded his head.

All The Spades got in position and waited for Officer Antonio to walk through the front door.

"Baby I got here as soon as I….." Officer Antonio paused mid-sentence when he barged through the front door and saw a black man holding a gun to his wife's head.

"So glad you could finally make it", Wolf said with a smirk on his face as he watched The Spades hold the cop at gun point and disarm him.

"What's going on here guys?" Officer Antonio asked nervously looking around.

"So you like killing black men I see," Wolf said walking up on the racist cop. "If it's one thing I can't stand is a coward who hides behind his badge," he said standing nose to nose with Officer Antonio. "You ain't shit and your death will be a warning to all your kind," Wolf told him. "You've been warned," he said as a Spades member crept up on the officer from behind and put a bullet in his head. Behind him Wolf heard another gunshot blast go off immediately and he immediately knew Live Wire had killed the wife.

"What's next?" Live Wire asked with his thirst for blood showing on his face.

"Y'all got the rest of the night off," Wolf announced.

"Good," Live Wire smiled. Now he could finally go and spend some time with Rosey and get him some loving.

"You did good today," Wolf said shaking Dice's hand. "I'll see you first thing in the morning." The Spades quickly exited the house and hopped back in the two vans and peeled off.

Later on that night Wolf drove around the city looking for some new drug spots that he didn't know about. There were so many drugs on the streets of New York that Wolf knew that taking down local and mid-level dealers would soon become a waste of time. It was time for The Spades to start targeting the connects and big time players. If the local and mid-level hustlers didn't have anyone to supply them, how and where would they get work from? With all the connects and Big Willies out of the picture, it would be much easier to get rid of the rest of the small fish. Wolf's mind was already made up. He would have half The Spades go after the lower level hustlers while him and the more higher rank Spades members would tackle the big fish. As Wolf cruised the New York streets, he came across a low key looking bar. He parallel parked in front. He figured why not have a few drinks? It wasn't like he had a home to go to. Ever since Wolf came home, he'd been sleeping in his Hooptie some nights while all the other nights he slept in the basement of the church. Wolf had more than enough money to get himself a crib, but his main focus was to get these businesses established so he could help the unemployment rate in the community.

Wolf hopped out his Hooptie and entered the bar. The place was dimly lit and the music was playing at a nice level, not too loud and not too low. Inside there were only seven other customers in this establishment. Wolf made his way to the bar counter and helped himself to a seat on a barstool. As Wolf waited for the bar maid to come down to his side of the bar, he checked out her merchandise and was pleased with what he saw. The bar maid wasn't no model or nothing. She was more on the average side of the fence. The bar maid favored the female rapper Diamond. She stood around 5'7 and looked like she weighed in at about 170 lbs.

"What can I get for you?" The bar maid asked with a pearly white smile.

"Vodka and orange juice," Wolf replied. The bar maid fixed his drink, handed it to him, and then moved on to the next customer. Wolf sipped his drink as his mind went on to think about how to accomplish his mission as soon as possible. New members were joining The Spades everyday and soon The Spades number count would be in the thousands. In the next few months Wolf expected The Spades to be a well house hold name. Five drinks later Wolf looked up and saw that he was the last and only one left in the bar.

"I'm sorry, but what time do y'all close?" Wolf asked the bar maid.

She smiled. "You good. We still got a whole forty-five minutes," she said sitting a bottle of Ciroc down on top of the counter. "Seems like you got a lot on your mind. Mind if I drink with you?"

Wolf nodded at the barstool next to him signaling for the bar maid to have a seat.

"Ivy," the bar maid extended her hand.

"Wolf," he replied as the tow shook hands.

"What kind of name is Wolf?" Ivy asked sipping her drink.

"I got the name because behind closed doors I'm known to be an animal," Wolf flirted openly. Since being released from jail this was the first real conversation that Wolf was having with a female. The alcohol had Wolf feeling good and caused his tongue to get a little loose.

"An animal, huh?" Ivy said with a raised brow. "I hear that," she said with her eyes focused down on Wolf's crotch. Wolf was just the type of man that Ivy went after. He was strong, black, handsome, and tall. "I bet you drive all the ladies crazy."

"Actually I haven't driven anybody crazy in a while," Wolf admitted. "At least not yet," he said undressing Ivy with his eyes as he sipped his drink slowly.

"Before I came over here it looked like you had a lot on your mind. Want to talk about it?" Ivy said smoothly changing the subject from sex to another topic. The last time Ivy had been with a man was over a year and a half ago and right now she was about ready to jump on Wolf and fuck his brains out. She wanted to fuck him like he'd never been fucked before. She wanted to fuck him like her life depended on it and like she was a seasoned porn star so changing the subject seemed like the best thing to do.

"Yeah I did have a little something on my mind," Wolf told her. "And you are the perfect distraction," he smiled putting his glass to his lips.

"So what do you do for a living if you don't mind me asking?" Ivy sipped her drink still trying to keep the conversation simple and regular, but that task was one that was going to be easier said than done. The sexual tension was definitely there, no matter how hard Ivy wanted and tried to ignore it. "If that's too personal, then you don't have to answer that."

"I want to eat your pussy," Wolf said seriously as he downed the rest of his drink.

"Excuse me?" Ivy replied with a shocked expression on her face. That last comment had caught her off guard, but at the same time it made her pussy very wet. "I don't know what you think, but....."

Before Ivy could finish what she was saying, Wolf quickly stood up and kissed her passionately as his hands massaged and cuffed Ivy's round plump ass. Ivy kissed Wolf for a few seconds before she pushed him away and walked off towards the exit in a hurry. Immediately Wolf thought he had went too far and that Ivy was leaving because she was scared of him or either going to find someone to escort him out of the bar for being so aggressive. Wolf looked on in shock as he watched Ivy walk to the exit and flip the sign on the door from open to close. Then she turned around and gave him a seductive smile that said be careful what you ask for as she locked the front door to the bar and head back over towards Wolf.

Wolf removed his shirt and flossed his incredible looking cut up body. All that time in jail working out had did his body good. Ivy looked at Wolf's six pack and couldn't control her hormones. Wolf and Ivy shared a loud long sloppy kiss while their hands roamed and explored each other's body. Low moans escaped Ivy's lips as she darted her tongue in and out of Wolf's mouth. As their tongues continued to gently wrestle, Wolf unbuttoned Ivy's jeans and smoothly slid her jeans down to her ankles. Ivy planted soft wet kisses on Wolf's neck as she stepped out of her jeans. Wolf effortlessly scooped Ivy up and sat her down on top of the counter where he removed her thong with his teeth. Once Ivy's thong was removed she spread her legs open wide exposing her slightly hairy pussy.

Wolf placed his face close enough to Ivy's pussy and sniffed it. It had been so long since he had smelled some pussy that he just wanted to cherish the moment for a second.

"Come eat this pussy," Ivy demanded in a sexual charged voice. Wolf did as she asked and buried his face in between Ivy's legs, making hungry noises as he kissed, licked, and slurped all over her clit.

"Yes...Yes baby...Yes!" Ivy moaned... She moaned from deep down in her soul. Her body was shaking while her hands were holding Wolf's face pulling him deep into her soaking wet pussy. Ivy was getting turned on by the slurping sounds that came from between her legs. She began gyrating her hips and grinding her pussy into and all over Wolf's face. Ivy made ugly faces and sounds like she was dying a slow death, like she was being murdered one lick at a time.

"Ahh...Ahhh...YES!" Ivy screamed as her legs locked around Wolf's neck as her body shook uncontrollably. She clawed at the back of Wolf's head as her orgasm came long, loud, and hard. As soon as Ivy stopped shaking, she quickly hopped up off the counter and pushed Wolf back a few feet, then melted down to her knees and aggressively pulled Wolf's pants down. She was glad when she saw that his dick was already hard. Ivy spit on Wolf's dick as she slowly jerked it with one hand while looking up in Wolf's eyes from down on her knees. "I'm about to suck the shit outta this dick," she said seductively. Ivy took Wolf in her mouth. She felt his hands in her hair while she felt his dick touch the back of her throat. Loud moans escaped from Ivy's lips as Wolf held the back of her head and began fucking her mouth, feeding her hard dick. Ivy gagged as saliva dropped from her chin as she let Wolf have his way with her mouth. Wolf aggressively fucked Ivy's mouth until it felt like he was about to explode. Ivy's mouth made a loud wet noise as Wolf removed his dick from her mouth. Then he guided Ivy over to a red chair. He helped position her in the chair with her back to him and her knees sinking into the cushion. Wolf grabbed a handful of Ivy's hair and pulled her head back forcing her to look at him while he entered her from behind at an easy and slow pace. He heard her breathing change from smooth to desperate to choppy. "Tear this pussy up!" Ivy growled looking into Wolf's eyes. Wolf squatted down at a low angle and came upward with hard and fast strokes. With each stroke he delivered, he watched Ivy's ass bounce and jiggle all over the place like JELLO. With her eyes closed tight and her mouth wide open, Ivy moved her head in pain and in pleasure while sweating as if she were in Africa.

"WOLF, WOLF, OH MY GOD, WOLF, SHIT!" Ivy's legs trembled. Then her entire body did the same.

"Oh shit, I'm about to come!" Wolf announced.

"No!" Ivy said pushing Wolf off of her as she spun around and sat in the chair facing him. "I wanna suck it out," she said looking up at Wolf with a devilish grin on her face. Ivy slowly sucked and slurped all of her cum and juices off of Wolf's dick.

"You want me to cum in your mouth?"

"mmm...hmmmm" Ivy moaned.

"You gone swallow it?"

"mmm...hmmmm"

"All of it?"

"mmm...hmmmm," Ivy moaned loudly as her head bobbed up and down a hundred miles an hour. The sound of her mouth was wet and her determination spoke even louder forcing Wolf to cum sooner than he wanted to. Ivy moaned when she felt warm cum shoot through her mouth. With her warm hands, she cradled Wolf's balls and held on to his erection making sure she sucked out every last drop before finally releasing him from her mouth.

"Damn!" Wolf huffed out of breath. Right now he felt like this was the best pussy he ever had in his life. It was either that or the fact that he hadn't had no pussy in such a long time. Either way, Wolf was satisfied and feeling good.

"How was it?" Ivy asked with a smile while squeezing back into her jeans.

"Delicious!" Wolf said as the two busted out laughing.

"You definitely are an animal!"

"I take pride in my work." Wolf smiled as he slipped back into his clothes.

"That's the first time I ever had sex with a man I barely even knew. I feel a little embarrassed," Ivy said looking over at Wolf while pouring herself another drink.

Wolf didn't believe a word she spoke for one second, but he played along. "It's nothing to be embarrassed about. We both are grown adults."

Ivy walked up to Wolf and planted a soft kiss on his lips. "Thank you. I really needed that."

Wolf and Ivy sat at the bar talking and getting to know each other better as they finished off the bottle of Ciroc. The more Ivy spoke to Wolf, the more she found herself liking him. Not only was Wolf a master lover when it came to laying the pipe down, but he was also very intelligent and well spoken.

Once they finished off the bottle, Ivy and Wolf exited the bar. Wolf stood over to the side while Ivy locked up the bar.

So you got a number I can reach you at?" Wolf asked while holding his cell phone and leaning up against his Hooptie. He'd enjoyed hanging out with Ivy and spending time with her. He looked forward to seeing her again in the near future. Ivy took Wolf's cell phone from his hand and stored her name and number inside then handed it back to him.

"Don't take my number if you not planning on using it," she said placing a hand on her hips. "You better call."

Wolf smiled "I got you," he said walking around to the driver side of his Hooptie.

"Where you think you going?" Ivy said standing in front of the driver's door blocking Wolf from entering his car. "I'm not letting you drive in this condition," she told him.

"I feel fine."

"Feel fine my ass," Ivy snapped hooking her arm around Wolf's arm and escorting him away from the Hooptie. "You're spending the night with me," she told him. "I only live right up the block and I promise I'll take good care of you and that dick," she added with a giggle.

Wolf and Ivy laughed, joked, and flirted while they took their time heading down the block. Wolf stopped joking when him and Ivy walked up on a homeless woman fishing through a garbage can for something to eat.

"Excuse me miss," Wolf called out getting the homeless woman's attention. "What seems to be the problem?" he asked nodding towards the garbage can.

"I don't have a motherfucking problem!" The homeless woman barked and continued to fish through the garbage can.

"Here," Wolf said removing a hundred dollar bill from his pocket and held it out towards the homeless woman. The homeless woman quickly snatched the bill from Wolf and held it up to the sky checking to make sure it was real. Once she was sure that the bill was in fact real, she turned and looked at Wolf. "What do I have to do for this?" she asked looking down at his crotch.

"Go get you something to eat," Wolf said ignoring the homeless woman's last comment. "What's your name?" Wolf asked while jotting down some information on a small piece of paper. When he finished writing, he held the paper out towards the homeless woman.

"Wendy," the homeless woman announced accepting the piece of paper from Wolf's hand.

"Come see me tomorrow at the church. The address is written on that piece of paper." He nodded down at the piece of paper in her hands. "How old are you?"

"Twenty-eight," Wendy answered with an ashamed and embarrassed look on her ashy face.

"Like I said, come see me tomorrow," Wolf said as him and Ivy walked off.

"That was very nice of you," Ivy smiled. "I heard of giving bums a dollar or two, but damn a hundred dollars."

"She needs it more than I do," Wolf replied. The twenty eight year old homeless crack head digging in the garbage was the main reason Wolf was determined to get drugs off the streets. He hated to see the effect that it had on his people. Seeing that young woman on drugs hurt his heart and made him angry. Five minutes later Ivy and Wolf entered her small one bedroom apartment. The place was small, cozy, and well decorated with a woman's touch.

"Make yourself at home," Ivy said. Then she disappeared inside the bathroom and seconds later she sound of the shower could be heard. While Ivy was in the shower Wolf gave himself a tour around the one bedroom apartment. When Wolf reached the bedroom, he flopped down on Ivy's soft comfortable looking bed and closed his eyes. He was mentally preparing himself for all the violence and blood that he knew was going to be spilled out on the streets. Wolf's eyes quickly shot open when he heard someone enter the bedroom. He looked up and saw Ivy standing in the doorway butt naked with a devilish grin on her face.

Chapter 7
"The Jamaicans"

The next day Wolf pulled up in front of the church and spotted the homeless woman Wendy sitting down on the curb looking like she had a lot on her mind and the weight of the world on her shoulders. When Wendy saw Wolf stroll up to the church, she quickly stood to her feet with a huge smile on her face.

"Hey," she said smiling. Immediately Wolf could see that the homeless woman had tried to fix her hair the best she could using her fingers as a comb.

"Hey wassup," Wolf returned the smile. "I'm glad to see you," he extended his hand.

"Hey," Wendy said again as the two shook hands. "Thank again for what you did for me last night."

"You are too young to be out here on the streets like this," Wolf told her. "That's why The Spades are here to help the people," he paused. "We gone get you all cleaned up and get you a job."

"Why would you do all that for me?" Wendy asked. She just couldn't understand why somebody would want to help her out when she was at her lowest point in her life.

"Why wouldn't I want to do all that for you?" Wolf answered her question with a question.

Wendy reached into her pocket and pulled out ninety dollars. "You see, I still got the money that you gave me last night," she said in a fast pitch voice. "I didn't blow it," she smiled as if she was proud of herself and had accomplished something major.

Wolf smiled as he led Wendy inside the church. He could see that Wendy was a good girl who just got caught up in a few bad situations. Wolf walked straight up to Pastor Anderson's office door and knocked lightly.

"Hey Wolf! How's everything going?" Pastor Anderson asked with a smile. Ever since he had agreed to let The Spades use the church's basement, Wolf had donated more than one-hundred thousand dollars to Pastor Anderson and the church so far and Pastor Anderson couldn't have been happier.

"I'm good," Wolf replied quickly. "This here is Wendy and I need you to help her get clean." He turned and headed down the stairs to the basement where over a thousand Spades members in all black awaited instructions from their leader.

Once Wolf had everyone's attention, he began. "It's time to start going after the more bigger fish out there," he announced.

"What about the little fish?" Dice asked.

"I'm going to assign half of The Spades to take care of the smaller players, but with the big players out of the game, there will be nobody to supply the more lower level hustlers," Wolf explained.

"Who's next on the hit list?" Live Wire asked excitedly.

"It's a crew out in Brooklyn that call themselves "The Crazy Jamaican's" and their leader goes by the name of Screw Face," Wolf said. "These clowns have several trap houses out in Brooklyn and they're known to be very violent so it's safe to say that we gone have to bust a few skulls on this mission."

Wolf went on and assigned ten Spades to take a van and ride out to each of The Crazy Jamaican's trap houses and wait for his word. Once the meeting was over, Wolf, Live Wire, Dice, and the rest of The Spades exited the churches basement and headed towards their destination.

****

Screw Face sat up in his Jamaican restaurant that he owned with several of the other Crazy Jamaican's. Screw Face had called a small meeting to discuss a small and minor problem that had potential to turn into a big problem; a real big problem.

"The Spades," Screw Face began. "Who are these fuckers?" He asked looking around the table for answers. Plenty of stories about this new organization had been floating around in the streets, but Screw Face wanted to hear it from his crew.

"A new crew out to clean up the streets by killing off all the drug dealers," Bobby Dread answered. He was Screw Face's right hand man and personal body guard. He was a handsome dark skin man who's dreads hung down to his ass. On his hip rested a 9mm with an extended clip. "But so far they have only been going after low level hustlers and workers."

Screw Face sipped his tea and then said, "Gather up a team and pay them a visit before they decide to pay us a visit first." He ordered as the bell above the front door rang signaling that someone was entering the restaurant.

"Looks like we got company," Bobby Dread said nodding towards the front door as he removed his 9mm from his waist and sat it on his lap. Screw Face looked towards the entrance and saw three men dressed in all black enter the restaurant headed in his direction. Immediately Bobby Dread hopped up from his seat standing in the path of the leader of the group. "That's far enough," Bobby Dread said. Wolf looked down at the gun that rested in Bobby Dreads hand, then back up into his eyes and he could tell that the man that stood before him wouldn't hesitate to put a bullet right between his eyes.

"My name is Wolf and we," he said sweeping his hand through the air, "Are The Spades and we need to have a word with Screw Face."

"Speak your piece," Screw Face said cockily. He felt safe and comfortable knowing that his best soldiers were close by, armed and ready to shoot.

"We come in peace," Wolf began. "All we ask is that you stop selling poison to my people and taking part in destroying our community."

Screw Face chuckled. "If I don't sell poison then how will I eat and feed my family?" He took another sip form his tea.

"The Spades have several businesses up and running," Wolf told him. "And we'd love to hire you as well as all of your friends and family. If y'all were to join The Spades, you would make more money helping us get rid of other dealers and you would be helping to clean up the community in the process."

Screw Face remained silent for a few seconds as if he was in deep thought. "As good as your offer sounds, I'm sorry, but I'm going to have to pass," Screw Face smirked. "I live, shit, eat, and breath drugs. Besides I don't like how y'all just busted up in my restaurant like y'all some fucking big shot, macho killers. Y'all should be lucky I don't have y'all dumb asses killed for pulling a stunt like this…. Now get the fuck up outta here." Screw Face flicked his wrist as if he was shooing them away. "Before I get mad!"

Wolf nodded his head. "You've been warned," was all he said as him and The Spades turned and left.

"Pussy boys," Screw Face said loud enough for The Spades to hear just as they exited the restaurant.

Back outside the restaurant Wolf, Live Wire, and Dice walked back over to the van. Wolf opened the side door and each man threw on a bullet proof vest and grabbed an automatic weapon as it suddenly began pouring down raining. Wolf quickly pulled out his cell phone and made the call giving all ten groups of Spades permission to run up in all of Screw Face's trap houses, kill everyone, and take all the money.

Wolf hung up and the trio slid ski masks over their faces as they walked straight up to the front of the restaurant and opened fire on it. The sound of loud machine gun fire filled the streets, followed by shattered glass, innocent people screaming, and car alarms blaring. Wolf was the first one to re-enter the restaurant. His eyes immediately locked on Screw Face who hopped up from his seat and tried to make a quick dash towards the back exit of the restaurant, but a shot to the back of his thigh slowed him down.

Wolf quickly took cover as Bobby Dread and two other soldiers returned fire in the middle of the restaurant.

Live Wire sprung up from behind a wall with his Tech-9 and dropped the two soldiers with shots to their head. Both toppled face down to the tiled floor, souls evicted from their bodies before they even realized what was going on.

Bobby Dread fired four shots in rapid succession before turning and dashing out the back exit.

"I got Screw Face," Live Wire announced as he watched Wolf and Dice run out the back exit after Bobby Dread.

Live Wire smiled as he slowly walked up on Screw Face, who was crawling on his stomach at a snail's pace leaving a long trail of blood behind. "Look at me, you faggot," Live Wire said using his boot to flip Screw Face over on his back.

"Wait," Screw Face said with his hands up and palms out as if his hands would be able to block bullets. "I got fifteen thousand dollars cash on me right now if you let me live; I'll give you whatever you …."

Live Wire's Tech-9 rattled in his hands as he squeezed the trigger silencing Screw Face forever. Live Wire then quickly searched through the dead man's pockets. He removed the fifteen thousand dollars from one of his pockets and stuffed it down into his own pocket. Live Wire swiftly moved over towards the cash register, opened it, and removed all the money and then made a bee line straight for the exit.

****

Wolf and Dice chased Bobby Dread down the street in the rain, popping shot after shot at him hoping to put a bullet in the man's dread locks. Bobby Dread flung his arm backwards and popped off a couple of shots until his clip was empty. Trying to avoid getting his head blown off, Bobby Dread dashed across the street causing cars to come to a screeching stop and collide with one another as several horns blared loudly. Bobby Dread quickly made a quick cut to his right and entered a dead end alley. He stopped in front of the chain linked fence and turned around to face his killers. If he was going to die, he planned on dying like a man and with integrity.

Wolf and Dice entered the alley and saw Bobby Dread standing in the middle of the alley with a murderous look on his face and fire dancing in his eyes. Wolf stood several feet away from Bobby Dread and aimed his gun at him. He pulled the trigger....click, click, click! Wolf quickly looked over at Dice.

"It's empty," Dice replied motioning down towards the .38 that rested in his hands.

Once Bobby Dread saw that both Wolf and Dice's guns were empty, he smoothly removed his wet shirt revealing his well cut up body and six pack. He then took a karate stance and motioned for Wolf and Dice to come get some with his hands.

Wolf and Dice both turned and looked at each other for a long second. From the stance that Bobby Dread stood in they could tell that the man had to know some kind of Kung-Fu, martial arts, or something.

"Come on!!" Bobby Dread growled as the rain drops bounced and splashed on his muscular body.

Wolf quickly charged Bobby Dread and threw two haymakers. Bobby Dread weaved the two punches easily and caught Wolf in his face with a round house elbow that sent rain drops flying from Wolf's head. After he landed the elbow, he caught Dice in the face with a powerful side kick that put Dice on his ass.

Wolf recovered quickly and charged Bobby Dread again. He threw punches from all angles. Each punch had bad intensions and the potential to knock any man out. Bobby Dread blocked each punch with ease and with a grin on his face as he watched Wolf tire himself out. Once Wolf punched himself out, Bobby Dread went into attack mode. He snapped off a left-right-left-right-double left-double right to the head, then finished Wolf off with Jean Claude Van Dam's round house to the head. That dropped Wolf face first in a puddle of dirty water. By the time Dice made it back to his feet, Bobby Dread grabbed the back of Dice's head with both hands, forcefully shoved his head down as he raised his knee up to his chest and violently smashed his knee into Dice's face. Dice was knocked out before he even hit the ground. Bobby Dread stood over Dice's unconscious body looking down at him. He was about to get on some Bruce Lee shit and jump and stomp Dice's head into the concrete, but the site of Live Wire entered the alley caused Bobby Dread to turn and run full speed towards the fence. When he reached the fence it took him three quick moves and he was over the fence and running down the other end of the alley. The way Bobby Dread hopped over the fence caught Live Wire off guard. He hadn't expected for the man to be able to move so fast and with so much agility. Live Wire quickly ran up to the fence and fired several shots down the alley, but he knew Bobby Dread was too far down along the alley to get a good shot. The shots were just to let Bobby Dread know that this shit wasn't over.

"Bitch ass nigga," Live Wire huffed as he turned and saw Wolf slowly crawling back up to his feet. He quickly helped Wolf get to his feet, then he moved on and helped Dice back up to his feet also. The trio then got as far away from the alley as possible before the cops decided to show up.

Chapter 8
"I'm About My Money"

"Fuck me Daddy! Yessss, Fuck me Daddy!" Tonya screamed with an unbelievable look on her face. She was on all fours in the back of a Yukon while one of her regular customers was hitting her from the back doggy style. Tonya faked and pretended like the John was tearing her pussy up when in all reality he wasn't big enough to hurt or tear up anything. Whether the man was packing or not, it was Tonya's job to make all of her customers feel like they were hung like King Kong and she was good at what she did and even better for the ego.

"Damn!" Tonya smiled once the John was done with her. "What you was trying to do; make me fall in love?" She giggled.

"You like that, baby?" Tonya said excitedly. "I felt that shit all up in my chest," she lied with ease. Lying was something Tonya had picked up rather easily ever since she began dealing with Champagne. Her job was to keep the customers happy and coming back and if she had to lie in order to keep getting that money then so be it!

"Make sure you come see me again Daddy, you hear," Tonya said over her shoulder as she slid out the passenger seat and walked back over to her post and waited and searched for her next customer. Tonya's hair hung down to her shoulders and she wore a bright red spandex slash elastic tight fitting dress. On her feet she sported a pair of red four inch heels that made her toned legs look even sexier. Her full lips were painted with bright red lipstick that she couldn't wait to get smeared.

Tonya looked up and down the street looking for her next potential customer when she spotted the last face she wanted to see. Tonya sucked her teeth and rolled her eyes. "What are you doing here?" She asked with much attitude.

Dice walked up and stood directly in front of Tonya. He was tired of waiting for Wolf and The Spades to come take care of this situation for him. Plus he knew there were much bigger and more important people on The Spades hit list that needed to be dealt with first. "Where's my son?"

"At my mom's house; DAMN!" Tonya huffed like Dice was becoming an annoyance. "Why don't you just leave me the fuck alone?"

"He's not at your mom's house. I already went there and checked," Dice told her. He couldn't understand why Tonya didn't want him to see his son. With all the dead beat dads out there, Dice thought Tonya would be happy that he was willing to step up to the plate and be there for his son, but he thought wrong. "Let me see my son and I swear I'll leave you alone."

Tonya sucked her teeth. "Yo stop sweating me," she said and turned on her heels and tried to spin off.

"Bitch stop playing with me!" Dice growled firmly grabbing Tonya by her forearm. He was seconds away from putting his foot in her ass. "I'm not going nowhere until I see my son and I'm going to make sure you don't make one dollar," he told her. "I don't care if I have to come out this motherfucker everyday!"

"Get off of me!" Tonya yelled jerking her arm free. She hated Dice and wished he would just leave and never come back. "Why don't you just leave me alone?"

"Bitch!" Dice barked. "I don't' give a fuck about you! All I want to do is see my son!"

"You're obsessed with me," Tonya said seriously. "You just can't stand that I don't want to be with you no more, can you?"

"You wanna play games and waste both of our time. Go right ahead. I don't give a fuck." He shrugged. "I promise you won't make another dime until I see my son."

"Hey baby, wassup? You working?" One of Tonya's regulars said as he pulled up to the curb with his passenger window rolled down. Before Tonya could reply, Dice was already at the passenger window.

"Yo, my man," Dice said looking the John straight in his eyes. "She ain't working right now. Come back later." He knew fucking with Tonya's money was going to piss her off. Not only that, but it would piss Champagne off as well.

"Why are you doing this?" Tonya huffed. "I finally got a real man and now you wanna get mad and come try to fuck up my money!" She rolled her eyes. "You a real clown!"

Dice ignored Tonya. He could care less what she was talking about. All he cared about was seeing his son and until then Tonya was going to be a broke motherfucker. As Tonya sat cursing Dice out, she saw two of Champagne's other hoes strolling down the street.

"Write your number down and I'll call you and we'll set up something so you can see your son," Tonya said in a fast pitched voice. The last thing Tonya wanted was for word to get back to Champagne that instead of getting that money, she was out entertaining her baby daddy.

"When you gone call?" Dice asked with a suspicious eye. He didn't believe a word Tonya said and he trusted her as far as he could throw her.

"Tomorrow! Now write your number down," she pressed. When Tonya looked up she locked eyes with Sparkle. Sparkle was one of Champagne's top money makers and Tonya's rival. Whatever Tonya did, Sparkle made it her business to top her and out shine her. And for some strange reason that Tonya couldn't figure out, Sparkle held a spot in Champagne's cold heart. Sparkle looked like the female rapper Nicki Minaj, but a low budget version. Sparkle even went as far as getting ass implants in her already huge ass. The ass shots just made her ass poke out even further. Not to mention with her good looks and horse ass, she began stealing customers from other bitches on the track.

"mmm....hmmmm!" Sparkle huffed. "I'm telling Daddy," she said tapping the screen on her iPhone and then placing it to her ear. Right then and there Tonya knew she was going to be in big trouble.

Tonya snatched the number from Dice's hand with an attitude. "I hope you know you just got me in a shit load of trouble." She looked down at her cell phone and had a text message from Champagne. The message said, "Bitch get your ass home now!"

"I don't give a fuck," Dice said coldly. "I'll be up here every day until you call me and allow me to see my son."

"I said I'll call you tomorrow," Tonya said quickly as she ran to the curb and flagged down a yellow cab. When a cab stopped, she disappeared into the back seat and the cab sped off.

All Dice could do was shake his head as he watched the yellow cab pull off and disappear around the corner. He couldn't understand why Tonya would stand outside all day and night selling her body just to give all the money to someone else. The more he thought about it, the harder it was to figure out. If that's what Tonya wanted to do with her life then so be it... All Dice cared about was seeing his son and if he had to come to the strip everyday and harass Tonya in order to see his son then that's just what he was going to do.

****

Tonya stepped foot in the five bedroom house that Champagne and all of his hoes shared with her head hung low. In the living room Tonya saw Champagne sitting on the couch and Sparkle was naked curled up in his lap with a smirk plastered on her face while the rest of Champagne's hoes all sat around and walked throughout the house butt naked. That was Champagne's only rule. While inside the house, all of his hoes were to be butt naked at all times. Tonya looked at Sparkle thinking how in the hell did she beat her home?

"Look who finally decided to join us," Sparkle said purposely causing everyone including Champagne to turn their focus on Tonya.

"Daddy I can explain," Tonya said quickly. "I swear....."

Champagne quickly raised his index finger up to his lips hushing Tonya before the lie she was getting ready to tell could roll off of her tongue. "So while everybody else is out getting that money, you out on the strip talking to your broke ass baby daddy all day, right?" Champagne said in a cool tone tapping Sparkle's fat ass signaling for her to get up as he slowly rose to his feet. Tonya was about to plead her case, but after giving it some thought she decided that her best bet would be just to keep her mouth shut and take her punishment like a woman.

"Didn't I tell you that I didn't want you talking to that clown again?" Champagne asked standing face to face with Tonya.

"Daddy I swear I was trying to get him to leave, but....."

"Bitch, where's my money?" Champagne said cutting Tonya off. He didn't have time for no excused and bullshit stories. All that mattered to him was his money.

Tonya pulled three hundred dollars from her purse and handed it to Champagne with an ashamed and defeated look on her face. Each of Champagne's hoes was to bring home no less than fifteen hundred dollars every single night, no matter if it was rain, sleet, or snow. Fifteen hundred dollars was always expected. Champagne took the three hundred dollars and looked at it like it had been rubbed in a pile of shit.

Champagne looked at the money closely. "That's it?"

"Daddy that's all I had a chance to make," Tonya replied.

"I understand," Champagne smiled. He faked like he was about to walk away, then quickly turned and punched Tonya in her mouth.

"Arghh!" Tonya screamed in pain. The swift punch caught her off guard. Her legs buckled and she hit the floor hard. She looked up at Champagne from the floor with fear in her eyes. Over in the cut she noticed Sparkle and a few of the other hoes cracking up dying laughing. "Daddy, I'm sorry!"

"Yeah you are sorry," Champagne agreed while slowly removing his belt from his jeans letting the buckle swing freely. "You a sorry, nasty, ungrateful bitch!" He growled as he swung the belt with all his might. The buckle of the belt whistled through the air and then connected loudly on Tonya's skin. Champagne beat and dragged Tonya's ass all throughout the house until she was barely conscious. "Stupid Bitch!" Champagne cleared his throat and hog spit in Tonya's face. If it was one thing Champagne couldn't stand was a bitch that didn't know how to listen. He disappeared in his bedroom and returned carrying a dog collar and leash in his hand. "Get over here Bitch!" He huffed placing the dog collar around Tonya's neck and then tying the end of the leash to the radiator. "Stay!" Champagne commanded like Tonya was an animal.

"Come on Daddy, let me get that stress up outta you," Sparkle laughed looking down at Tonya curled up in the corner in a fetal position. Sparkle grabbed Champagne's hand and gave him soft wet kisses before the two disappeared inside the bedroom.

Tonya laid on the floor with a dog collar around her neck like some kind of animal as tears streamed down her cheeks. All the hoes in the house walked pass Tonya like she was invisible. Not one of them asked if she was alright or even if she needed anything. As Tonya lay on the floor crying, the sound of Sparkle screaming and the head board beating against the wall could be heard loud and clear. The more Tonya cried, the louder Sparkle screamed and the louder the head board banged against the wall at a fast steady rhythm. As Tonya lay on the floor, she thought that this can't be what she was put on this earth for; to be at the mercy of someone else. Right then and there she began thinking of ways she could make her great escape.

Chapter 9
"I Need Mines"

Live Wire stood in his apartment wearing nothing, but a pair of Polo boxers as he counted out twenty-five thousand dollars in cash. He received the cash on a job that him and a few of the other Spades did the other day. Instead of dropping the money off at the church like he was supposed to, Live Wire decided to keep the money for himself. Live Wire felt that Wolf was putting too much money back into the community instead of their own pockets. Live Wire was all for helping out the community, but first he had to help himself.

Rosey lay across Live Wire's bed butt naked with a blunt in her hand and a pair of expensive sun glasses on her face. "You like these glasses?" Rosey asked taking a long drag from the blunt, then extending her arm.

"Fuck them glasses," Live Wire said taking the blunt from Rosey's soft hand. "I'm over here thinking about how I'mma get a million dollars and you talking about some stupid ass over priced glasses." He shook his head, then took a few pulls form the blunt.

"Well if I talk too much, then why don't you come put something in my mouth," Rosey said seductively licking her lips staring at Live Wire form behind her shades.

"I gotta run," Live Wire said. That's gone have to wait until I get back."

"Oh hell no," Rosey said with much emotion. The last time Live Wire had told her that she didn't' see him again until two days later and she wasn't letting him off that easy this time. Rosey turned on all fours on the bed, buried her face in a pillow, stuck her big ass high up in the air, and spread her ass cheeks open with her hands. "Come get this pussy," she said in a sexually charged voice. "Your pussy be missing you so much while you gone. Please Daddy... I need some of that dick," she whined. "Come tear this pussy up!"

Live Wire looked at Rosey laying across his bed on all fours with her ass cheeks held open and couldn't resist. Her pretty, pink, wet, juicy pussy was staring him in the face. Live Wire took another pull from the blunt and removed his boxers. He joined Rosey on the bed and rubbed his hard dick up and down Rosey's wetness teasing her, causing her to moan in anticipation. Not able to take it anymore Rosey reached behind her and slipped him into her wetness. "Damn," she screamed looking back at what was going in and out of her.

"Spread them ass cheeks apart," Live Wire demanded as he planted one foot down on the bed and began fucking Rosey like he hated her. Greedy sounds came from Rosey as Live Wire pulled her hair and smacked her on the ass.

"This what you wanted?" Live Wire growled as he watched Rosey's ass bounce and jiggle with each powerful stroke he delivered.

SMACK!

"This my pussy!?"

"Yes baby, yes!"

SMACK!

"You gone give my pussy away!?"

"No baby!" Rosey shouted "Never!"

"I can't hear you!"

SMACK!

"No baby, I'll never give your pussy away!"

Live Wire held Rosey's waist firmly with two hands as her ass made loud slapping sounds each time it bounced off his torso. Rosey arched her back and released a long drawn out orgasm, her moans never ending.

"I wanna taste it," Rosey moaned. Live Wire pulled out of Rosey's pussy and stood straight up on the bed and watched as Rosey took him in her mouth with small slow thrust that quickly turned into big fast thrust. Her mouth felt like a wet tight vacuum as Live Wire exploded and filled her mouth with fluids.

"And you better swallow all of it!" Live Wire huffed with a smile as he quickly slid off the bed and started to put his clothes back on. He headed for the door. "Yo, I'll be back in a few hours," he yelled over his shoulder on his way out the door.

"I got a few things I gotta take care of myself so I will call you later," Rosey walking towards the bathroom.

"Say no more," Live Wire said as he closed the door behind him. He was running late and knew that Wolf and the rest of The Spades were waiting for him. Live Wire hopped in the new black Lexus Coupe he'd just purchased and headed straight towards headquarters.

****

Wolf and Pastor Anderson walked down several blocks that were known for being drug infested and unsafe depending on what time of night it was. Pastor Anderson smiled as he saw kids riding their bikes, girls jumping rope, and several other kids playing without a care in the world. "I see you and The Spades have been doing a good job cleaning up these streets," Pastor Anderson pointed out. "This used to be one of the worst neighborhoods in the city."

"Used to be," Wolf smiled. He was proud and happy to see kids able to play freely and not have to worry about drug dealers standing on the corners at all times of the night or rival drug crews beefing over corners. Beside it was good for the kids to see positive instead of negative all the time. "I got a few more businesses I want to buy so I'm going to need you to find me some more people's names to put them in."

"I'll get on it first thing in the morning," Pastor Anderson said. So far The Spades had taken all the money they got from drug dealers and opened up ten businesses and even brought into two McDonald's. As Wolf and Pastor Anderson walked down the street, several woman and even a few men came up to Wolf and shook his hand and told him how much of a good job he was doing. They told him how they were loving the new community and how safe it now was for the kids.

Twenty minutes later Wolf and Pastor Anderson made it back to the front of the church. Wolf was in the middle of saying something, but paused when he saw Live Wire pull up in a brand new Lexus Coupe bumping Fabolous' new mix tape at its highest volume.

"Excuse me for a second," Wolf said walking over to meet Live Wire at the car. "What the fuck is this?" he asked nodding towards the Lexus.

"This that new Lexus thing," Live Wire smiled. "Shit fly right?"

"I pay you and the more experienced Spades members a little more than the others," Wolf said in a hushed voice. "But that don't mean to go out and buy one hundred thousand dollar cars and flash it in the other's faces."

"I'm a fly, smooth, flashy nigga! What you expect?" Live Wire said nonchalantly. "Don't I look like the type of nigga that's supposed to be riding around in a one hundred thousand dollar car?"

"You missing the point," Wolf pressed. "It's all about....."

"It's all about the community, I know," Live Wire said finishing off Wolf's sentence for him. "I'm all for taking care of the community, but I also feel as if we should be taking care of ourselves at the same time," he told Wolf. "I mean we out here risking our lives for the community so, it's only right that we reap the benefits too. Don't you agree?"

"We gonna have our time to shine, but right now the main priority is the community. We started this movement for a specific reason and that reason wasn't too we can ride around in luxury cars. Soon all of our businesses will be making us so much money that we ain't even going to know what to do with all of it; right?" He paused looking at Live Wire's eyes. "Just be patient; aight?"

"You got it," Live Wire said giving Wolf a pound. "Who's next on the hit list?" he asked curiously.

"Some clown on the streets called Prince," Wolf told him as he watched the big smile spread across Live Wire's face. "I know you and Prince had a little run in at the club a few weeks ago so I wasn't moving on this one until you got here," Wolf smiled. "You ready to do this?"

"I was born ready," Live Wire replied as him and Wolf entered the church to inform the rest of The Spades of who was next on the list.

Chapter 10
"The Prince"

Prince stepped foot out of the new Brooklyn Nets Arena with a light skinned chick that he barely knew by his side. The chick was beautiful and she wore a shiny black expensive looking weave that hung down to her ass. In front of Prince was a seven foot beast who was paid to hold him down at all times. The streets knew him as Tall Man. Tall Man wasn't a very talkative person, instead he was the type to let his hands and guns do the talking for him.

As Prince, Tall Man, and his lady friend strolled through the parking lot, Prince rubbed the scar on the side of his face where Live Wire had cut him at. Every time he looked in the mirror Prince thought about killing and torturing Live Wire. Prince didn't know too much about The Spades and quite frankly he didn't give a fuck about them. All he cared about was getting revenge on Live Wire for scarring him for life.

"Any word on this Live Wire fucker?" Prince asked. Pauleena was the Queen of the streets and he was the prince and him walking around with a scar on his face didn't sit well with him and it didn't look good. Everyone knew that the streets talked and the streets were waiting to see and hear what Prince's reply would be.

"Not yet," Tall Man answered scanning the parking lot for any signs of trouble. "I got all my peoples out on the streets looking for him as we speak."

"One of my home girls told me that she fucks with some guy named Live Wire. I don't know if this is the same Live Wire y'all talking about though," Prince's lady friend said.

"What's your friend's name?" Prince asked quickly.

"Rosey," his lady friend replied.

"When you get back to the house, make sure you text me her address," Prince told her. If this was in fact the same Live Wire, Prince planned on painting the streets red with is blood. As the trio strolled through the parking lot Prince spotted a filthy man with long dirty looking dread locks and a black trench coat on that came down to his calves leaning up against his Range Rover. Prince's hand instantly slid down to his waist and gripped the handle of his 9mm with the extended clip that held 32 rounds.

"Yo, my man!" Tall Man's voice boomed. "Step the fuck away from the vehicle!"

"Bobby Dread," the man said in a calm tone. "I need to have a word with the prince."

"Yo Dread what's good? You know me from somewhere or something?" Prince asked removing his 9mm from his waist band and letting it hang freely down by his waist. If the Jamaican said something stupid, Prince's mind was already made up. He was going to clap him.

"I work with Screw Face," Bobby Dead said. "I need to speak to Pauleena. It's an emergency," he said with urgency in his voice. Prince was the one who dropped off the work to everyone in the city for Pauleena so he knew exactly who Screw Face and The Crazy Jamaicans were.

"Pauleena's on vacation right now and won't be back until the end of the week," Prince told him. "She left me in charge until she returns. How can I help you?"

"My whole crew is dead," Bobby Dread said. "The Spades came and sneak attacked my whole crew....killed everyone!"

"Word?"

"Yes, a few of The Spades had me trapped in an alley and I fought my way out," Bobby Dread told Prince. "Two on one and I could of killed two of them with my bare hands if a third Spades member didn't show up."

"Don't worry; me and my peoples are on the job," Prince said with a smile on his face while sticking his 9mm back into his waist band. He loved a challenge and The Spades were definitely looking like a challenge.

"It's too many of them," Bobby Dread said. "We all going to have to come together if we plan to take The Spades out and I think you need to get Pauleena on the phone and let her know that she needs to come back from vacation early."

"Like I told you, Pauleena will be back at the end of the week," Prince said. "Until she returns, I'm in charge and I'll take care of this small problem."

Bobby Dread shook his head. "It may be over a thousand of them. Maybe even more... I know you the prince of the city, but these guys are for real. The Spades are not fucking around!"

"You scared of these niggas or something?" Prince spat tired of hearing about how strong and dangerous these Spades were.

"Me not scared of no man," Bobby Dread replied with a serious look on his face. "I just think we should all come together and even the odds out a little bit.... If y'all not with that plan then I'll just have to go hunting after The Spades alone," Bobby Dread said pulling his trench coat back revealing the A.K. 47 that he hid inside the long coat. "I'm not fucking around with these pussy boys!"

Prince and Tall Man busted out laughing at Bobby Dread. Prince loved how serious the Jamaican was about getting revenge on The Spades organization.

"Something funny?" Bobby Dread asked. He was getting more and more pissed off with each passing minute.

"Yeah, I don't have a problem with you teaming up with us until this matter is resolved," Prince told him. "First thing tomorrow we going hunting, but tonight we are parting," he announced. Prince's younger cousin was the hottest unsigned rapper in the streets right now and tonight he was performing at some club downtown that Prince had been hearing a lot of buzz about. "My cousin is performing tonight and we gotta go check him out."

"Who your cousin, Snow?" Tall man asked.
Prince nodded.

"Who he signing with?"

"He hasn't decided yet," Prince answered. "This supposed to be the biggest party in the city so you never know. Maybe we might bump into The Spades inside the club." A smirk danced on his lips as him, Tall Man, Bobby Dread, and his lady friend hopped in the Range Rover and headed downtown towards the club.

****

"I'm pulling in the club's parking lot now. Where y'all at?" Prince said into his iPhone as he looked out the tinted window searching for his cousin.

"Pull up to the back entrance and you can't miss us," Snow said ending the call. In front of the back entrance of the club Snow stood outside along with his thirty man entourage. Each man in his entourage had a felony and sold drugs to make a living. Not to mention, twenty-eight out of the thirty members of the entourage was strapped including Snow. Snow and his best friend Trouble built a team of drug dealers and guys who lived to sell drugs and make as much money as they could before Snow's mix tape set the streets on fire. Snow and Trouble's team called themselves M.O.E. which stood for "Money Over Everything" even though the music thing was about to take off, Snow still had a little work out on the streets.

"Yo, y'all coming in or not?" A big bald headed bouncer's voice boomed.

"Yo, hold on a second. We waiting for my cousin real quick," Snow told the bouncer. Every member in his entourage wore all black with the three letters M.O.E. written across their chest in white letters. Snow also wore all black and dark shades. Three iced out chains rested around his neck and on one of his wrist was a diamond studded iced out bracelet and on his other wrist was an expensive looking watch. In one of his hands, he held a bottle of Rosay and in his other hand he held a blunt. "There go Prince right there," Snow announced once he saw the Range Rover pull up.

Prince hopped out the Range with a smile on his face. He felt good when he saw his cousin's movement playing out before his eyes. He remembered fronting Snow and Trouble their first one hundred grams and now to see all the people wearing M.O.E. shirts made Prince feel good.

"I see you," Prince smiled as the two cousins gave each other dap followed by a hug. "I was just listening to your mix tape on the way over here... That shit fire!"

"Good looking," Snow smiled. "Thanks for coming out and partying with your baby cousin."

"Nigga, I'm twenty-nine and you only two years younger than me," Prince pointed out as he gave Trouble a pound. Trouble got his name because every time he came around trouble was always close behind.

"Come on, we gotta go inside before these faggots start bitching," Snow said leading his entourage inside the back entrance of the club. "Yo, y'all chill right here while I talk to this promoter nigga and make sure he got my bread together," Snow said disconnection himself from his entourage for a second so he could talk business with the club's promoter. While Prince and Tall Man laughed and got drunk with the M.O.E. crew Bobby Dread stood over to the side with a suspicious look on his face. He made sure he kept his trench coat opened slightly just in case something jumped off, he would be able to reach his A.K 47 with record breaking speed. Bobby Dread wasn't with all the flossing and showing off. He only had one thing on his mind and that was killing The Spades.

Twenty minutes later Snow and his entourage hit the stage. The beat dropped to a song he had called "Don't Play With Me." The crowd went crazy when they heard the beat drop. Snow walked on the stage with a microphone in one hand and a bottle of Rosay in the other. A few members from the entourage threw M.O. E. shirts out into the crowd.

Bobby Dread stood in the background on the stage watching the men before him act a fool. While the entire club recited Snow's lyrics Bobby Dread scanned the crowd hoping and praying that he saw anyone who he even thought belonged to The Spades organization so he could handle his business. He shook his head as he watched Prince toss stacks of money out into the crowd like his money grew on treas.

Snow walked to the edge of the stage and rapped his lyrics as he felt several female hands grabbing and pulling at his dick and jeans. Prince smiled like a proud parent as he watched his cousin work the crowd. As Snow stood on stage rapping, a cup full of ice flew up on the stage from out the crowd. Seconds later Snow and Prince laughed as they watched Snow's entourage jump down off the stage into the crowd and search for the ice thrower. Seconds later a scuffle broke out as Snow's entourage stomped the ice thrower out until several bouncers broke up the scuffle and tossed everyone involved out of the club.

****

After the performance several beautiful women made their way around to the parking lot in the back of the club where Snow and his entourage stood talking shit and getting drunk and high. As Snow sat talking to two bad bitches, loud gun fire erupted followed by screeching tires.

Prince ran and tackled Snow down to the ground as several women and men wearing M.O.E. shirts dropped down to the ground from bullet wounds. A black car coasted at a slow speed as two masked shooters hung out the window firing machine guns, shooting and killing any and everybody who stood around.

Once Bobby Dread heard the familiar sound of a semi-automatic weapon being fired, he was the first one to jump in the gun battle. Bobby Dread flapped his trench coat open and grabbed his A.K. all in one quick motion lie he had been practicing that move for years. Bobby Dread aimed his A.K. at the black car and squeezed the trigger lighting up the streets making it sound like a war zone. The A.K. bullets ripped through the car like it was wet paper. The car swerved then crashed into another parked car. Once the car came to a crashing stop, Prince, Trouble, Tall Man, and several M.O.E.

members opened fire on the black car. Out of nowhere a motorcycle zoomed past with a gun man hanging off the back of the bike firing an Uzi followed by a black van. The van came to a screeching halt, the side door slide open, and out jumped five Spades all firing at anything moving.

Prince returned fire as him and Snow back peddled to his Range Rover. Prince's main concern was getting Snow out of harm's way. His younger cousin had a future ahead of him and he'd never be able to forgive himself if Snow got hurt behind sore bullshit he was caught up in the middle of. Tall Man covered Prince while Prince and Snow hopped in the Range Rover and pulled off. Tall Man, Bobby Dread, Trouble, and the rest of Snow's entourage continued to shoot it out with The Spades until the loud sounds of sirens could be heard.

Immediately both crews retreated back to their vehicles and all that could be heard was the sound of tires burning rubber and a motorcycle gunning its engine. The only thing that was left behind was over two hundred empty shell cases left on the concrete.

Chapter 11
"The Bahamas"

Pauleena laid in her beach chair on the beach with a red two piece bikini on and a pair of oversized expensive sunglasses that were protecting her eyes from the sun while she got her tan on. Pauleena had been out in the Bahamas for a month and a half now and was enjoying her much needed vacation. She needed a break from all the drama and chaos that her way of living caused. While on vacation Pauleena left her iPhone powered off in her hotel suite. She knew Prince was more than capable of running things in her absence until she returned. Pauleena's body as well as her mind needed the vacation more than anything, but with each passing day Pauleena was getting more and more home sick. Malcolm and several other Muslim body guards stood on the beach burning up in their all black suits. Their job was to protect Pauleena even if it meant losing their own lives and each man took their job serious.

Pauleena's peace was disturbed when she heard a familiar voice calling her name. Pauleena sat up and saw Malcolm and her team of security about to ball a Spanish man up and throw him in the trash can literally. All Malcolm was waiting for was the word form Pauleena.

Pauleena removed her sunglasses from her face so she could get a better look at the Spanish man. "Psycho?"

"Yo, wassup baby?" The Spanish man smiled. "I know that was you over here," he said looking at Pauleena form head to toe. "A body like that is one I'll never be able to forget."

"He's cool," Pauleena called out to Malcolm as he watched her security part like the Red Sea and let Psycho pass. Psycho walked up and hugged Pauleena tightly as his hands slid down and palmed Pauleena's plump round firm ass. When Malcolm saw the Spanish man's hands slip down to Pauleena's ass, he looked as if he wanted to detach the man's head from his body. No Pauleena wasn't his woman, but Malcolm just felt like it was his job to protect her to the fullest like in a father figure sort of way.

Pauleena quickly slapped Psycho's hands away and stepped back a few inches. "What you doing out in the Bahamas?" She asked curiously. The last time she saw Psycho was almost five years ago when she entered their home and caught him in the bed with another woman. Without thinking twice, Pauleena shot the woman dead in cold blood. Over the years Pauleena did her best to stay away from Psycho so she wouldn't kill him. Ever since their relationship fell apart, Pauleena stayed away from relationships as well. Psycho was a killer. He killed people for a living... Contact killing was his specialty and it was something he enjoyed doing.

"I came out here to make sure that you were okay," Psycho told her. "I heard that you might have been in danger so I flew out to New York to try and find you, but after twisting a few arms I was told you were out here on vacation so I came out here to see for myself that you were okay."

"Why wouldn't I be ok?" Pauleena said not understanding what Psycho was talking about. She hadn't seen him in over five years and now he just popped up out the blue looking worried and asking her if she was okay.

"I heard about some new group who calls themselves The Spades out in New York trying to clean up the streets by killing all the drug dealers," Psycho said. "And I just wanted to make sure you wasn't caught up in the middle of that shit."

"The Spades?" Pauleena repeated with a dumb founded look on her face. All of this was new to her. For the past month and a half she had cut off all communication with the underworld and needed to be updates.

"Ummm, You haven't been in contact with your peoples back in New York?" Psycho asked with a raised brow.

"Nah," Pauleena answered. "Put me on," she said giving Psycho her undivided attention.

"I was out in Florida when I kept on hearing about all of these drug dealers being killed out in New York on the news. Knowing that you were now operating out of New York, I did my research and found out that a large organization call The Spades have been out killing drug dealers everyday for the past month and a half, talking about they trying to clean up the community..... Shit crazy," Psycho shook his head. "A bunch of jail niggas out on some Robin Hood shit!"

"Word?" Pauleena smirked as he processed the information that Psycho had just given her. "So all this is going on in New York right now?"

Psycho nodded. "That's why as soon as I heard about what was going on, I flew straight out to New York."

"Flew straight out to New York for what?"

"I had to make sure nobody was fucking with my baby!"

"I'm not your baby," Pauleena quickly corrected him.

"You gone always be my baby," Psycho said trying to sneak a kiss, but Pauleena quickly jerked her head back before their lips got a chance to connect.

"I appreciate you coming all the way out here to make sure I was okay, but I'm a big girl and more than capable of taking care of myself and handling my business," Pauleena stated in a matter of fact tone. The truth was that she still loved Psycho, but hated him at the same time for what he did to her and for abusing her trust.

"I'm coming back to New York with you," Psycho announced. "At least until this Spades situation is taken care of... I'm not taking no for an answer. I wouldn't be able to live with myself if something happened to you."

Pauleena, Psycho, and her team of security headed to her suite. A group or an organization out to fuck with her money didn't sit well with Pauleena. After all the shit she had to go through to keep her spot, if The Spades thought for one second that Pauleena was going to fold under pressure then they were in for a rude awakening.

Pauleena reached her suite and turned and faced Malcolm. "Let me speak to Psycho alone for a second."

Malcolm nodded as he watched Pauleena and Psycho enter her room and close the door behind them. Malcolm didn't trust Psycho nor did he feel comfortable leaving Pauleena alone in a room with the stranger, but Pauleena was the boss and what she says goes.

Once Pauleena entered the room, she walked straight over to her desk and powered up her iPhone and iPad. She searched the web reading clips about the recent killings of several drug dealers and drug crews. Pauleena became even more upset as she listened to all the different voicemails that were left on her phone complaining about The Spades.

"I did my homework on The Spades and they seem to be the real deal," Psycho said helping himself to a drink. "I know you don't really be liking help and be wanting to do things on our own, but I think you might need as much help as you can get on this one."

"I'll be fine," Pauleena said disappearing inside the bathroom and seconds later the sound of the shower could be heard. A million thoughts ran through Pauleena's mind as the hot water and strong pressure massaged her body. If it wasn't one thing, it was another. All Pauleena wanted to do was make money and enjoy the fruits of her labor, but it seemed like every time Pauleena was trying to chill, some dumb shit presented itself and caused her to have to get on her bullshit. Pauleena let the shower water rinse the soap off of her body when she heard the bathroom door open and then close. Then suddenly the shower curtain was snatched open and Psycho stood on the other side of the curtain butt naked holding his erection in his hand. Before Pauleena got a chance to protest, Psycho grabbed the back of her head and kissed her. His kiss was rough, sloppy, loud, and filled with old emotions. Psycho roughly spun Pauleena around forcing her to bend over and hold the wall in the shower as water splashed and ricocheted off of her sexy flawless body.

Psycho bent down and sucked on Pauleena's clit from the back. He firmly gripped Pauleena's thighs and licked away at her wetness. Pauleena's moans came from a place deep inside her soul. It had been five years since she had been touched by a man and her body couldn't take it as she moaned and came at the same time.

"Oh yes baby! Yes, eat this pussy," Pauleena moaned loudly while gyrating her hips and grinding her wet pussy even further onto Psycho's tongue. Once Psycho got done eating her pussy, he spread Pauleena's ass cheeks apart and slowly licked her ass crack like it was an envelope. As Psycho licked Pauleeena's ass clean, he moaned loudly like he was the one getting pleased instead of her. He was moaning like her ass was the most delicious thing he had ever tasted in his entire life. He was moaning like he had the devil in him as he forced Pauleena to come for him again.

Once he was done with that, Psycho stood up and rubbed his erection up and down Pauleena's wetness. Then he went inside her so hard that it made her scoot away a little. Psycho firmly grabbed Pauleena's waist to keep her from running as he long dicked her, talked shit, and slapped her ass all at the same time. Pauleena made curt sounds like mmm... and ahhh... then she came violently. Psycho stayed behind her. He dipped to get a good angle. He had Pauleena's breast flat against the wall while he was thrusting deep, steady, and strong strokes in and out of Pauleena. All you could hear was wet skin slapping against wet skin as the two shared moans until Psycho quickly pulled out and let his semen swirl down the drain.

Once the love session was over, Pauleena turned and hugged Psycho tightly while resting her head on his shoulders. "I missed you so much," she admitted.

"I missed you too baby," Psycho said scooping Pauleena up in his arms like she was a baby. He carried her out of the bathroom and gently laid her down on the bed. "I love you Pauleena," Psycho said looking in Pauleena's eyes. "Losing you was the worst thing that I ever did in my life and

I had five long years to realize that without you, I'm not complete!"

"How am I supposed to trust you?" Pauleena asked seriously. "I did everything in my power to keep you happy and that still wasn't enough... What's going to be different this time around?"

"I can show you better than I can tell you," Psycho countered sincerely with his words coming straight from his heart. "After all the shit we been through, I think we both deserve a second chance at love."

Pauleena took a few seconds to take in what Psycho was saying before she replied. "I don't know about all that. Right now I'm only thinking about getting back to New York and getting the streets back in order... I'll deal with you later."

Before Pauleena and Psycho got dressed and headed to the airport, they got it in one more time for old time sake.

Chapter 12
"Shots Fired"

Wolf sat at the table in the soul food restaurant that he owned. He wanted to check out the spot to see how business was doing so he invited Ivy to join him for dinner at his new restaurant. Lately Wolf and Ivy had been spending a lot of time together. Wolf even brought a new house in a low key location and asked Ivy to move in with him. After explaining to Ivy what The Spades were all about and represented, Ivy wanted to join the organization. There were already a few female Spades members so Wolf told her that he would get back to her with his decision about joining the organization but she didn't hesitate to move in with him.

"So you came up with this whole Spades idea while you were in jail?" Ivy asked shoveling a fork full of mac-n-cheese in her mouth. Ivy loved Wolf dearly and wanted to spend as much time as she possibly could with him, but she knew he was a busy man and she was just happy to be around him whenever he had time.

"Yeah," Wolf smiled. "I was in there for long enough so I had to come up with some type of plan."

"I love your mind," Ivy told Wolf. "I think you are brilliant."

"You're good for the ego, you know that," Wolf said looking down at his phone. He had just received a text message from Live Wire. "I have to make a quick run over to Live Wire's house to pick up something. You feel like riding with me or you just want to meet me back at the house?"

Ivy gave Wolf a look that said you gotta be kidding me. "Of course I want to go with you." Ivy knew if she let Wolf out of her sight that she wouldn't see him again for at least a day or two; that's how busy The Spades kept him.

Wolf tossed a few bills down on the table as him and Ivy stood up to leave.

"You know I love you right?" Ivy said sliding in for a kiss. As the two kissed, Ivy rubbed Wolf's back and felt that he was wearing a bullet proof vest. "Is everything alright?" She asked with her face full of concern.

"I love you too," Wolf replied ignoring her last question as the two made their exit. Wolf zoomed out of the parking lot and headed to Live Wire's crib. The dress that Ivy wore had Wolf ready to do some things so he planned on seeing Live Wire for a few and then heading back home so the two could get their romance on.

Wolf pulled up in front of Live Wire's apartment and found a parking spot. Wolf angled the car perfectly as he began the process of parallel parking. Wolf got the tail of his car into the parking spot when he heard a car pull up to a screeching halt right next to him. Wolf glanced out of his window and saw the window of a black car rolled down and Prince holding a .45 in his hand.

"OH SHIT!" Wolf yelled as he ducked down as seven loud shots blasted off in a rapid succession. BOOM! BOOM! BOOM! BOOM! BOOM! BOOM! BOOM! Wolf quickly covered Ivy with his body as broken glass rained down on top of them. Wolf reached over and opened up the passenger door as he felt three powerful bullets rip into the back of his vest causing him and Ivy to spill out the passenger door down onto the concrete.

Once Wolf and Ivy was down on the ground, Tall Man put the pedal to the metal as Prince hung half way out the window and shot out all the windows in the front of Live Wire's apartment before the black car disappeared down the block and around the corner.

Once Wolf was sure that the gun men were gone, he rolled off of Ivy who he noticed was bleeding. "Where you hit at?" Wolf asked wincing in pain. His back was on fire. It felt like he had been tossed down several flights of stairs.

"My leg," Ivy cried with her eyes closed. The pain was so intense that she just knew she was going to die right there on the curb.

Seconds later, Live Wire came running outside shirtless with a gun in each hand. "Yo, what happened?" He asked with his voice full of panic and concern.

"Call an ambulance," Wolf said squirming around on the concrete in obvious pain. Live Wire pulled out his phone and called for an ambulance then rudely stepped over Ivy and tended to Wolf's wounds. He lifted up Wolf's shirt and noticed the vest. "Thank God for this vest," he said as he helped Wolf sit up and remove the vest. By now Rosey had made her way outside.

"Oh my God," she screamed covering her mouth with her hand.

"Here take this shit in the house!" Live Wire yelled handing Rosey Wolf's bullet filled vest and his two guns.

"Hold up," Wolf said in pain. He reached into his waistband and removed his 9mm and held it out. Rosey took the gun from Wolf's hand and then disappeared back inside the apartment.

Live Wire slowly helped Wolf up to his feet. He paid Ivy no mind. His main concern was making sure Wolf was okay. "Did you see who the shooter was?"

"Prince," Wolf announced. "It was Prince."

"Don't worry, I'll take care of it," Live Wire promised as the ambulance and several police cars showed up making a noisy arrival.

"They wasn't coming for me. They were here for you!" Wolf said doing his best to stand straight up so the cops or paramedics wouldn't know he was involved in the shooting.

"Here for me?" Live Wire said confused. "But how did they…"

"Rosey," Wolf said cutting Live Wire off as the paramedics rushed to Ivy's aid. Rosey was the only one who knew about his whereabouts besides Wolf.

"Don't worry, I'll take care of it," Live Wire said with a smirk. He was just starting to like Rosey, but she betrayed him and The Spades. Whether it was on purpose or not, it didn't matter to Live Wire. He was a team player. Wolf gave the call so she had to go and no questions asked.

"I'mma get up with you in the morning," Live Wire yelled as he watched Wolf take his time stepping up on the back of the ambulance trying to down play the amount of pain he was really in. Once the ambulance took off, Live Wire turned and headed back inside.

Live Wire stepped inside the apartment and saw Rosey step out the bathroom butt naked rushing towards the bedroom. "Where you going?" he asked curiously.

"I'm going to the hospital with you to make sure your friend and his girl are alright... Don't leave without me. I'll be ready in a second." Rosey disappeared inside the bedroom. Right then and there, Live Wire knew that Rosey didn't give up his whereabouts, at least not knowingly that is. But whether it was on purpose or not, her mistake had caused Wolf and his girlfriend to get shot and for that reason alone, Rosey had to be dealt with. Live Wire grabbed his .45 off the coffee table and hid it behind his back as he entered the bedroom. He stepped inside the bedroom and saw Rosey quickly getting dressed.

"What is this world coming to?" Rosey said. "I can't believe somebody would just let all off all of them shots in front of your crib like that."

"I know that shit crazy, right?" Live Wire said as he slowly snuck up behind Rosey. "Niggas be wilding around here, right?"

"You ain't never lied. I was just thinking..."
Live Wire swiftly grabbed the lamp off the dresser and busted Rosey over the top of her head with it. He watched as she fell awkwardly down to the floor as blood leaked from a gash left from the lamp. Rosey looked up from the floor and saw Live Wire aiming the barrel of a big gun in her face. "Baby?" Rosey whispered. "What are you doing?" She asked holding her bloody head.

"You told them motherfuckers where to find me," Live Wire accused.

"Never baby," Rosey said as tears began to roll down her cheeks. "I would never give you up to anybody."

Live Wire wanted to believe her, but her story just wasn't adding up. None of it made sense to him. "Stop lying!"

"Baby," Rosey said looking up in Live Wire's eyes. "I would never do anything to hurt you.... Never.... I love you.... And, I'm....." She paused for a second. "I'm pregnant!"

Live Wire snatched a pillow from off the bed and pressed it over Rosey's face and pressed the barrel of his .45 into the pillow. He held the pillow firmly as Rosey struggled and fought for her life.

Live Wire fired a shot into the pillow and ended Rosey's struggle once and for all. Live Wire quickly got dressed, grabbed anything that could link him to the apartment, and exited the apartment leaving Rosey's body behind to be found by the police. He felt a little bad about what he had just done, but he told himself that he did what he had to do. Live Wire hopped in his Lexus and headed to the nearest strip club. Right now he needed some attention; the type of attention that only a stripper could give.

Chapter 13
"Pimping Ain't Easy"

Two days later Wolf sat down in the basement of the church getting his thoughts together. He sat in the basement with his new 24/7 bodyguard. His bodyguard was a big former nightclub bouncer who went by the name of The Big Show. The Spades came to the conclusion that Wolf needed a bodyguard around to protect him at all times. The Spades were making so much noise out in the streets that Wolf knew sooner or later that the police or worse, the F.E.D.S. would be knocking at their front door. Wolf still felt sharp pains in his back from the bullets that had exploded in the back of his vest the other night.

"I heard Pauleena is back in town," The Big Show said looking at Wolf.

"Word?"

"Yeah, heard her team had a big welcome back party for her last night," The Big Show added. Wolf didn't reply. He had a lot on his plate at the moment. Not to mention, his girlfriend was still laid up in the hospital. Several Spades members were still out on the streets taking down low and mid-level hustlers and organizations every day. The Spades had so much money that Wolf was running out of places to stash the money that they took from all of the street dealers.

"You think we should go after Pauleena before she gets back in her comfort zone?" The Big Show asked.

"Nah, not yet," Wolf replied. "But she is definitely on the hit list… When her name comes up, it's on."

The Big Show was about to reply, but quickly pulled his Tech-9 from its holster and spun around with the swiftness of a cat when he heard the basement door open.

"Take it easy," Dice said holding his hands up in surrender. "It's just me."

"He's cool," Wolf said. The Big Show slowly lowered his weapon. The first thing Dice noticed when he stepped foot in the basement was that Wolf was wearing a bullet proof vest.

"Dice, what's up? How can I help you?" Wolf asked motioning with his hand for Dice to have a seat.

"I need a favor," Dice said coming straight out with it. "I'm sorry to bother you at a time like this. I heard about what happened to you the other night."

"That shit wasn't about Franks," Wolf said brushing the attempt on his life off as if it was no big deal. "Now about this favor you need?"

"Well you were supposed to get back to me about the situation concerning my son," Dice said. "I still haven't seen him since I've been home," he paused. "My son's mother is with this nasty pimp who won't let her let me see my son. Now I know we down the hit list, but is there any way we can push this motherfucker Champagne's name up on the list... This is an emergency!"

"I forgot all about that," Wolf admitted. "Why didn't you remind me?"

"I know you a busy man and all that."

"I don't give a fuck how busy I am... Family comes first," Wolf told him. "This pimp Champagne, do you have an address for him?"

Dice reached down in his pocket and handed Wolf a piece of paper with an address on it.

Wolf took the paper and slid it down in his pocket. "Let me do this interview for YouTube real quick to let the world know what The Spades are all about," he said as The Big Show pulled out his iPhone and gave Wolf a head nod signaling that he was recording.

"Hello world," Wolf began sitting behind an oak desk wearing his usual all black.

"My name is Wolf and I am a representative for The Spades," he paused and looked directly in the camera. "The Spades are an organization out to protect and serve the community... If you don' know who we are you will real soon. Our main objective is to clean up these streets so our children can have a better place to live and grow up... We are against drugs and anything negative in the community," Wolf said. "Anyone interested in joining The Spades or interested in helping out the community, you can get in touch with me on my twitter page. I just set it up. Hit me up at @TheRealWolf," Wolf said giving the camera a salute before The Big Show stopped recording.

"How long will it take to upload that video on YouTube?" Wolf asked as he noticed Live Wire enter the basement smelling like a mixture of weed and a woman's perfume.

"It will be available for the world to see in less than three minutes," The Big Show replied with a smile.

"What's shaking down here?" Live Wire asked giving each man dap.

"We about to go take care of some fake pimp in a minute," Wolf told him. "But what's up with you coming through drunk, smelling like weed, and being seen out with a different woman every night?"

"What you mean?" Live Wire shrugged. "I'm living my life. I'm young, handsome, and the waviest nigga out right now. I'm supposed to have a different woman every night."

"You are one of the leaders of The Spades and you should be leading by example, don't you think?" Wolf asked with a raised brow. He didn't understand why Live Wire had to be on front street all the time and so flamboyant about everything he did or was involved in.

"Loosen up," Live Wire huffed removing his .45 from his waistband and checking the magazine, making sure it was fully loaded. "I'm just having fun and enjoying myself... What's the big deal?"

Wolf decided to leave the conversation at that. He knew talking to Live Wire sometimes was a waist of breath, time, and energy. So, like it or not, that was his partner.

"What's this pimp's handle?" Live Wire asked as him, Wolf, Dice, and The Big Show piled into a black van.

"Champagne," Dice answered with hatred in his eyes. He had no idea how this night was going to turn out, but the one thing he knew was, he was damn sure about to find out.

"Oh word?" Live Wire asked with a smile. "I heard that nigga stay with some bad bitches." For the rest of the ride all four men rode in complete silence while Live Wire sat in the back of the van on his cell phone having phone sex with one of his many woman. All Wolf could do was shake his head as he had no other choice but to hear Live Wire's conversation.

"Word? That pussy wet right now?" Live Wire said in a smooth voice into the phone.

"Yeah, you got my dick mad hard right now; word," Live Wire licked his lips. "Tell me how bad you wanna suck this dick.... Mmm.... Let me hear you suck on it." Then Live Wire put his phone on speaker phone so the entire van could hear the woman on the other line making loud sucking noises with her mouth.

"Ignorant nigga," Dice mumbled under his breath as he and everyone else in the van was forced to listen to Live Wire and his lady friend have phone sex.

Twenty minutes later, The Spades black van pulled up in front of a nice sized house. Each man filed out the van one after another and walked straight up to the door. The Big Show took a step back and came forward with a hard strong kick. It took three kicks before the front door broke off the hinges.

****

Tonya sat on her hands and knees still chained to the radiator for talking to Dice instead of getting that money. Champagne had been treating her like an animal for the past week and a half. This was a side of Champagne that Tonya had never seen before. Usually he was nice to her. In the beginning Champagne had promised Tonya the world. Tonya's dream of riding off in the sunset with Champagne was quickly turning into a nightmare. As Tonya sat tied to the radiator like a dog waiting for its owner to return out of a store, she could hear Champagne and the rest of his hoes laughing and enjoying themselves. Tonya smelled the smell of McDonald's floating through the air. The smell reminded her that she hadn't eaten all day. "Daddy!" She called out. She had to call Champagne at least ten times before he finally showed up.

"What you want bitch?" Champagne said as if Tonya calling his name was annoying him.

"Daddy, I'm hungry."

"Why the fuck should I let you eat? Huh?" Champagne asked looking down at Tonya like she was garbage.

"I know I've been a bad girl Daddy," Tonya said. "But I promise if you give me another chance to make things right, I swear you won't have another problem out of me again…. I don't want to be in the pit anymore."

"You bitches gotta get out there and make a difference…… And the only way you bitches gone make a difference is if you make a move," Champagne paused. "So you don't make a move if it ain't gone make a difference…. Understand!"

"Yes Daddy," Tonya nodded her head. When Champagne began talking that pimp talk for some reason it turned Tonya on. Tonya watched as Champagne walked over to his cat named Fluffy.

"Move Fluffy," Champagne shooed the cat away as he bent down and picked up Fluffy's bowl. He dumped whatever food that was inside the bowl into the garbage, then sat the bowl down in front of Tonya not even bothering to rinse the bowl out. "Here bitch!" Champagne grabbed a grease stained McDonald's bag from off the counter and filled the bowl with a few chicken nuggets and some fries. "Eat up," Champagne said then returned to the living room to join the rest of his hoes.

At that moment Tonya felt like shit, like a real loser. In her heart she knew she deserved better, but her problem was that she didn't know how to get better and didn't believe she was really worth better. Not having any other options, Tonya buried her face in the cat bowl and began eating her food without using her hands out of fear of getting into even more trouble. Just as Tonya finished her food, she noticed Sparkle walk up butt naked with her bright read pedicured toes stopping directly in front of the cat bowl.

"Did you eat all of your food like a good girl?" Sparkle asked with an evil smirk plastered across her face.

"I'm not in the mood right now," Tonya said shooting Sparkle an evil look. "Don't you got some dick to go suck or something?"

Sparkle chuckled. "I just came by to make sure you got something to drink." She bent down and filled the cat bowl with Sprite. "Drink up," she said as she turned to walk away. Sparkle took two steps and then stopped and turned back around like she left something behind. "Oh and by the way I think I will take your advice and go suck some dick," she smiled. "While you drinking out of a cat bowl like an animal, I'll be in the bedroom sucking MY daddy's dick.... Have a nice day; you raggedy ass bitch!" Sparkle laughed as she walked out of the kitchen and disappeared inside the living room. Tonya stared a hole in Sparkle's back as her big perfect fake ass bounced and jiggled with each step she took.

"I can't stand that bitch," Tonya mumbled looking down at the Sprite that sat in the cat bowl with little pieces of French fries, chicken nugget crumbs, and a piece of hair or two floating around in the Sprite. Just as Tonya was about to take a sip out of the bowl she heard three loud booming noises followed by the front door crashing open. Dice was the first one in the house and immediately their eyes locked. Dice was the last person Tonya wanted to see her like this; tied to a radiator with a cat bowl in front of her. Dice quickly kneeled down and untied Tonya's leash from the radiator while Wolf, Live Wire, and The Big Show entered the living room.

"Fuck is you niggas?" Champagne asked dryly. He sat on the leather sofa with his arms draped around two women; one white and the other Spanish.

"The Spades," Wolf informed him. "I'm here to ask that you stop brainwashing, misleading, and using our women for your own selfish gain and profit," Wolf told him. "If you need work, we have several different jobs for you to choose from. We could use a smart guy like you on our team. Instead of doing evil, why don't you try doing some good for once in your life?"

Champagne and all of his hoes busted out laughing like they had just heard the funniest joke in the world. "Thanks for the offer, but you can take your jobs and stick them up your ass!"

Before Wolf could reply he saw two of Champagne's hoes reaching. He quickly raised his arm and put a bullet in the first woman's head. Before he could train his 9mm on the second gun woman, several bullets ripped through her body leaving her body riddled with bullets as smoke eased out of her body at the spot where the bullet holes were.

Wolf then turned his gun on Champagne. "You've been warned!"

"No, wait!"

Wolf turned around and saw Tonya standing there naked. Dice stood behind her with a hand on her shoulder.

"I want to kill him," Tonya volunteered walking up to Wolf with her hand held out. Wolf paused for a second then sat that 9mm in the palm of her hand. Tonya stood directly in front of Champagne and aimed the hammer at his forehead.

"Bitch!" Champagne growled. "Give me that gun right now before I put my foot so far up your ass that you'll be burping shoe polish!"

Tonya remained silent with the 9mm still aimed at Champagne's head. The more she heard Champagne talk, the more she hated him.

"Listen here bitch," Champagne smiled. "You got three seconds to give me that gun or else…"

POW! POW! POW! POW! POW! POW!

Tonya kept firing until she was sure that the pimp named Champagne was dead. She felt like a bird had let her out of her cage as she looked at Champagne slumped over on the couch. Wolf slowly eased the gun out of Tonya's hand, turned and looked at Dice. "Get something to cover her up with and put her in the van."

Once Tonya was out of the house, Live Wire went down the line and fired a bullet in each one of Champagne's hoes head. Live Wire stopped when he reached the last hoe. She didn't beg for her life like the rest of the women did nor did her eyes show any hints of fear. Live Wire looked at the Nicki Minaj look alike up and down. His eyes resting on her big huge horse ass that made her look like she was sitting on a booster seat. "What's your name?"

"Sparkle," she answered rolling her eyes.

"Go get dressed," Live Wire said with a smirk. "You coming with me," he said as he watched Sparkle's fat ass disappear in the bedroom.

"What the fuck you doing?" Wolf lightly scolded. "You know the rules. No witnesses!"

"Did you see that ass?" Live Wire said looking at Wolf like he was crazy. "What you expect me to let all that ass go to waste?"

The Big Show shook his head with a disgusted look on his face. He was looking at Wolf for the word. Before Wolf could reply, Sparkle returned from the bedroom wearing a white wife beater, a pair of white Good2Go leggings with the red writing, and a pair of flip flops. Her hair was pulled back in a loose ponytail and he bang stopped right above her eyebrows. In her hand she held a Louis Vuitton duffle bag.

Wolf stuck his 9mm back into his waistband. "She's your problem," he said as him and The Big Show exited the house leaving Live Wire and Sparkle alone in the house full of dead bodies.

"Are you going to kill me?" Sparkle asked.

"Nah," Live Wire answered quickly. "I'm about to give you the opportunity of a life time."

"And that is?" Sparkle asked curiously.

"I'm about to let you see what it's like to be with a real boss," Live Wire told her. "That nigga Live Wire about to be running this whole shit in a minute," he said speaking of himself in the third person.

Sparkle couldn't front, she was definitely feeling Live Wire's confidence and not to mention his swag was on a thousand. "No you about to see what it's like to be with a real boss bitch," Sparkle said applying gloss to her sexy lips. Live Wire smiled. "Come on, we outta here."

****

"Thank you so much. I appreciate everything you've done for me and my family," Dice said shaking Wolf's hand.

"Don't mention it! You family," Wolf said. "Now go get her inside and get up with me tomorrow."

"You already know." Dice smiled as he watched the black van pull off. Dice turned around and saw Tonya standing there wearing a T-shirt that barely covered her ass and nothing else. Dice looked down and saw that her bare feet were filthy. "Come on," he said sticking his key in the front door and entering his nice four bedroom house.

"Wow," Tonya said when she stepped foot inside of Dice's house. He had an average size house, but it was the nicest house that Tonya had been inside of her entire life. "You live here alone?" She asked her voice full of doubt.

"Yeah," Dice replied dryly. He wasn't really in the mood for talking right now. "Yo, it's three bathrooms in here. Pick one and go get yourself cleaned up." Dice walked into the kitchen and poured himself a strong drink as he watched Tonya slowly make her way upstairs searching for a bathroom. Honestly Dice didn't want Tonya in his house, but he figured he'd let her stay here for the night. Then first thing in the morning he would drop her off at the nearest shelter. During the ride to Dice's house, Tonya gave Wolf Champagne's mother's address and Wolf promised to deliver Little Dice to the house first thing in the morning and that's all Dice cared about. Tonya wasn't his problem and after the way she had treated him and denied him the right to see and spend time with his son, he couldn't wait to shit on Tonya. He wanted to let her see how it felt to be shitted on and treated like trash. Ever since Dice started dealing with Wolf and The Spades, he saw his life do a 360 right before his eyes. Dice never had money, cars, and a house until he started dealing with The Spades and he never planned on going back to the way he used to live; no matter what. Fifteen minutes later Tonya came strutting down the stairs butt naked.

"Yo, wait right there," Dice said stopping her half way at the top of the stairs. "Follow me," he said leading Tonya to his bedroom where he gave her a pair of sweatpants and a wife beater to put on.

Tonya quickly threw on the sweats and wife beater and stopped Dice before he could leave the bedroom. "Can I talk to you for a second?" Tonya looked like a totally different woman without her makeup on her face and fancy designer clothes on her back.

"We don't got shit to talk about," Dice said with anger in his tone. If looks could kill, Tonya's neck would have been ripped off her shoulders.

"Can you please just hear me out? Please?" Tonya pleaded with tears building up in her eyes.

"Ohhhhh," Dice said excitedly. "You not charging me to talk to you tonight?" He asked sarcastically.

"Dice, I'm sorry!"

"You wanna know what's so crazy," Dice said. "That if the tables were reversed, I would of never treated you the way you treated me."

Tonya slammed the bedroom door and stood in front of it so Dice couldn't leave the room. "Dice, I'm sorry. Champagne had me brainwashed and he held my son hostage to make sure I didn't stray away from him and continued to do whatever he asked me to do," she told Dice.

"Sounds like a personal problem to me," Dice said coldly.

"Dice I don't have nothing and nowhere to go," Tonya cried. "You have to help me. I don't have nobody else."

"And why the fuck should I help you?" Dice growled. "Give me one good reason why I should help you... One good reason?"

Tonya stood quiet for at least a minute or two with a stupid look on her face. Dice was right; she couldn't give him one good reason why he should help her. Especially after how mean and nasty she was to him when all he was trying to do was see and spend time with his son.

"That's what I thought!" Dice shook his head. "You outta here first thing in the morning." Dice pushed Tonya from out front of the door and headed downstairs leaving Tonya upstairs in the bedroom crying her eyes out.

Chapter 14
"Money Don't Sleep"

Snow sat in the back of his Hummer alongside Trouble while two members from his M.O.E. entourage sat up front as the Hummer cruised the highway. Snow sipped a strong drink as him and his crew bobbed their heads to a new instrumental beat that he had just purchased from a super producer. Snow bobbed his head, but his mind was still on the attempted hit on his life. He didn't know much about The Spades, but when and wherever he bumped into one of them at, it was sure that the end results would be flooded all over the internet and all the gossip sites. The word on the streets was, Snow and his M.O.E. crew had beef with The Spades and for his image and street credibility to stay intact; he had to handle his business on-site whenever he saw anyone who represented The Spades. Snow may have been a rapper now, be he still had ties in the streets. Unlike a lot of rappers out, Snow really lived his raps. He really sold drugs. He really spent nights in the trap. He really had shoot outs in the streets in broad day light and not only that, his cousin was Prince.

"You gone have to go crazy on this beat," Trouble said passing Snow the blunt.

Snow bobbed his head and accepted the blunt. "I'mma kill it," he said confidently, then took a long drag from the blunt. Right now Snow was the hottest rapper out in the streets and he knew it. Record labels were having bidding wars over who would sign the rapper the streets called Snow. Snow was making so much money from doing shows from the tracks from his mix tape that he had the streets and clubs going crazy so he didn't rush into signing anything. He decided he wanted to wait and see which label came with the best offer.

"You fuck with this Terminator nigga like that?" Trouble asked.

"Nah," Snow answered quickly. "This gone be my first time meeting him tonight," he said as the Hummer pulled into the Madison Square Garden garage.

"So what happen? His people just reached out to you and offered you money to escort him out to the right tonight?" Trouble asked curiously. Snow was his right hand man and felt that it was his job to protect Snow at all times.

"Basically," Snow answered. "$50,000.00 not to mention all the publicity I'm going to get from this shit. Millions of people gone be watching this fight tonight." Snow smiled as him and is crew hopped out the Hummer and walked towards the V.I.P. entrance. Each man wore a M.O.E. shirt with major ice on their necks. Their crew stood for "Money Over Everything" and when you saw Snow, he looked like money.

"V.I.P. passes?" A black police asked blocking the entrance. Snow and his entourage pulled out their passes and presented them to the police officer. "Listen up," the police officer said in a stern tone. "I know you rappers like to carry guns and risk your freedom to prove absolutely nothing," he said looking directly at Snow. "But there are no weapons allowed pass this door so if y'all packing, I suggest that y'all go stash y'all heat in the car. The only people that are allowed to carry guns is your security and he has to provide a license to carry a firearm."

"Snow don't do security," Snow said cockily as him and his crew headed back to the Hummer and stashed all of their weapons. Snow and his entourage returned back towards the entrance, got patted down, and walked through a metal detector. Then they were finally allowed to enter the arena. A petite blond hair woman escorted Snow and the M.O.E. crew down towards The Terminator's dressing room. As Snow walked through the arena he noticed the weird and funny looks he received from the few white people he passed. It was if they hated to see a black man with more or as much money as them and all that did was make Snow want to floss even more just to make them even madder.

After a three minute walk, Snow and his entourage reached a door that said "The Terminator" in big bold letters. In front of the door stood a 6'9 two hundred and sixty pound bald headed security guard.

Once Snow reached the front of the dressing room, he could hear Drake's song "Crew Love" blasting from inside the dressing room.

"Snow, what up? The Terminator is expecting you." The security guard gave Snow dap like him and Snow were child hood friends or something.

Snow stepped foot in the dressing room and immediately a smile formed across his face. Music was blasting and over in the corner five beautiful women sat on a red couch singing along with Drake's music getting drunk. Several bottles of wine and liquor rested on a table right next to a bucket of ice. The entire atmosphere felt good and comfortable. Snow looked over to his right and saw The Terminator sitting backwards on a chair getting his hands wrapped. He wore a pair or orange leather trunks along with the orange boxing shoes to match. A pair of Ray Ban sunglasses covered The Terminator's eyes while a dark skin lady in her mid thirties with a nice size ass massaged the Champion's shoulders while he got his hands wrapped.

"Snow is here," The Terminator's assistant said bringing it to his attention. Once The Terminator finished getting his hands wrapped, he introduced himself to Snow and his M.O.E. crew.

"So glad you could make it." The Terminator smiled. "I love your music."

"Thanks for paying me in advance," Snow replied. He had seen The Terminator many of times on T.V. and most of the time, The Terminator was talking shit, bragging, and boasting, but to be able to see and talk to the champ up close and in person was a total different story.

"When I walk to the ring I want you to perform your song "Party Hard", that's my shit. I listen to that shit all the time while I'm training." As The Terminator spoke, the dark skin woman who was massaging his shoulders was now rubbing baby oil on The Terminator's chest, arms, and six pack. "I told my assistant that I had to meet you and tell you to keep up the good work."

Mr. Wilson sucked his teeth as he slipped The Terminator's orange gloves over his fist and tied and taped them up. He hated the company that his fighter kept around. The Terminator needed to be a hundred percent focused and Mr. Wilson felt that with all the women, rappers, and entourages hanging around that they weren't doing nothing but distracting his fighter. The Terminator had blown up and it was way too late to bring him back down to reality. In The Terminator's eyes, he was the greatest thing to ever put on a pair of gloves and he didn't believe there was a man on the planet who could whip his ass. As far as he was concerned, he was getting paid to show up, break a sweat, and collect a big check.

"Yo, I'm having a victory party after the fight. Come fuck with me so we can chop it up," The Terminator said giving Snow a fist bump as Mr. Wilson helped The Terminator slip inside his robe. On the several T.V.s that was posted up in the locker room, The Terminator's opponent was making his way to the ring. His opponent was an African man who the boxing world called Lucky Lefty.

A security escort banged on the dressing room door. "It's time to go!"

The Terminator and everyone in the dressing room exited the doom and made their way towards the ring entrance. As Snow walked side by side with The Terminator he could feel the entire building vibrating from the thousands of hyped up fans anticipating a good fight and possibly The Terminators first professional loss. They were at least three minutes away from reaching the ring entrance and the crowd was chanting loudly. The same petite blonde woman from earlier ran up and handed Snow a microphone.

"Good luck baby. Go do ya thing," Snow yelled in The Terminator's ear. He replied with a head nod as they waited at the entrance for their security escort to give them the word that it was okay to head to the ring.

"You focused?" Mr. Wilson yelled in The Terminator's ear. "This motherfucker out there wants to be you! He's willing to die out in that ring in order to take your spot at the top... You gone let this African motherfucker take your spot!?"

The Terminator's hood to his robe covered his head and he had his head down in deep thought. He looked up and stared at Mr. Wilson and Mr. Wilson could see his reflection in the sunglasses that covered The Terminator's eyes. "I got this," was all The Terminator said as the beat to Snow's song "Party Hard" blared loudly through the speakers.

Snow followed the security guards out of the tunnel and rapped the lyrics from his song as raging fans yelled and screamed out all kinds of shit. Snow walked down to the ring side by side with The Terminator. As Snow rapped, he had to slap several fans hands away as they broke their neck just to touch him and The Terminator. Two camera men walked backwards making sure they were capturing Snow and The Terminator's every move. The Terminator walked with a slow bop down towards the ring bobbing his head to Snow's lyrics. When they reached the ring, two men wearing suits held open the ropes so The Terminator, Snow, Mr. Wilson, and the M.O.E. crew entourage could enter the ring.

"Go in there and kill that nigga," Snow whispered in The Terminator's ear as the ring announcer announced the two fighters. The crowd was on fire and ready to yell and scream at any sign of excitement. The referee asked everyone to leave the ring and ordered both fighters to meet in the middle of the ring.

"I want a nice clean fight," the referee said sternly. "When I say break, I expect you to break immediately." He then eyed both fighters' trunks. "Anything under here is a low." He pointed below the belt line. "Have a good fight and touch gloves."

Both fighters touched gloves and then went to neutral corners. The crowd went crazy anticipating the bell to sound signaling the first round to begin.

"Let's go. It's time to take care of business!" Mr. Wilson yelled over the crowd as he kissed The Terminator on the cheek. "Watch out for his left," he yelled over his shoulder and then exited the ring. The Terminator stood in his corner staring across the ring at his opponent who looked to be in great shape. Determination was written all over the African's face. He wasn't just fighting for himself, but he was also fighting for his country. The African stared at The Terminator with a murderous "I'm going to kill you" look in his eyes.

As The Terminator bounced up and down in place like a pit-bull waiting to be let off his leash, he smiled and winked at the African.

Ding! Ding! Ding!

The crowd went wild as the two fighters squared off in the middle of the ring. The African's game plan from the beginning was to apply as much pressure on The Terminator as possible. He knew trying to out box the champ wouldn't be a wise move. The Terminator landed two clean jabs that snapped the African's head back. The African fired back with two sweeping hooks that The Terminator blocked easily with his gloves and forearms. The Terminator tried to dance away, but the African cut the ring off and trapped The Terminator in the corner. The Terminator slid into his Philly Shell Defense stance, the same defense style that made Floyd Mayweather, Jr. famous. The African fired an eight point combination at The Terminator that caused the crowd to erupt with loud yells and cheers. The Terminator smiled as the blows bounced off his gloves and shoulder. He quickly caught the African with a counter right hook, then tied him up and slipped away in two quick body shots before the referee separated them. The Terminator landed a jab followed by a straight right hand just as the bell sounded ending the first round.

The Terminator sat on the stool in his corner as the same dark skin woman who was massaging him in the dressing room held a bottle of water up to his lips.

"You see what I see?" Mr. Wilson asked kneeling down directly in front of his fighter.

"What you see?" The Terminator asked as he looked out in the crowd and saw Pauleena standing up in the front row with several men wearing dark suits with bow ties standing behind her. Pauleena stood clapping with the rest of the crowd with an evil smirk on her face.

"You hear me!?" Mr. Wilson yelled in The Terminator's face. "This African motherfucker leaves his right hand way too low. He's open for a check hook all day... Let me see a few of those," Mr. Wilson said hopping out the ring as the bell sounded again. The two fighters met in the middle of the ring.

"Back the fuck up!" The Terminator huffed as he landed a stiff jab in the middle of the African's face.

"Fuck you!" The African kept coming forward applying pressure.

"Shut the fuck up!" The Terminator landed another jab in the middle of the African's face then smiled. The African threw another flurry of punches. The Terminator blocked five out of six blows then fired two hard body shots of his own. The body shots slowed the African man down a little bit. As the African lunged forward firing a jab, The Terminator side stepped the jab and caught the African with a lightening quick check hook. The punch stunned the African and caused his knees to buckle. Sensing blood, The Terminator moved in for the kill as the crowd cheered and stood to their feet anticipating a knock out.

The Terminator forced the African in the corner and sent full throttle. He fired off a quick left-right-left-right combo and then landed two hard clean upper cuts. After that, the African was out off his feet. The referee quickly jumped in the middle of the two fighters and stopped the fight. The Terminator reached over the referee's shoulder and landed one last punch that violently snapped the African's head back. Seconds later the ring was filled with camera men, promoters, and members from both fighters team.

Mr. Wilson smiled from ear to ear, and then gave The Terminator a big bear hug. "Job well done!"

"Easy work," The Terminator said as he turned to one of the commentators who stood in the ring waiting to interview the champ.

"How do you feel?" The commentator asked holding the microphone up to The Terminator's mouth.

"I feel good!" The Terminator smiled while slipping his dark shades back over his eyes.

"You seemed well prepared for this fight," the commentator said. "Did that come from you watching a lot of tape on your opponent?"

The Terminator looked at the commentator like he was crazy. "Nah, I don't watch tapes on my opponents," he lied. "I'm just that much better than everybody else," he boasted.

"The question all of your fans want to know is.... Who's next?"

"Anybody can get it," The Terminator said arrogantly. "My job is to keep killing the competition and that's just what I'm going to do."

"Have you thought about fighting Brutus the Russian Sensation?" The commentator said knowing the question would catch the champ off guard.

The Terminator smiled. "Brutus the Russian Sensation and I are in two different weight classes, but if we were in the same weight class I would whip his ass too."

"Well, we've spoken to Brutus' team and they say they're willing to come down to fight you at a catch weight… I think that's what the boxing fans want to see. You two are the only two remaining undefeated fighters left out there… How much will it take to make this fight happen?" The commentator asked placing the microphone up to The Terminator's mouth.

"I leave things like that to my management team. I wanna thank everyone who tuned in tonight and showed up to watch the fight... I love y'all. I'm gone," The Terminator said as him and his team exited the ring and headed back to his dressing room. He couldn't believe the nerve of the commentator asking him about Brutus the Russian Sensation. Everyone in the boxing world knew that the Russian man was on steroids and not to mention he was a natural born hard heavy hitter. The Terminator had been offered thirty-five million to fight the Russian superstar boxer, but Mr. Wilson quickly turned down the offer.

"Good fight," Snow said giving The Terminator a pound. As The Terminator reached his dressing room, he saw Pauleena standing in front of the dressing room with an entourage of Muslim body guards along with a Spanish man with a smooth looking ponytail that came down to the middle of his back, another man stood next to Pauleena that The Terminator didn't know personally, but he did know that his name was The Prince.

"Congrats," Pauleena said.

"Thanks," The Terminator said. On the inside he was nervous, but on the outside he played cool. The last time he had saw Pauleena she had one of her crazy shooters shoot up his gym and several of his sparring partners.

"We need to talk," Pauleena said as her, Psycho, Prince, and Malcolm entered the locker room.

"Yo listen, I don't want no trouble," The Terminator said wiping the sweat off of him with a towel.

"I didn't come here to bring you any trouble... I'm willing to let bygones be bygones," Pauleena told him. "But, the million dollars I lost I'mma need that back."

"We'll have the money to you first thing Monday morning," Mr. Wilson said jumping in the conversation. He knew firsthand how Pauleena got down and didn't want or need those kind of problems for his fighter.

"Thank you," Pauleena smiled as she walked over and shook Snow's hand. This was her first time meeting Prince's cousin. She had met and done business with Trouble plenty of times. "Nice to finally meet Prince's talented cousin."

"Pleasures all mines," Snow blushed. To him Pauleena was a drug God and he was just honored to be in her presence.

"The Terminator's having a victory party," Snow informed Pauleena. "Y'all coming through?"

"Not tonight," Pauleena replied quickly. "I got a few things that need my immediate attention and I have to rid up to Clinton Correctional Facility and visit Knowledge," she said. "Let him know that we appreciate everything he did to help us get to where we are today."

"I respect that," Snow said looking over at Prince. "What about you? You partying with us tonight?"

"You already know," Prince smiled. The night life and partying was his thing.

"I'm outta here." Pauleena turned to leave. "Congrats again," she told The Terminator and then her and her crew disappeared out of the dressing room.

"You owe me," Prince said walking up on The Terminator. It was him who had talked Pauleena out of doing something to the champ.

"Thanks! I appreciate that," The Terminator said as he hit the showers and changed his clothes. He had some partying to do.

****

Live Wire pulled into the clubs parking lot in his new black B.M.W. with his music bumping at an extremely loud volume making a grand entrance like always. Live Wire hopped out the B.M.W. looking like a superstar alongside him was a new recruit named Bills. Bills was a former drug dealer who was fresh home from jail with a chip on his shoulder and a serious attitude problem. In front of the club twelve other Spades members stood awaiting Live Wire's arrival. Live Wire knew Wolf didn't want him or other Spades members out partying and indulging in any foolishness that might lead to them going to jail. But, he didn't give a fuck. In his eyes he was young and had one life to live.

Live Wire slipped the bouncer at the door a few hundred dollars to allow him and his crew to enter the club without having to wait in the long line. The only problem was they weren't allowed to enter with any weapons. Live Wire and Bills stepped foot in the club and saw that the club was off the hook. 2 Chainz new album bumped through the speakers and it had the club going crazy. As Live Wire squeezed and snaked his way through the crowd, several men and women just felt the need to show him love. The men shook his hand and the women hugged him. The entire city was beginning to recognize The Spades and they appreciated what their organization stood for and represented. Live Wire soaked up the love as a big bouncer escorted Live Wire and The Spades over to the V.I.P. area that awaited them. Over in the section next to Live Wire he noticed two men chilling and enjoying a few drinks while chit chatting with a few half naked women. "Yo, who that in the V.I.P. section next to us?" Live Wire asked the bouncer yelling over the loud music.

"Some author nigga named Silk White," the bouncer answered.

"Word?" Live Wire smirked. While Live Wire was locked up he had read plenty of books by the author and enjoyed his work. Live Wire walked over and leaned over the divider and introduced himself. "Yo Silk, what up? I read mad books of yours," Live Wire yelled over the music. "Keep doing ya thing. I respect ya pen game."

Silk White sat leaned back with a drink in his hand and two beautiful women who looked like they weren't up to no good on each side of him. He wore his dreads in a ponytail and a black and gold Pirates fitted hat rested on the top of his head. A snug fitting black tee hugged his arms and chest, below he wore a pair of black jeans, and a pair of Construction Timbs on his feet. Across from him was a tall man with dreads. He too wore all black except the white words on his shirt that read "Buck .45."

"What's good fam? What's ya handle?" Silk White asked smoothly giving the man that stood before him dap.

"Live Wire, you heard," Live Wire told him. "I just wanted to come over here and let you know I was loving the books... You should put me and The Spades in the next Tears of a Hustler series," he chuckled.

Silk White smiled. "I heard about what you and The Spades out here doing... That's real shit. Keep up the good work and be safe."

"You already know... One of my hoes loves all your books too. She was telling me something about some movie you got out," Live Wire asked.

"Yeah, yeah. The movie is called "Black Barbie". When you get a chance, check that joint out," Silk White said and then sipped from his drink.

"I got you," Live Wire smiled. "Keep up the good work... Before you and ya man get up outta here, come have a drink with me and The Spades."

"I got you. You already know," Silk White said as he felt his iPhone vibrating on his hip. He looked down at his phone and saw Kesha's name flashing across the screen. "I'mma get up with you before I leave," Silk White told Live Wire as he answered his phone and headed off to the bathroom so he could hear.

Bills handed Live Wire a bottle of Coconut Ciroc as other members of The Spades allowed several ladies to join them in the V.I.P. section. Live Wire bobbed his head to the new Young Jeezy song that bumped through the speakers when he felt somebody bump him from behind causing him to spill a little Ciroc on his shirt. Live Wire turned around and saw a brown skin chick with a nice set of titties and a nice ass standing in front of him.

"My bad," the brown skin woman said with a giggle.

"That's funny?" Live Wire smiled at the woman. "This my favorite shirt."

"I said I was sorry."

"Sorry is not good enough," Live Wire licked his lips. "What's your name?"

"Coco," the brown skin woman answered with a smile. Coco knew this was the biggest party of the year and knew it wouldn't be hard to catch the attention of a baller especially since she was now single.

"My shirt is ruined," Live Wire said removing his shirt and tossing it to the floor. He stood in front of Coco shirtless with two chains hanging from his neck. "You owe me a new shirt Coco." Live Wire took a swig from his bottle.

"I think I like you better without the shirt on," Coco flirted openly with who she knew was one of the leaders of The Spades movement that the whole New York state was talking and buzzing about.

"Is that right?"

"Yup, that's right," Coco smiled. Live Wire took another swig from his bottle and pulled out his iPhone 5 and handed it to CoCo. "Throw your number in there before I don't want it no more."

Coco laughed, but she still stored her number in his phone. "What's your name?"

"Live Wire"

"Did your mother name you that?" Coco asked.

"Actually she did," Live Wire lied as he pulled Coco into his body and let his hand slide down to part of her hips and part of her ass.

"Damn you smell good!" Live Wire sniffed her neck and then kissed her neck softly. "Get up outta here before I turn you out." Live Wire leaned back up against the rail and took another swig from his bottle. French Montana's new song bumped through the speakers and turned the club up. Coco walked up to Live Wire and pressed her soft ass up against his crotch. She pressed her soft ass up against his crotch and grinded her ass all over him while riding the beat all at the same time.

****

While The Terminator stepped out the stretch Hummer along with Snow, immediately the women who were outside the club went crazy. The Terminator's security had to hold the women off. At least twenty men stood in front of the club wearing M.O.E. shirts awaiting Snow's arrival. He didn't do security. His security was his Glock and his entourage. When Snow and The Terminator stepped foot inside the club, they stole all the attention. All eyes were on Snow, Prince, The Terminator, and the M.O.E. entourage as security pushed them through the crowd over towards the vacant V.I.P. section

The Terminator was used to all the attention and loved every second of it. Once they were situated, The Terminator gave one of his security guards the word to let some women join them in their private section.

"I'm proud of you," Prince said draping his arm around Snow's neck. "Soon you gone have the rap game in a choke hold." He turned and faced his younger cousin. "I don't want you fucking around in this drug game no more," he said sternly. Your job is to focus solely on the music and the music only."

"I got you," Snow said turning the bottle of Rosay he held in his hand up to his lips and taking a swig. "I ain't even gone lie. That shit that went down between us and The Spades... I still feel a certain type of way about that."

"You ain't heard?"

"Heard what?"

"I clapped the leader of The Spades," Prince bragged.

"Some soft nigga named Wolf."

"Word?"

"You know I don't play," Prince said as he eyed this nice little Spanish thing that stood over in the cut swaying back and forth to the music that blared through the speakers. "But now that Pauleena is back from vacation, The Spades have been quiet."

As Prince and Snow sat talking and drinking, Trouble interrupted the two's conversation.

"Yo, one of the bouncers just told me that Live Wire and a few other Spades are up in here," Trouble announced knowing revealing that information would lead to some shit jumping off.

At the mention of Live Wire's name, Prince immediately rubbed the scar on his face as murderous thoughts clouded his mind and had him seeing red.

"Where them niggas at?" Prince asked removing the chains from around his neck and then stuffing them down into his pocket.

"Them niggas is right over there," Trouble said pointing towards the V.I.P. section over on the other side of the club.

****

Live Wire sat on the couch with a glass of Coconut Ciroc in his hand and Coco curled up sitting on his lap whispering a bunch of sexy shit in his ear.

"Is that a foreign object in your pants or are you just happy to see me?" Coco giggled with a drunken slur. She was really feeling Live Wire. Even though she had only known him for a hour or two, she already knew that if he wanted the pussy that it was his to have.

"Foreign object?" Live Wire echoed. He was smacked (drunk). "Yo listen, I told you to get up outta here before I turn ya little sexy ass out," Live Wire said discreetly slipping his hand up under Coco's dress. He slid her thong over to the side and couldn't believe how wet Coco's pussy was.

"Is it wet enough for you? Huh?" Coco seductively whispered in Live Wire's ear while spreading her legs open and grinding her wet pussy on Live Wire's hand.

Coco moaned in Live Wire's ear as he played with her wetness. Live Wire's fingers moved underneath Coco's dress like he was a D.J. scratching a record.

"Oh my God... Oh my God!" Coco moaned and yelled. Her moans were getting louder and louder as she grinded even harder on Live Wire's hand until she purred out in ecstasy and came long and hard.

"I wanna ride that dick," Coco whined. "Let's get up outta here."

"Yo, we got company," Bills came over and informed Live Wire. Live Wire got up, wiped his fingers off with a napkin, and then followed Bills to see what was going on and who was interrupting him from getting his freak on. Live Wire looked out into the crowd and saw Prince, a rapper named Snow who he had seen a few times on World Star, and a gang of men all wearing shirts that read M.O.E. on the front.

Three big bouncers stood in front of the V.I.P. section that The Spades occupied. Refusing to let Prince, Snow, Trouble, and the rest of the M.O.E. members get to The Spades. The last thing they wanted was for the two crews to tear up the club.

"What up!?" Prince yelled up to Live Wire. "We got some unfinished business... We can do this inside or we can take it outside. What you wanna do?"

"Shut the fuck up!" Live Wire spat and tossed a drink down in Prince's face. From there all hell broke loose. Rosay, Ciroc, and Hennessey bottles flew throughout the club as the two crews clashed. Live Wire and Prince went at it like boxers. Each man giving as good as he received. Just as Live Wire began to get the upper hand on Prince, he felt a bottle shatter overt the back of his head. With his adrenalin pumping, Live Wire kept on fighting as blood dripped from his head down to his face.

Snow and Trouble stomped a Spades member out like they were trying to stomp out a fire. Out of nowhere Bills came to his fellow Spades member rescue. He clothes lined Snow and then turned and snuffed Trouble. Trouble's head violently snapped back as his fitted flew off his head. The club looked like a Royal Rumble. It took ten minutes for the bouncers to separate the two crews and push everyone outside. The only reason the brawl didn't continue when the two crews got outside was because there were way too many cops outside the club and the last place niggas wanted to be was in jail especially during the weekend.

Live Wire hopped in his B.M.W. and peeled out the parking lot like a bat out of hell. The next time he saw Prince, he promised himself that he was going to kill him right where he stood.

Live Wire pulled into the driveway of his new house and parked his B.M.W. in the garage and then entered the house through the garage door. Live Wire stepped foot in the door and saw Sparkle standing in the kitchen wearing nothing but a pair of black fishnet stockings pouring herself a drink. When Sparkle heard the door open and close, she turned around and saw Live Wire standing there with dried up blood on his face and ear.

"What happened to you?" Sparkle asked sitting her drink down with her voice full of concern.

"Had to get it on with some nondescript niggas," Live Wire said as if the dried up blood on his face was no big deal. He walked over to the counter, grabbed Sparkle's drink, and took a gulp. "Yo, my waves still there?" Live Wire asked with his head bent down so Sparkle could take a look.

"Boy!" Sparkle rushed Live Wire over to the kitchen sink so she could rinse, clean, and bandage up his head. "You over here bleeding half to death and you worrying about some stupid ass waves." She shook her head. At first Live Wire had kept Sparkle around just for the sex, but after a little bit of time he realized that Sparkle was one of the realest women he had ever dealt with. She didn't lie, behind closed doors she was super freak and knew just how to please him, and most importantly she was about her money. Live Wire had a few Spades robbing all the ballers who thought they had a chance at getting some of that pussy. The two made the perfect team.

"Wait right here while I run upstairs and grab you a towel," Sparkle said disappearing upstairs. Live Wire walked over and flopped down on the couch and grabbed the remote and cut some music on. Yo Gotti's mix tape, Cocaine Music 6 bumped through the speakers sending vibrations up the wall. Live Wire bobbed his head to the beat and removed all of his clothes and sat on the couch butt naked with a drink in his hand.

Sparkle returned downstairs carrying a towel. A smile spread across her face when she saw Live Wire sitting on the couch naked with a drink in his hand. "What about your head?" Sparkle asked.

"Huh? What you said, you want some head?" Live Wire smirked with a drink in one hand and his dick in the other hand. He was still horny from the little episode he had in the club with Coco and now he planned on taking it out on Sparkle and her big fat ass. "Get over here and come ride my face!" Live Wire demanded. He smiled as he watched Sparkle drop the towel down to the carpet, wiggle out of her fishnet stockings, and stand up on the couch looking down at him.

"Tell me how bad you wanna eat this pussy," Sparkle said in a sexually charged voice biting down on her bottom lip.

"Baby I'm gonna eat that pussy so good! I PROMISE!" Live Wire said looking up at Sparkle and her freshly waxed pussy.

"Beg me!" Sparkle demanded.

"Come feed me that pussy before I smack the shit outta you," Live Wire countered with a wisk of a smile.

"Damn," Sparkle moaned. "You know that kind of talk turns me on," she admitted as she began getting wet. Sparkle turned around and squatted down placing her big fat ass in Live Wire's face. Live Wire didn't play with that big ass. He licked Sparkle's clit flicking his tongue back and forth like a rattle snake.

"Ewww...," Sparkle moaned as the feel of Live Wire's tongue made her squirm and send shivers up her spine. Her legs tensed and her breathing did the same. She was getting turned on by the slurping that came from between her legs. Sparkle moaned deep and her body was shaking. Wildness invaded her while the convulsions her body was having had her grabbing and squeezing her firm breast as she began lightly bouncing up and down on Live Wire's face and tongue. She was giving his face a nice, wet, and slow ride. "Yes, yes... Ahhh... Ahhh..." Sparkle yelled then came violently.

Live Wire then made Sparkle stand up with her legs spread out. He then ordered her to bend over and grab her ankles as if she was stretching and getting herself prepared for a 40 yard dash. Live Wire dipped down to an angle and entered Sparkle's wet slice from behind. He moved deeper inside her and held her waist tight. He held it there for a minute. He tried to fill her up. Live Wire fucked Sparkle aggressively as if he hated her and was purposely trying to hurt her. All Sparkle could do was hold onto her ankles while Live Wire plunged in and out of her walls. All that could be heard was loud moans and skin violently slapping against skin. Sparkle held her ankles, bit down her bottom lip, and tried to swallow her rising moans. Live Wire then pulled her down on the couch where Sparkle continued to bounce her big fat ass violently up and down forcing Live Wire to explode.

"Yes! Oh, oh, oh yes!" Sparkle screamed at the top of her lungs as she felt her legs tremble. Then her entire body did the same. When Sparkle was done moaning, she stayed on top of Live Wire and caught her breath.

"Damn!" was all Sparkle could say. It has been a long time since she had felt feelings like this towards a man. Sparkle hated to admit it, but she was starting to fall in love with Live Wire. She loved everything about him.

"Yo, get off me," Live Wire said as he gently pushed Sparkle off of him. The two laid down on the plush carpet on the living room floor and thought about the experience they had just endured. Within minutes, both of them were sound asleep.

Chapter 15
"Face Off"

"You alright?" Wolf asked sitting a glass of Orange Juice and a bag of Doritos down on the coffee table that Ivy had her foot propped up on. Wolf still felt bad about getting Ivy caught up in his bullshit. She didn't have nothing to do with nothing, but still winded up taking a stray bullet to the leg.

Ivy sat on the white leather sofa with a laptop across her lap. "Ye baby, I'm fine." She smiled to let Wolf know that she was really okay. "Damn!"

"What?"

"Guess how many views the video you put up got?" Ivy said with a smirk on her face.

"How many?" Wolf asked excitedly.

"Three million, two thousand, two hundred, and thirty-eight," Ivy told him with a smile.

Wolf smiled also. He knew The Spades message was loud and clear. They were out to clean up the streets by any means necessary. Ever since Wolf uploaded that video on YouTube, The Spades numbers had increased. In total now there were almost 20,000 Spades members. There were so many members that Wolf had to break The Spades down into groups and assign each group one leader. The way Wolf saw things was within the next six months, The Spades would pretty much have New York under control and move then move on to the next state.

Ivy got up from off the couch and limped over to the bathroom. Wolf wanted to give her a hand, but knew she would decline his offer so he just remained seated and watched her closely. Wolf's cell phone vibrated on his hip. He looked down at the screen and saw Pastor Anderson's name flashing on the screen. "Yo, what up?" he answered.

"When you get a chance, I'm gonna need you to swing by my office. I have something I think you would be interested in hearing," Pastor Anderson said in a voice that let Wolf know whatever it was, it was bad.

"I'm on my way," Wolf said and ended the call. "Baby I gotta make a run real quick. You need anything while I'm out?"

"No baby. I'm good," Ivy said while coming out the bathroom. She kissed Wolf on the lips. "Just make it back home in one piece."

Wolf smirked as he looked at Ivy's ass poking out in the skirt that she wore. "Put some clothes on before I come back and bust that ass! Bad leg and all…" He smacked Ivy on the ass, spun on his heels, and headed for the door.

"I wish you would bust my ass!" Ivy yelled at Wolf's departing back. "My leg is injured… Not my pussy!"

All Wolf could do was laugh. When he made it out to the front of his estate, he spotted The Big Show and a few other Spades members who he paid to make sure no trespassers were allowed onto the property. Ever since the attempt on Wolf's life, he decided to beef up his security. From now on wherever ever Wolf went, so did four armed bodyguards. They were paid to follow his every move and stay closer to him than his own shadow. Not only that, four more Spades members were paid to escort and follow Ivy everywhere she went also. Ivy didn't like the idea of having to be followed and shielded by bodyguards everywhere she went, but she agreed to it knowing that her having a bodyguard would give Wolf a piece of mind.

Wolf stepped foot out of the black Navigator and his Spades bodyguards immediately surrounded him and escorted him inside the church. A block away in a black Crown Vic sat Agent Michael Starks. Starks was one of the best agents in the world. He was in Washington D.C. minding his own business when a YouTube video was presented to him. After watching the YouTube video, Agent Starks was curious and wanted to know more about Wolf and The Spades organization. After doing a little research Agent Starks realized that ever since The Spades organization was formed, the murder rate seemed to have sky rocketed to an all time high. A long list of mid-level and low rank drug dealers were turning up dead all over the city and Agent Starks wanted to blame Wolf and The Spades for all the killings, but what he lacked was evidence. After getting the green light from his boss, Agent Starks was sent to investigate and gather up as much information as he could on The Spades and build a case on them. Agent Starks snapped several pictures of Wolf and his bodyguards as they entered the church.

****

"I have some disturbing news to break to you," Pastor Anderson said sitting on the edge of his desk.

"I'm all ears."

"It's about Live Wire," Pastor Anderson began. "I'm afraid that he's been stealing money from the family," he said looking at Wolf closely to see if his face would show any emotion or reveal how he felt.

Wolf remained straight faced as he let Pastor Anderson's words marinate for a minute. From all the flossing that Live Wire was doing, Wolf had already suspected Live Wire of doing something on the side, but stealing was a no, no in Wolf's book. He planned on dealing with Live Wire sooner than later, but first he had to make sure Pastor Anderson was positive about the information that he was giving him. "You got concrete evidence that Live Wire's been stealing?" Wolf asked with a raised brow.

Pastor Anderson nodded to the computer screen on his desk. Wolf quickly walked around Pastor Anderson's desk so he could see the monitor.

Pastor Anderson played a tape of Live Wire stealing money. "He looked directly at the camera and smiled while he took the money," Pastor Anderson added. "And I don't have any hidden cameras. The camera is very visual. He knew he was on camera, but didn't care."

"I'll take care of it." Wolf stood up and headed for the door. He couldn't believe the audacity of Live Wire. If he was going to steal, he could have at least had the decency to be a little more discrete about it. It was obvious that Live Wire didn't give a fuck and for his actions Live Wire had to be punished.

Outside Wolf and his group of bodyguards quickly walked to the curb and hopped in the all black Navigator. Wolf didn't know what he was going to do about Live Wire and his sticky fingers, but he knew he would have to do something. This kind of behavior wasn't what The Spades represented and it wouldn't be tolerated.

"What was that all about back there?" The Big Show asked nosily.

"Pastor Anderson caught Live Wire stealing," Wolf said shaking his head.

"I been told you that Live Wire is out of control," The Big Show said. "And quite frankly I don't trust him... If I was you, I would watch my back."

Wolf chuckled. "That's what I pay you for," he pointed out.

"You can't trust a nigga that steals," The Big Show added.

"I think we're being followed," the driver announced peeking back at Wolf through the rear view mirror.

"What is it looking like?" Wolf asked curiously looking straight ahead so whoever was following him wouldn't know that Wolf was on to him or them.

"Black Crown Vic... Police or detectives, my guess," the driver said. Seconds later, the driver saw flashing lights in the rearview mirror signaling for him to pull over.

Agent Michael Starks stepped out the Crown Vic and cautiously walked up on the Navigator. From what he knew about The Spades, they were an extremely violent organization. Agent Starks reached the driver's window and peeked inside the vehicle.

"What seems to be the problem officer?" The driver asked ice grilling the cop. Agent Starks shined the bright light from his flash light in the driver's face and then on all the faces of each man inside the vehicle.

"Wolf step out of the vehicle," Agent Starks ordered. His voice was stern and serious.

The Big Show gave Wolf the "give me the word and I'll gladly shoot him look."

"It's cool," Wolf assured The Big Show as he slowly stepped out the Navigator with The Big Show close on his heels.

"Wassup?" Wolf said. Him and Agent Starks stood face to face.

"First off, let's get one thing straight," Agent Starks hissed. "I don't like you," he said. "I think you are a piece of scum and give black people a bad name." Agent Starks paused for a second as him and Wolf eye boxed with one another. "I'm here to let you know that I'm on your ass now so you better act like Spike Lee and do the right thing."

Wolf smirked, "That's it?"

"You think this is funny?" Agent Starks pressed. "You think going around murdering people is funny!?!" He yelled. "You might think you and your posse are cleaning up the streets, but all y'all idiots are doing is killing your own people! Y'all doing the same thing the dealers are out here doing, but you try to justify it by giving a few jobs to these people who out here struggling... You might be able to fool them, but you can't fool me!" Agent Starks said in a matter of fact tone. "I'm the best that ever did this shit... You hear me? And just know that it's only a matter of time before I lock your stupid ass up and throw you under the jail where you belong!"

Wolf smiled. He knew him smiling was pissing the Agent off so he did it on purpose. "I'm going to tell you this one time and one time only." Wolf paused to make sure he had Agent Starks undivided attention. "If we ever cross each other's path and its game time you better shoot to kill, cause if you land in my cross hair I won't hesitate or think twice about pulling the trigger... You've been warned!"

The look on Agent Starks face told Wolf that he was ready to shoot him dead right then and there, but Agent Starks knew him and the man the streets called Wolf would be crossing each other's paths again. "You fucking with me. You fucking with the best," Agent Starks said. "I am the best and I will bring you down; dead or alive; one way or another... You think you and your crew are just going to go around killing people just because you say they're bad people? That's what the legal system is for."

"Fuck you and the legal system. How about that?" Wolf snapped. He was sick and tired of listening to Agent Starks trying to belittle him and his movement. Wolf knew it wouldn't be long until the police caught on to him and The Spades. First the police and up next was the media. That was just the publicity The Spades needed to become a household name all across the world.

"Fuck me?" Agent Starks repeated. "No, you just fucked yourself," he said then turned and left. He hopped back in his Crown Vic, made a U-turn, and sped off in the opposite direction.

"He looks like he is going to be a problem," The Big Show said out loud as he watched the Crown Vic's tail lights fade into the night.

"We just have to be a little smarter, that's all," Wolf replied as him and The Big Show hopped back inside the Navigator. For the rest of the ride back to his estate Wolf thought long and hard about what Agent Starks had said. Deep down inside he didn't want to cross paths with the Agent again, but he knew him and Agent Starks going head to head was something that couldn't be avoided no matter how hard Wolf tried.

Chapter 16
"Fuck That"

Snow pulled into a parking spot in front of the studio in downtown Manhattan in his cocaine white 750XI B.M.W. Since his name was Snow he made sure everything he owned was all white. He had white cars, a white iPhone, white furniture in his home, and every now and then you might even catch him with a white chick or two. In the passenger seat sat Trouble and in the back seat sat two light skin chicks. Snow ran through women like basketball players ran through sneakers. In the back seat weren't just two regular women, they were the two new girls that Trouble had recruited to transport drugs out of town to North Carolina, but the two girls weren't transporting shit until Trouble introduced them to Snow like he promised. For the past twenty-four hours Snow and Trouble locked themselves in a hotel room and took turns having their way with both women. Snow hopped out the B.M.W. with a bottle of peach Ciroc in his hand and three chains hanging form around his neck with large diamond pieces attached to them. The diamond pieces on the chains bounced off the chest of his white t-shirt that had M.O.E. written in black letters.

"That new track you put out dissing The Spades got the streets on fire right now," Trouble said. He was still hype about getting it on with The Spades at the club a few weeks ago. The first stage was hand to hand combat and everyone knew that if or when it reached the second stage there were sure to be shots fired.

"Fuck The Spades," Snow said dryly. He would deal with The Spades when that time came, but right now him and his lawyer were trying to figure out how they would get out of having to pay all the people who were suing him claiming false injuries that occurred during the brawl in the club between Snow, his M.O.E. crew, and The Spades. "I ain't thinking about them clowns," Snow replied. "I think it's time to start putting together this album."

"Did you decide on who you going to sign with yet?" Trouble asked curiously.

"Nah, not yet," Snow told him. In front of the building that the studio was in, Snow noticed a man wearing a hoodie leaning up against a parked car. Snow took a swig from his bottle of peach Ciroc and then turned his gaze on Trouble. "Yo peep son with the hoodie on." He nodded towards the hooded man.

"I'm already on it," Trouble said with his hand gripped around the handle of his .357.

"A, yo Snow!" The hooded man called out just as Snow, Trouble, and their two lady friends were about to enter the building.

Snow cautiously stopped in his tracks and turned his gaze on the hooded man. "What's up?"

The hooded man smiled. "That mix tape you just put out was trash! You rap niggas is crazy!" He chuckled. "Stay rapping about a life y'all are too scared to live!"

"Yo fam, you know me from somewhere?" Snow asked with his face crumbled up as him and Trouble inched their way over towards the hooded man.

"I'm the last person you wanna get to know; trust me," the hooded man said sternly. "Cause unlike you fake rap niggas, I'm really bout that life," he said convincingly.

"This nigga must have bumped his motherfucking head," one of the chicks said in the background juicing up the situation.

Snow smirked. "A, yo my man, I'mma tell you like this…."

"I don't wanna talk!" The hooded man growled cutting Snow off. "I'm done talking."

Snow took a gulp of peach Ciroc and spit it in the hooded man's face. "Shut the fuck up!"

The hooded man lunged towards Snow with murderous intensions. Snow quickly took two steps back as

Trouble hit the hooded man on the side of the head with his .357 dropping him right where he stood.

"That's right! Fuck his ass up!" The two chicks screamed from the sideline as they watched Snow and Trouble stomp the hooded man out.

Snow then violently tossed the Ciroc bottle down. Trouble smiled when he saw the Ciroc bottle shatter on the hooded man's face. "You ain't gone talk shit now; right!" Trouble shouted pressing the barrel of his .357 into the hooded man's bloody forehead.

"Drop your weapon!" Agent Starks yelled appearing out of nowhere. He held his 9mm in a firm two handed grip and the barrel was trained on Trouble's head. Agent Starks had showed up to the studio to let Snow and his M.O.E. crew know that just like The Spades, he was on to them as well. Agent Starks didn't have a problem with rappers or rap music. It was the shoot outs and killings that he had a problem with.

Trouble hesitated for a second. He thought that Agent Starks was with the hooded man until he saw Agent Starks' badge attached to his belt. It was only then that Trouble slowly laid his gun down on the ground.

"On the ground now!" Agent Starks barked inching his way over towards the foursome. He quickly kicked Trouble's .357 out of arms reach then called in for backup and an ambulance. Agent Starks let the two women go and shoved Snow and Trouble in the back seat of his unmarked car as he watched the paramedics place the hooded man in the back of the ambulance.

Agent Starks stuck his key in the ignition and made the car come to life. Immediately Snow's voice hummed through the speakers at a low volume. Agent Starks bobbed his head as he pulled away from the curb.

Agent Starks cut the radio off and then looked at Snow through the rearview mirror. "All that talent you got and you want to be hanging around scum like that," he nodded towards Trouble. "I know every single song on your mix tape by heart," Agent Starks said. "You've been given a gift from God.... Don't throw it away."

"Fuck you!" Snow spat staring blankly out the window. He wasn't in the mood for this reverse psychology bullshit. Snow came from a family of drug dealers and gang members and that's just what it was. As far as he was concerned Agent Starks could kiss his ass.

"What's going on with y'all and The Spades?" Agent Starks asked again peeking at Snow through the rearview mirror.

"My man said fuck you!" Trouble snapped. "You ain't hear him the first time... Motherfucker!" He shook his head. He couldn't stand cops. He didn't even like crossing guards because their uniforms looked similar to the police uniforms.

"And you," Agent Starks said placing his gaze on Trouble. "You call yourself a friend, but instead of telling Snow to stay away from the trouble makers and stay focused... What you do? Huh? You encourage him to do negative instead of positive... Some friend..."

Trouble sighed loudly. "This nigga blowing my shit," he huffed.

"From what I'm hearing, The Spades are really shutting down the streets," Agent Starks said with a smirk. "I respect The Spades and think they are really out to do good... My only problem is all the shootings and killings!"

"Nigga!" Trouble barked. "Nobody don't give a fuck about that bullshit you talking about! You gone make me go in ya mouth if you keep it up," he threatened.

When they arrived at the precinct Agent Starks shoved Trouble over towards another officer. "Hey Jim, put that big mouth in the pin with the three Spades members that we picked up tonight," he said with a smirk as he forcefully shoved Snow down into a metal seat.

"Fuck you! You bitch ass nigga!" Agent Starks heard Trouble's voice yell from down the hall.

"Listen up," Agent Starks said looking down at Snow. "You have the potential to be a leader so I don't understand why you out here following these knuckleheads...

You have everything you could possibly want. What more could you want?"

Just as Snow was getting ready to reply he heard some loud banging noises coming from down the hall and the familiar sound of more than one man rumbling followed by loud moans and groans. Immediately Snow recognized Trouble's voice.

"You put him in a pin with The Spades; for real?" Snow asked wide eyed.

A smirk danced on Agent Starks lips. "Like you told me in the car... Fuck you and fuck him!" Agent Starks laughed as he spun off leaving Snow alone in his thoughts.

Chapter 17
"Let's Wake the Neighbors Up"

Malcolm pulled the all black Escalade up in front of a new lounge that The Spades had just opened up. The lounge was to give working people in the community a place to go get a drink and unwind after work. "Don't have me waiting out here all night either," Malcolm huffed with an attitude.

"Shut the fuck up," Psycho spat as him, Prince, and Bobby Dread all slide out the S.U.V. and entered the lounge. Psycho couldn't stand Malcolm and wanted so badly to put a bullet in the big man's head, but the only thing that stopped him was Pauleena. He knew if he did anything to Pauleena's head bodyguard that he would surely have to hear her mouth. Psycho hated the fact that Malcolm took his job too seriously. Not only that, but Psycho also knew that Malcolm was mad and jealous the he was back in Pauleena's life and most importantly her bed. Even though he never showed it or spoke on it Psycho knew that Malcolm loved Pauleena.

Inside the lounge Prince and Psycho stood close to the exit checking out the atmosphere. Prince smiled. The place wasn't too bad. It wasn't a place that he would hang out at, but the place was nice and packed. As he looked around, everyone inside seemed to be having a good time and enjoying themselves.

Bobby Dread walked up to the bar and took a seat on an empty stool. He ignored all the weird stares and looks people gave him as he ordered a Heineken. Bobby Dread was the only man sitting at the bar wearing a trench coat with a mean and angry look plastered across his face. Bobby

Dread turned the Heineken up to his lips and took a deep swig. In one quick motion, Bobby Dread turned and shattered the green Heineken bottle over the man's head who sat next to him. He then hopped up to his feet, pulled his trench coat open, whipped out his A.K. 47 with the hundred round drum, and opened fire out into the dance floor. Bobby Dread yelled at the top of his lungs as he held down on the trigger waving his arms back and forth. The A.K. rattled in his hands as empty shell cases spit out the top of the assault rifle back to back sounding like nickels hitting the floor.

"Told you this Jamaican nigga was crazy!" Prince smiled as he nudged Psycho. When all the gun smoke cleared, the only man left standing was the bartender. Psycho slowly walked up to the bartender and slapped him like he was nothing more than a cheap whore.

"Listen to me and you listen to me carefully," Psycho growled while grabbing the bartender by his collar. He moved in closer as he spoke. "You are Pauleena's new message boy... You do know how to deliver a message; right?"

The bartender nodded his head up and down nervously with a scared look on his face and fear in his eyes.

"You tell that bitch ass nigga Wolf that Pauleena said fuck up her money and she's going to fuck up his life and destroy every and anybody he loves," Psycho huffed. "Tell him don't fuck with us or anymore of our peoples and we'll be nice and think about letting him keep his life... Got it?"

The bartender nervously nodded his head up and down again.

"You have a number where I can reach Wolf at?"
The bartender shook his head no.

"So how do you get in touch with Wolf then?" Psycho growled.

"E-mail"

Prince slid a napkin and a pen over to the bartender. Psycho watched closely as the bartender scribbled Wolf's e-mail address down on the napkin. Once he put the pen down, Psycho head butted him; knocking the bartender out cold.

Once the trio had what they had come for, they quickly fled for the exit.

Chapter 18
"Trust Issue"

Dice stood in the living room with a drink in his hand looking down at Lil Dice who lay sleeping on the couch. A smile spread across Dice's face. He was so happy to have his son back in his life where he needed to be. Since Lil Dice came back into Dice's life, Dice made sure he spent as much time with his son as possible. The only problem Dice had was Tonya. She was currently living in a shelter out in Brooklyn and still working his nerves. During the day Dice watched and took care of Lil Dice, but some nights when he had to work he allowed Tonya to come over and spend the night. It was no way he was letting Tonya take his son to no shelter. So nights when he had to work Tonya stayed at his house to watch Lil Dice. Lately Dice had been noticing a change in Tonya for the better. Ever since Dice had rescued Tonya from Champagne, it seemed that Tonya had a serious change of heart about her way of living. Dice didn't know if Tonya was pretending to turn over a new leaf or if she was really serious about becoming a better person, but either way Dice didn't trust Tonya... Not even a little bit.

Dice refilled his glass with Hennessey when he heard a light knock at the front door. Dice walked over to the door and peeped through the peep hole. He opened the door and stepped to the side. Tonya walked through the front door dripping wet. She had got caught out in the rain.

"Yo, where your umbrella at?" Dice asked looking at Tonya like she was crazy.

"I didn't know that it was supposed to rain," Tonya replied innocently.

"Go put your shit in the dryer... I gotta get ready to go in a minute." Dice took a sip from his drink.

"I need to speak to you about something before you go," Tonya said walking over towards the laundry room.

"Whatever... Just make it quick cause I gotta be out!" Dice headed upstairs to his bedroom to grab his gun and a few other things he needed for the job that him and a few other Spades had been assigned to. Dice stepped in the closet and grabbed a light jacket. When he stepped out the closet he saw Tonya standing in the doorway of the bedroom wearing a pink lace see through bra with the pink thong to match. Even her nails were painted pink.

"Can I speak to you for a second?" Tonya asked.

"Not right now," Dice said trying not to take in Tonya's curves and sex appeal. Not to mention her perfume was intoxicating. "Whatever you have to say is going to have to wait."

Tonya stepped inside the bedroom and closed the door behind her. "I promise it will only take a second."

"What is it now?" Dice huffed not hiding his dislike for Tonya.

"Damn! Why you gotta say it like that?" Tonya snapped back. "Like I'm getting on your nerves or something."

"What is it?"

"Well I wanted to be the first to tell you that Wolf got me a job at one of The Spades restaurants." She smiled. "I've been working there going on six weeks now and guess who got employee of the month?" Tonya smiled striking a pose.

"Who?" Dice asked dryly

"Me," Tonya beamed. "Aren't you proud of me?"

"Congrats," Dice said faking a yawn while peeking down at his watch. "Listen I gotta go. Take care of my crib while I'm gone."

Tonya stood in front of the door declining Dice access to leave.

"Come on move. I don't got time to play." Dice sucked his teeth.

"No, fuck that," Tonya spat. "I got something to say and you going to hear me out." She rolled her eyes and folded her arms across her chest.

Dice sighed loudly, walked over to the bed, and took a seat giving Tonya the floor.

"Thank you," Tonya began. "Now like I was saying ever since you saved my life, you have to admit that I've been doing good," she smiled. "And I was wondering maybe if it was okay with you, I could possibly join The Spades."

"Join The Spades?" Dice chuckled. He was proud that Tonya was trying to get her life together, but joining The Spades... He wasn't sure if she was ready to be a part of the organization. "Nah, I don't know about all that."

"Why not?" Tonya asked.

"Cause"

"Cause what?"

"Cause I said so," Dice told her exhaling loudly. "Why don't you just go on about your business? Like why you keep on trying to hang around me?'

"Because," Tonya said. "I want to prove to you that I'm a brand new person and it's all because of you," she smiled. Tonya slowly walked towards the bed and rested a hand on Dice's shoulder. "I know I fucked up baby, but..."

"I'm not your baby," Dice said quickly cutting Tonya off.

"Sorry," Tonya apologized. "I know I fucked up, but I love you... And think you should give me a chance to make things right."

"You can't make things right," Dice said quickly. Some things just aren't forgivable."

"Baby... I mean Dice, I can show you better than I can tell you. All I'm asking for is a second chance." She paused. "If not for me, do it for our son and our family."

Dice stood up to his feet. He was done listening to this foolishness. In his eyes Tonya was just trying to get back on his good side because she didn't have nowhere else to turn to or nowhere else to go. "Listen I gotta get going. Take care of my house while I'm..."

Tonya roughly grabbed the side of Dice's face and pressed her lips against his as the two shared a long sloppy drawn out kiss. Dice pushed Tonya off of him. "What the fuck you doing?"

Tonya kissed Dice again while massaging his dick through his jeans. She smiled when she felt how hard Dice was and how his manhood still responded to her touch. "You want me to stop?" Tonya spoke seductively with her mouth still attached to his mouth. "Huh?" She darted her tongue in and out of Dice's mouth as their tongues did a slow dance. "Or you want me to suck the shit out of your dick?" She asked slowly while undoing Dice's jeans. Before Dice could answer, he felt his jeans and boxers drop down to his ankles.

"Can I please suck on this big dick?" Tonya asked in a sexually charged voice looking into Dice's eyes as she stroked his manhood slowly with both hands. "Can I.... Please?"

"Yes," Dice moaned with his eyes closed. It was something about Tonya that Dice just couldn't resist.

Tonya slowly melted down to her knees. She was looking at Dice's manhood as she placed soft wet kisses all over the head. She then slowly took him into her warm wet mouth. A loud drawn out moan escaped Tonya's lips as she moved her mouth up and down on Dice's dick taking more and more of it in until she got the whole thing in. Dice looked down and admired Tonya while she sucked hard, slurped loudly, and slowly glided her head up and down. Tonya was moaning loudly as if she was pleasing herself while pleasing Dice all at the same time. She deep throated Dice's dick until she could feel his balls slamming up against her wet chin with each thrust. Dice moved his hips and went deeper inside Tonya's mouth. He grabbed the back of her head as he continued to dick feed her until he couldn't take it any longer and exploded in Tonya's mouth.

"Ooooh Shit!" Dice groaned breathing heavily. Tonya didn't stop there. The sweet taste of Dice's cum only made her head bob up and down even faster. It made her suck even harder, slurp and moan even louder, and it made the beast inside her wake up.

Once Dice's dick was standing back at attention, him and Tonya went at it like animals. Dice pulled her hair and fucked her long and hard. He fucked her like he hated her, like he was trying to kill her, like he was trying to pay her back for all the times she did him wrong. Dice made Tonya stand up and touch her toes while eh fucked her senseless.

"OH YES... YES... AHHH, AH.... Oh I missed this dick so much!" Tonya moaned loudly. "I'm about to cum!" She screamed as her legs began to shake uncontrollably. Tonya arched her back and came a long drawn out orgasm as her body glistened with sweat.

"Oh my God!" Tonya said with her eyes closed as she lay sprawled out across the bedroom carpeted floor breathing heavily. "I love you Dice and I promise to be the best I can be and make you proud of me... You'll see; watch.... I promise!"

Dice laid back on his king sized bed butt naked staring up at the ceiling. He knew he had just made a mistake and was pretty sure he would be paying for it sooner than later. He just hoped and prayed that the cost would be reasonable.

Chapter 19
"You've Been Warned"

Wolf laid across the bed on his stomach while Ivy straddled his lower back and slowly pressed down on Wolf's back giving him a nice oiled massage. Ever since Prince shot Wolf in his back, he had been having major pains all throughout his back.

"Aw yeah, right there," Wolf moaned while wincing in pain.

"You need to go to the doctor and have them take a look at your back," Ivy suggested. You should have let them take a look at it the same night it happened.

"Why go through all that when I got my own personal masseuse right here," Wolf smiled. Him and Ivy had been getting along great and their love was growing and getting stronger with each passing day. When Wolf and Ivy first hooked up he never would have thought that the two of them would be where they are today. Ivy even joined The Spades. She was a rider and wanted to help her man out as much as possible and any way she could.

"I am your personal masseuse," Ivy agreed. "But what happens when I'm not around and your back starts hurting? Then what?"

"I'm fine baby," Wolf said as he heard his iPhone buzz. "Now get ya fine ass up and get me something to drink."

Ivy eased up off the bed. Her leg was feeling much better and now she walked with a slight limp, but nothing serious. She wore a tight fitting white wife beater and nothing else. "What you want to drink?"

"Orange juice," Wolf replied as he looked at the home screen on his iPhone and saw that he had an e-mail. "Oh and one more thing," he said stopping Ivy just as she was about to exit the bedroom.

"Wassup?" Ivy said craning her neck back inside the room looking back at Wolf.

"I love you baby," Wolf said looking at Ivy's big ass as she smiled. She told him she loved him more and then disappeared downstairs. Once Ivy was out the room Wolf pressed the e-mail icon on his iPhone and saw that he had an e-mail from Pauleena. "Fuck this bitch want?" He said out loud as he opened the e-mail and read it.

From: Pauleena Diaz
Subject: The Spades?
Date: September 16, 2012
To: Wolf

Hello Wolf, my name is Pauleena and I've been hearing a lot about you and your Spades organization. Now I'm not sure if you've been informed or not, but this is my city... And nothing goes on without me knowing about it and from what I've been hearing you and The Spades call yourselves cleaning up the streets... LOL I don't have a problem with you and The Spades trying to clean up the streets... But, what I do have a problem with is you fucking with my money... Mr. Wolf don't fuck with my money and I won't destroy your entire life and everyone's lives around you... I'm sure you will see things my way, so the losses I've taken so far from you and The Spades I'll chalk it up to you not knowing any better... In the future just please make sure not to fuck with nothing or no one that belongs to me... Have a nice day Mr. Wolf.

Wolf read the e-mail twice and then quickly hit the reply button. Who the fuck did this bitch think she was?

From: Wolf

Subject: Your City?
Date: September 16, 2012
To: Pauleena Diaz

Ms. Pauleena thank you for your e-mail and I'm sorry I didn't know that this was "your city" and that I had to get permission from you before and after every move I made... I'm replying to your e-mail to let you know that me and The Spades are out to clean up the streets by any means necessary so if you don't want no problems then I suggest that you find a new occupation and a different and more positive way to make money because if you haven't heard, The Spades are running the streets and this is our city now. People who want to sell poison aren't allowed and will be dealt with sooner than later... Read this e-mail carefully because I'm not the one for a whole lot of talking... Have a nice day Ms. Diaz.

Almost instantly there was a response.

From: Pauleena Diaz
Subject: You talking real tough!
Date: September 16, 2012
To: Wolf

Mr. Wolf if I didn't know any better, I'd might of mistaken you for being a real live gangster... LOL You talking real tough over this computer... I hope you're not one of those computer gangster's that I've been hearing about. The bottom line is this is MY city and I happen to "love" my occupation... What I don't like are people who don't know shit about me thinking they can just come and push me around... Mr. Wolf I'm not the one you want to fuck with. Actually I'm the last person on this earth that you want to fuck with... And I'm not the one to do a lot of talking either. I'd rather let my guns do the talking... Mr. Wolf if I was you, I would back the fuck up before you get clapped the fuck up...

From: Wolf
Subject:I talk tough cause I do tough things!
Date: September 16, 2012
To: Pauleena Diaz

Listen I don't' have time to keep going back and forth with you. Either you stop slanging poison or deal with the consequences... And please don't think that because you are a woman that I will feel sorry for you for one second or even think about taking it easy on you... You continue to sell poison in my community, then you deal with the consequences... Have a nice day Ms. Diaz.

From: Pauleena Diaz
Subject: The Consequences
Date: September 16, 2012
To: Wolf

Wolf I'm going to keep this short and sweet... Fuck you and fuck your consequences... When you see me, you know what to do!

From: Wolf
Subject: You've Been Warned
Date: September 16, 2012
To: Pauleena Diaz

You have a real filthy mouth for a woman. I just hope that your bite is as loud as your bark... I've asked you nicely to stop slanging poison to my people. You refuse so now me and The Spades will respond accordingly... Ms. Diaz you've been warned!

From: Pauleena Diaz
Subject: Fuck You!
Date: September 16, 2012
To: Wolf

Mr. Wolf just by reading your e-mails I can tell that you are a clown and I look forward to running into you. All I ask is that you keep the police out of this... It started in the streets so let's keep it there... This is how I feed my family. This is how all my people feed their families so if you think for one second that I'm going to lay down, you my friend are in for a rude awakening. This is what I do. This is what I been doing and this is what I'm going to continue to do... Like I said, I look forward to running into you Mr. Wolf. Just know there will be shots fired on site.... You've been warned!

Wolf looked down at his iPhone and knew that shit was definitely about to get real, real fast. Wolf did his research and knew all about Pauleena and how she got down. There was only one name on the hit list before Pauleena's. Once that was taken care of, Pauleena was up next.

"You alright baby," Ivy asked re-entering the room carrying two glasses of juice in her hands.

"Yeah I'm good baby," Wolf replied with a smile.

"How's your back feeling?"

"Much better now." Wolf stood up and walked over to his closet and began getting dressed.

"Awww, you have to leave already?"

Wolf nodded his head. He knew Pauleena was the real deal and figured he might as well start planning on how he would get rid of the Queen of the city and all of her followers.

"Be careful out there baby," Ivy kissed Wolf on the lips as she watched him walk out the door.

Wolf stepped outside and saw The Big Show along with several other Spades standing around popping shit. "Yo, we got one more mission to take care of and then Pauleena is up next."

The Big Show smiled. "It's about fucking time! I can't stand that bitch!"

"Well let's get this done so we can get down to the real deal," Wolf said as him and The Spades hopped in the black van and peeled off.

Chapter 20
"Let the Games Begin"

Agent Starks sat camped out in his car taking pictures of all of the high rank Spades members and the license plates of all of the nice cars lined up on the block. Wolf and The Spades threw a block party for the community before the weather got too cold. Eight blocks were taped off for The Spades to enjoy themselves. Music bumped through the big speakers that were set up throughout the blocks. The women Spades members were in charge of serving the food and drinks. Agent Starks loved what Wolf was doing for the community and how he was able to bring the people together and keep it peaceful. Agent Starks' only concern was keeping it peaceful. Once he was done taking pictures of The Spades, he hopped out and decided to take a closer look. He was the type that needed to be up close and in the mix of things.

Wolf stood over in the corner smiling, kissing babies, and shaking hands like he was the President. The whole city came out to show The Spades love and to let them know that they highly appreciated their efforts in the community. Wolf took several pictures with the people who supported him and The Spades movement. Wolf glanced over at Ivy who was over at the table with the rest of the women serving the people.

Ivy shot Wolf a private glance and silently mouthed the words "I love you" to him. She knew Wolf was solely out to serve and help the people, but she couldn't help but notice all the women, single mothers, and even elder women who were all smiling up in Wolf's face every chance they got; which seemed like every second! Ivy did her best to pay the women no mind. She knew she was Wolf's woman, but she wanted the world to know that she was his one and only queen. Wolf always kept Ivy away from things and never acknowledged her as his woman in public in fear that one of his enemies would harm her in order to get back at him. Ivy understood Wolf's logic, but she still wanted all the women who were all grinning up in his face to know that he had a good woman at home who would stand by his side no matter what. Wolf and Live Wire were becoming celebrities so to speak. Ivy was happy for Wolf, but in the back of her mind she knew that the more famous Wolf became, the more women would be out to steal her spot and take her man. That's what scared Ivy the most.

"Don't even pay them women no mind," Pastor Anderson said creeping up on Ivy from behind placing a friendly hand on her shoulder.

"I'm trying my best, but it looks like it's some serious competition out here," Ivy said forcing a smile on her face.

"I'm going to give you a little food for thought," Pastor Anderson said. "Know your place," he told her. "It's a reason why you have keys to Wolf's house and not none of them other women... Once you figure out why you've been chosen and not all those other women, you'll feel much better, but only you know the answer to that."

Ivy smiled. Pastor Anderson was always good at uplifting people's spirits and making them feel much better about themselves. "Thanks Pastor."

"Anytime," Pastor Anderson said then frowned when he saw Live Wire show up with some big booty girl wearing a pair of red Good2Go leggings. He shook his head with a disgusted look on his face. "I hope this fool don't start no mess," Pastor Anderson mumbled, smiled at Ivy, then spun off.

Live Wire bopped coolly with Sparkle by his side. He had just finished busting her ass right before they arrived at the block party. Three chains hung from Live Wire's neck, a bottle of Coconut Ciroc was in his hand, and from the bulge under his shirt it was evident that he had a gun on him. By his side, Sparkle wore her hair out, a red top that her breast threatened to bust out of at any moment, red Good2Go leggings, and a pair of black red bottom heels. Sparkle had an attitude and a slight frown was plastered on her face. She didn't really care for all the extra attention that women were showing her man. Sparkle didn't understand and she didn't have as much class or the patience that Ivy had. She was ready to explode at any second. Once Live Wire got done smiling and taking pictures with all the people, Sparkle dug into his ass.

"Do you have to take a picture with every bitch that grins up in your face," Sparkle huffed.

"Don't start!" Live Wire shook his head and then took a swig from his bottle.

"Don't start my motherfucking ass!" Sparkle capped back. "Live Wire don't play with me cause I will embarrass you out here," she warned. "If it was me smiling up in other men faces, I bet it would be a problem."

"Why you hoe talking?" Live Wire hissed. "Don't hoe talk... If you wanna go smile up in other niggas faces then go ahead," he flicked his hand dismissively.

"Fuck you mean, why I'm hoe talking?" Sparkle snapped. "You know what I don't even have the energy to argue with you right now," Sparkle huffed as she pulled out her cell phone and pretended like she was looking at something important.

Live Wire shook his head and took another swig from his bottle. He didn't understand women. You could give them everything and they would still be jealous for no reason. As he looked around, he had to admit it was some serious competition out at the block party. Women wore skimpy outfits and close to nothing. The women who were out looked as if they were dressed for a night club instead of a block party. Just as Live Wire was about to assure Sparkle that she had nothing to worry about, he saw Coco walking up with a smile on her face. Coco wore her hair in a ponytail and she had on an all black tight fitting outfit and a pair of four inch black pumps.

"What up superstar?" Coco asked holding her arms out for a hug. Sparkle quickly looked up from her phone and over at Live Wire and Coco. Live Wire hugged Coco a little too intimately for Sparkle's liking. Live Wire paid Sparkle no mind and ignored her evil looks. Live Wire hated the fact that Sparkle was so jealous, but he kept her around because out of all of the women that he ever been with, Sparkle was the realest. She always kept it real with him and he knew that Sparkle would ride with him through thick and thin whether he was wrong or right... She was a keeper.

"Damn, you smell mad good," Live Wire said releasing Coco from his embrace as he took another swig from his bottle.

"Why you ain't never call me?" Coco asked.

"My bad; I been mad busy," Live Wire looked over Coco's shoulder and at Sparkle who was staring a hole through Coco. "But listen, I'mma call you tonight though," he said trying to get rid of Coco before things got ignorant.

"What you trying to get rid of me or something? What your girl out here or something?" Coco asked suspiciously. Honestly she could care less if Live Wire's girl was out there or not. She could tell that Live Wire was feeling her. Coco was the baddest chick walking the planet if you asked her and she was confident that she could steal any man away from any woman.

"Nah, I ain't trying to get rid of you. It's just a lot of eyes out here." Live Wire took another swig. "But, I'mma definitely hit you up tonight. Ya number still the same; right?"

Before Coco could reply, Sparkle walked up and joined in the conversation.

"Hello. How you doing?" Sparkle said loudly making her presence known. "What's up with all this whispering going on over here?"

"Obviously we didn't want everybody hearing what we had to say," Coco said slyly knowing it would piss Sparkly off. Sparkle was competition and it was no wrong in love or war. "You got my number baby. Call me later when you are free." Coco smiled, kissed Live Wire on the check, and then walked off. Coco didn't have as much ass as

Sparkle, but she had enough to turn heads. Live Wire's eyes followed Coco's ass as she walked off.

"Damn!" Sparkle yelled snapping Live Wire out of his trance. "You see something you like over there!?"

Live Wire smiled and then took another swig from his bottle.

"That's funny?" Sparkle snapped jumping all up in Live Wire's face. "You think that's funny!? These whack ass bitches all up in ya face and you think that shit is funny?"

"You wilding right now," Live Wire said while taking another sip from his bottle. "You Od-ing right now over nothing."

"Okay well I'mma go smile up in some niggas faces and see how funny you think it is…"

"There you go hoe talking again," Live Wire sighed. Then with the quickness he turned and smacked the shit out of Sparkle. Her neck jerked violently and her ear-ring went flying off. The slap shocked and stunned Sparkle for a second. As soon as the reality of what just happened set in, Sparkle lunged at Live Wire swinging wildly and cursing loudly.

Live Wire grabbed Sparkle and violently slammed her down to the ground. Several Spades members quickly stepped in between the couple separating them.

"Get that bitch up outta here before I hurt her." Live Wire growled.

"Yo, my man," a tall Spades member said aggressively. "That's a female," he said looking at Live Wire like he wanted to get it popping. "Ain't no man got the right to put their hands on a female."

"Word?"

"Word," the tall Spades member replied. Live Wire reached for his waist. How dare this peasant speak to him like that? Before Live Wire could pull out his strap, Wolf quickly stopped him.

"Don't even think about it," Wolf warned draping his arm around Live Wire's neck. The two walked out of ear shot before Wolf spoke again.

"What the fuck is your problem?" Wolf asked. "We supposed to be out here making the community a better place to live and you was just about to shoot one of our own... What's been going on in your mind lately?"

"If niggas violate, then I'm putting them in they place," Live Wire replied. "I don't care who it is."

"You don't get it do you?" Wolf asked. The nonchalant look on Live Wire's face made him want to rip his head off. "Ain't no man bigger than the mission."

Live Wire chuckled. "You need to take your own advice."

"What's up with you stealing money?" Wolf asked coming straight out with it.

"I don't call it stealing," Live Wire told Wolf. "I call it doing what I gotta do... Straight up, I'm the one out there risking my life while you sitting in the office pretending to be a business man... You are living in a fantasy world. This shit is real out here... I love money... Fuck the community," Live Wire said as he noticed The Big Show walk up.

"You a real piece of shit; you know that?" Wolf said looking Live Wire dead in his eyes. "You are no longer a Spades member and if I ever catch you anywhere around any of my people, The Spades will be given the green light to take you out on site... Do I make myself clear?"

"Crystal," Live Wire countered. The thought of backing down never crossed his mind. Wolf was his man and all that, but if Wolf decided to get fly out the mouth with him then he had no problem putting hands and feet on his partner.

"Get the fuck up outta here before I get upset," Wolf barked.

Live Wire took another sip from his bottle and smiled at Wolf. "Talk to me like that again and I'll bust this motherfucking bottle over your head," he threatened.

"Excuse yourself," Wolf said in a stern and firm tone. "I'm not going to ask you no more."

Before things could get out of hand, Agent Starks walked up right on time. "Gentleman," he said. "Nice little event y'all got going on over here." Agent Starks turned and faced Live Wire. "I don't think we've met... Agent Starks," he extended his hand.

Live Wire looked at Agent Starks like he was crazy and turned and walked off.

As Live Wire walked off, he saw an African man standing in front of a cooler selling water.

"Yo fam, let me get a water," Live Wire said tossing the bottle of Ciroc down to the ground. He was smacked (drunk) and badly needed some cold water.

The African man grabbed a bottle of water from out the cooler and held it out towards Live Wire. "One dollar"

"Nigga give me one from the bottom of the cooler," Live Wire barked. "Fuck you tryna give me that warm shit..."

"Hey man, I don't want no trouble," the African man said placing the bottle of water back inside of the cooler.

In a quick motion Live Wire raised his foot and kicked over the cooler spilling ice and bottles of water all over the ground. The African man thought about responding violently, but decided against it. He didn't want no trouble with The Spades so he just let it ride.

"Faggot ass nigga," Live Wire huffed as he spun off. He hopped in his Benz and pulled off in a dramatic fashion. As Live Wire drove, he knew the next time he bumped into Wolf it was sure to be a problem. He didn't like how Wolf had just tried to style on him out in public like he wasn't a shooter, like his gun didn't go off, and like he want' bout that life. Live Wire had love for Wolf, but he wasn't just gone let Wolf talk to him any ole kind of way. Live Wire pulled up in front of one of his Spanish chick's house. He was still mad at Sparkle for acting like a jealous fool out in the street so he wasn't quite ready to go home yet. Live Wire was still contemplating on if he should smack the shit out of Sparkle again when he got home or not. He stumbled out of his Benz and pointed his key fob at the luxury car, locking the doors and activating the alarm. He walked up to the front of the house and froze when he felt cold steel being pressed to the back of his head. Live Wire immediately knew he had been caught slipping. He knew he was about to die, but he refused to give his killers the satisfaction of hearing him beg for his life.

"Don't move!" Tall Man ordered as Psycho walked up and removed Live Wire's gun from his waist. Once Live Wire was unarmed, two Muslim men kicked the front door open. Tall Man forced Live Wire inside the house as he watched the two Muslim men run up the stairs and drag his Spanish chick and her daughter down the stairs and hold them at gunpoint.

Live Wire was forced to watch the Muslim men hog tie his Spanish chick and her thirteen year old daughter up. "What's this all about?" Live Wire asked quickly sobering up while looking around at the house full of men.

"You know exactly what this shit is about," Pauleena said stepping through the front door with Prince bringing up the rear. Pauleena wore a navy-blue skirt suit with an expensive pair of navy-blue four inch pumps. Pauleena pulled her hair back into a ponytail and then removed her suit jacket exposing two 9mm's that hung under her arms in the shoulder holster. "Wolf's address... I want it!" Pauleena said standing face to face with Live Wire. "And I want it now!" Live Wire smiled as he gave Pauleena a quick once over. "I don't know anybody named Wolf." Live Wire looked from Pauleena over to Prince and blew Prince a kiss.

"You must not know who I am," Pauleena said returning Live Wire's smile.

"Maybe I don't give a shit who you are," Live Wire countered.

Pauleena quickly snapped one of her 9mm's out of its holster and let it hang freely down by her side. "You should give a shit," she said and then walked straight up to the Spanish chick and pressed the barrel of her 9mm into the woman's forehead and pulled the trigger... POW!

Live Wire yawned loudly. "Was that supposed to impress me?" He shook his head. "I barely even knew her," he shrugged.

"So you ain't afraid to die?" Pauleena walked back over towards Live Wire with a smile on her face. She loved a challenge.

"I'm a Spades," Live Wire said proudly. "We're all prepared and ready to die at any given moment."

Pauleena nodded her head. "I see," she said and then walked over to the teenager and pressed the barrel of her 9mm into the young girls forehead.

"Pauleena wait!" Psycho said stopping her. "No children!"

"This ain't Scarface," Pauleena replied and pulled the trigger... POW!

Live Wire smiled. "So you're Pauleena?" He had heard plenty of stories about the drug Queen pin, but this was his first time running into her face to face. "It's a pleasure to finally meet you... I apologize for my rudeness. I didn't know who you were."

"Wolf's address," Pauleena said sternly. "I want it now," she demanded.

"I can do you one even better. I can tell you where he's at right now," Live Wire told Pauleena.

"Where?"

"What's in it for me?"

"You get to keep your life," Pauleena said aiming her 9mm at Live Wire's head.

"I want in," Live Wire said seriously. "There's a lot of money out there on them streets and I want in... Make me a partner."

"Fuck you," Psycho said jumping in the conversation. Off the rip he didn't like or care for Live Wire.

"Right now there are over 25,000 Spades running around the city willing to kill and die for what Wolf believes in and Pauleena's name is up next on The Spades hit list," Live Wire told them. "I have around three to four thousand Spades members under me that I can cross over to your team with... I'm talking about four thousand niggas that's all about money. We can form us a real live get money team," Live Wire smiled. "The soldiers up under me are The Real

Spades and trust me, you going to need all the fire power you can get."

"How do I know I can trust you?" Pauleena asked raising a questioning eyebrow. In her book trust was something that had to be earned.

"You don't," Live Wire smiled. "This is a money relationship... As long as the money is coming in, we straight... All the blocks that The Spades have cleaned up, me and The Real Spades will flood them back with drugs... What do you say? Do I have a new connect or what?"

Pauleena stood silent for a moment in deep thought thinking over Live Wire's proposition. "Welcome to the team," Pauleena said extending her hand.

"Nah, you too sexy for a hand shake," Live Wire said leaning down giving Pauleena a nice tight hug. "Damn, you smell mad good," he said purposely trying to piss Psycho off.

"Nah fuck that!" Prince huffed. "This nigga cut my face. He ain't getting off that easy!"

"You still crying about that?" Live Wire shook his head. "Stop being a bitch and get over it!"

"Nah, nah... I ain't going for this shit," Prince spat. He couldn't see himself working with someone who tried to take his life on more than one occasion. "Fuck that! Something gotta give..."

"I said he's on the team and that's that," Pauleena said sternly turning her gaze on Prince. "I don't want to hear shit else about this. Do I make myself clear?"

"Nah, fuck that," Prince hissed. "I want to kill this nigga right now!"

"Aight, Fuck it! Y'all got five minutes to get this shit out of y'all's system," Pauleena said looking from Prince to Live Wire. "After that, we will all be working together as a team."

Prince removed his .45 from his waistband and handed it to Tall Man. Then he cracked his knuckles.

"This light work," Live Wire said removing his chains from around his neck and stuffing them down into his pocket. Pauleena, Psycho, Malcolm, Tall Man, and the rest of Pauleena's Muslim security formed a circle around Prince and Live Wire. Live Wire removed his shirt and sat it down on the coffee table. "Don't wanna get no blood on my shirt," he said with a smile.

Pauleena sat back and watched Prince and Live Wire go at it like animals tearing up the entire house in the process. She thought it was stupid for the two to be fighting one another, but she knew it would be worse if they didn't get it off their chests. Ten minutes later Live Wire had a busted lip and Prince had a bloody nose. The living room looked as if a tornado had hit it. After the fight was over Pauleena made the two shake hands. Prince and Live Wire weren't friends, but for now they would have to get along. If not for Pauleena, then for that almighty dollar.

"Now where can we find Wolf at?" Pauleena asked handing Live Wire a rag filled with ice.

****

"I love you," Wolf said hugging Ivy from behind and planting a kiss on her neck. He had been so busy entertaining the people that he hadn't showed Ivy any attention all day.
"Oh you remember little ole me?" Ivy spoke with a hint of jealousy in her voice. She knew she couldn't have all of Wolf's time and she was working on not being so selfish when it came to sharing his time.

"Don't act like that baby," Wolf smiled. He knew Ivy was mad that he was getting so much attention from the women or the hoes as she called them. Even if it were just innocent dialog, he knew Ivy would automatically think otherwise. "You know I only got eyes for you baby!"

"Mmm…hmmm," Ivy hummed playfully. "You better, or else!"

"Or else what?" Wolf playfully challenged.

The block party was still popping and everyone seemed to be having a good time and enjoying themselves. Wolf was proud of himself for doing something positive and help worthy. Wolf and Ivy's conversation was interrupted when Dice and Tonya walked up wearing smiles on their faces. Wolf was glad to see the two back together and working things out.

"What's good?" Dice said giving Wolf dap.

"I had to cancel Live Wire's contract," Wolf told him.

"Word?"

"Word," Wolf replied. "The nigga was stealing money, wilding, buying fancy cars, and partying every night... He was bugging. He was giving The Spades a bad name and making us look bad."

"What's wrong with that nigga?"

"I don't know," Wolf shrugged as it began to pour down raining out the blue. "Meet me at my crib. I got a few things I want to run by you," he told Dice as he watched hundreds of people run trying to hurry and get out the rain. The Big Show and four Spades quickly surrounded Wolf and Ivy and quickly escorted them to their awaiting Range Rover. A Spades member sat behind the wheel with the windshield wipers working overtime. Wolf and Ivy slid in the back seat. Once The Big Show was sure they were safely inside the Range Rover, he hopped in the passenger seat and the Range Rover quickly pulled off.

"I hate being out in the rain," Wolf complained.

"What you made of sugar or something?" Ivy joked. She was just happy to be sitting down especially since she had been on her feet all day. She was happy to be a part of The Spades, but she had to admit that it was a lot of work.

"Hush," Wolf said playfully. "I'm happy that Dice and Tonya got back together and are trying to work things out."

"Me too," Ivy agreed.

"Yo, get down!" The Big Show yelled as he saw two vans come to a screeching stop right in front of the Range Rover blocking its path. Wolf and Ivy quickly ducked down as loud gun fire erupted. Broken glass rained down on top of Wolf and Ivy's head as bullets riddled and rocked the Range

Rover from side to side. Wolf covered Ivy with his body not wanting her to get shot again because of him.

The Big Show pulled out his Dessert Eagle and returned fire hoping the gun shots would keep the killers at bay for a second or two so him and Wolf could gather their thoughts.

Before the killers could move in for the kill, three black vans pulled up full of Spades members. Before the killers got a chance to retreat, The Spades quickly turned the one sided gun battle into a nasty shootout.

"Stay here!" Wolf ordered and then slid out the Range Rover to join the gun battle. He was the leader and had to be out there in the trenches right along with his troops.

Wolf shot two of the would be killers before the sound of sirens filled the air. He looked around and saw that each of the shooters that came to kill him were sprawled out on the concrete dead. The Big Show quickly took Wolf's gun and handed it off to another Spades member. No matter what The Big Show's job was to keep Wolf alive and out of jail by any cost and any means. The Spades member gathered up all The Spades weapons and tossed them in the back of one of the black vans and hopped behind the wheel and peeled off right before several cop cars pulled up to the scene.

"Get Mr. Goldberg on the phone," Wolf said as several cop cars surrounded him and the bullet filled Range Rover.

****

Snow pulled his white B.M.W. onto the big estate and was immediately greeted by two huge armed men that had security written across their chest in white letters. Snow showed his pass to the security guards and then was allowed entry onto the property. Tonight was The Terminator's birthday and he was throwing a big party in his mansion and only the who's who, the popular, and the famous was allowed on the premises.

"It better be some hoes up in here," Trouble said form the front seat. In the back seat sat two other M.O.E. members.

Snow looked at the expensive fleet of luxury cars that were lined up back to back. The section of parked cars looked like a foreign car dealership. Snow parked his B. M. W. next to a red drop top Porsche. Just by looking at all the vehicles that were lined up in the parking area Snow could tell that only people with money were here at the mansion. When Snow and his M.O.E. entourage showed up at the front door, they were searched and then allowed to enter the mansion. Snow stepped foot in the mansion and immediately a smile spread across his face. The mansion was filled with rich looking men dressed in expensive clothes and sexy women all dressed in close to nothing. The mansion was packed wall to wall with people. The women easily outnumbered the men. There were even several women walking around the mansion wearing lingerie with five inch heels and nothing else. Snow looked up towards the ceiling and saw naked women swinging on swings that hung from the ceiling with their faces covered by masquerade mask.

"This the type of shit I'm talking about," Snow said with a wide smile on his face as him and his crew made their way through the crowd. Nicki Minaj's song "Beez In The Trap" bumped loudly through the speakers causing all the women to move their bodies like strippers to the beat. Snow grabbed a flute of champagne from the tray of a passing waiter. Over in the corner Snow spotted The Terminator. The Terminator sat over in the cut shirtless with a pair of Ray-Ban's covering his eyes. An iced out chain hung from around his neck and both of his wrist were glittering with so much ice that it looked like the diamonds on his wrist were dancing. Down below he wore a pair of basketball shorts with his iPhone clipped and attached to his waist, and a pair of black socks and some Nike slippers. Over the past few months ever since The Terminator's last fight him and Snow had begun to hang out a lot and became good friends.

Several naked women surrounded The Terminator, his entourage, and his body guards while the champion enjoyed his birthday with all of his rich celebrity friends. "Yo, my nigga what's good?" The Terminator yelled when he spotted Snow flanked in jewelry.

"You know I wasn't gone miss the party of the century," Snow smiled and gave The Terminator dap. "I see some nice things running around in here."

"You know I stay with the best women the world has to offer," The Terminator boasted.

"Let me know which one of these hoes is yours so I can stay away from her," Snow smiled rubbing his hands together.

"They all mines," The Terminator laughed loudly. "Nah, you know I don't own none of these beautiful women... Take your pick."

The party went crazy when Snow's street anthem came blaring through the speakers.

Trouble draped his arm around Snow's neck. "Them labels gone have to come correct with that paper if they want to sign you... You got the motherfucking streets on fire right now!" He yelled over the loud music looking at how the crowd reacted to the song.

Snow grabbed another champagne filled flute form off the tray of another passing waiter as he bobbed his head to his own lyrics with a smile plastered across his face. His buzz was blowing through the roof and he knew soon he would have to choose a label to sign to. So far all the major labels were in a bidding war over the hottest unsigned artist in the streets right now. As Snow bobbed his head to the music, a huge fat ass caught his attention. "Damn," he mumbled. This was the biggest ass Snow had ever seen in his life. Snow sipped his champagne and continued his conversation with The Terminator all the while keeping his eyes on the sexy Nicki Minaj look alike that stood only a few feet away.

"Is Pauleena coming through?" The Terminator asked sipping on a bottle of water. Even when he wasn't in training, The Terminator still didn't indulge in alcohol or drugs.

"Yeah she's on her way right now... Her and her new boyfriend Psycho... Excuse me for a second," Snow said. He just had to holla at the Nicki Minaj look alike before she disappeared on him. He walked up on Nicki and grabbed another flute of champagne form the tray of another passing waiter and held it out to Nicki. "Drink?" Sparkle sucked her teeth and rolled her eyes when she saw who was standing in front of her. "Can't you see I already have a drink?" She nodded towards the glass flute in her hand.

"My bad ma. No need to get all ugly," Snow smiled. "What's your name?"

"Sparkle; why?" She snapped. Sparkle had seen Snow on T.V. and on the internet a few times and quite frankly she wasn't impressed with him or his raps.

"Why?' Snow huffed looking Sparkle up and down like she was crazy. "You must got your period or something cause you acting like..."

"No I don't have my period, but I do have a man," Sparkle said cutting Snow off.

"Fuck ya man go to do with me?" Snow asked confused. "I was just trying to make conversation and you starting bugging... Ya man here with you or something?"

"No! You lucky he ain't here right now," Sparkle said in a matter of fact tone. "Cause if he was here, he probably would of smacked the shit outta you by now!"

Snow smiled and looked in Sparkle's face to see if she was bullshitting or if she was dead serious. After a few seconds, Snow realized that Sparkle was indeed dead ass serious. "Yo ma, do you know who I am?"

"Yeah I know who you are," Sparkle hissed. "You a fake wanna be rapper who only make videos for YouTube... Yeah, and?" She said louder than necessary calling herself styling on Snow.

"Listen bitch," Snow began. "I don't know what the fuck your problem is, but your best bet..."

"What this bitch over here talking about?" Trouble said jumping into the conversation.

"Bitch?" Sparkle echoed giving Trouble the evil eye. "You bum ass niggas don't want me to call my man," she threatened. "Cause I'll have him come up here and air this whole shit out!"

"Who ya man?" Snow asked curiously.

"Live Wire," Sparkle announced proudly. "He's the leader of The Spades and trust me you don't want them kind of problems cause once them crazy niggas get here..." SPLASH!!

"Bitch burn it up!" Trouble said in a disrespectable manner as he tossed a drink in Sparkle's face.

Sparkle slowly wiped the liquid from her face using the back of her hand and forearm and then lunged at Trouble. Before Sparkle could reach him a M.O.E. member snuffed her from the blind side dropping her right where she stood.

Sparkle hit the floor hard, but she was still conscious. Before she got a chance to get up off the floor, two big security guards picked her up off the floor and escorted her out of the mansion kicking and screaming.

"This shit ain't over with!" was the last words the party goers heard from Sparkle before she was tossed out onto the front lawn like a piece of garbage.

Chapter 21
"No More Warnings"

Ivy hopped out of the shower and heard a bunch of voices coming from downstairs. Ivy threw on a black silk robe and headed downstairs to investigate who the voices she heard belonged to. Ivy and Wolf never had company over like that so to hear all those different voices made Ivy curious. When Ivy made it downstairs she saw at least thirty-five Spades in the living room loading machine guns and loud talking as if they couldn't wait to take someone's life.

"Um Wolf can I have a word with you for a second?"

Wolf sat his Tech-9 down on the coffee table and then quickly joined Ivy upstairs. "Don't ever come downstairs wearing nothing like that again," he mildly scolded her. "Now what's on your mind?"

"What's going on downstairs?"

"We taking Pauleena down today," Wolf told her.

"Oh my God!" Ivy exhaled with a worried look on her face. "Baby please be careful." She heard about Pauleena and all the violent stories that were connected to her name. After how easily Pauleena had the Range Rover that her and Wolf were inside shot up, Ivy was really worried. She already knew she would be a nervous wreck until Wolf returned.

"I got you."

"After this Pauleena thing is over can you maybe let somebody else run The Spades for a while so we can go on a vacation and do some things that normal people do... Like start a family, invest in stocks and bonds, go horseback riding, and things like that... You know baby, normal people stuff."

"Ain't nothing about me normal," Wolf reminded Ivy. "This my life baby and the people and the community come first."

"Even before me?" Ivy asked with her brows rising on their own. She couldn't believe Wolf would or could say something like that.

"Man listen," Wolf sighed rubbing his waves. "When I met you this is what I was doing and ain't nothing change, but the year and the range," he said slyly. "This is a movement and when you're a Spades, you're a Spades for life."

"So you willing to throw us away and throw everything you've accomplished so far away for the community and the people?"

Wolf didn't reply. He just stared at Ivy like she was retarded.

"I love you! Do what you wanna do; just be careful!" Ivy stormed off with an attitude. She didn't understand Wolf. What more could he give to the community or the people, but his life and his freedom. Ivy didn't want to argue or upset Wolf before such a big job so she walked back into the room and gave Wolf a kiss and apologized to him for her outburst.

"Either you in it until the end or you ain't in it at all," Wolf said as he heard a pinging sound signaling that he had an e-mail. "I love you baby and we will talk about this when I get back." Wolf pulled out his iPhone and went straight to his e-mail.

From: Pauleena Diaz
Subject: You can run but you can't hide!
Date: September 28, 2012
To: Wolf

It's only but so ling you can hide from me… I tried to reason with you, but you wanted to do things the hard way.

SMH   And to think I thought you and your team was official… Silly me.

Wolf read the e-mail and all he could do was smile. He had to admit, he liked Pauleena's style.   It was just a shame that she was on the opposite team.   He quickly tapped the reply button.

From: Wolf
Subject: Who's hiding?
Date: September 28, 2012
To: Pauleena Diaz

That little stunt you pulled was cute, but a little on the amateur side for me… Ms. Pauleena I promise I will look you in your eyes as I listen to you beg for your life before I kill you… Like I told you in the last e-mail… You've been warned.

From: Pauleena Diaz
Subject: Don't talk me to death!
Date: September 28, 2012
To: Wolf

Less talking and more action Mr. Wolf… My track record speaks for itself… I guess I'll leave the talking to you. When you ready to turn the city up, you know where to find me. Until then… Suck my dick… Clown.

From: Wolf
Subject: Action is my middle name!
Date: September 28, 2012
To: Pauleena Diaz

If action is what you want, its action you gone get…
See you soon Ms. Pauleena

PS. Keep the cops out of this.

Wolf pressed send and slide his iPhone back down into the clip on his waist and headed back downstairs. Pauleena's e-mails had pissed Wolf off and made him just want to kill her even more. He quickly rounded up all The Spades and headed out the door. The Spades next stop was Pauleena's mansion.

Chapter 22
"Shots Fired"

Psycho sat on the bed counting a huge pile of twenties as Young Jeezy's T.M. 103 hummed through the entertainment system. Being Pauleena's man definitely had its benefits. Psycho already had his own money, but now he was making more money than ever. Inside Psycho was really in love with Pauleena and would die before he let or allowed anything to happen to her. He knew soon The Spades would be trying to retaliate and he planned on doing everything in his power to keep his woman out of harm's way. Pauleena had put Psycho in charge of her O.T. (Out Of Town) customers. Money was rolling in from every direction even with The Spades interfering with a few of their spots.

Pauleena stepped out the bathroom butt naked smelling like fresh strawberry body wash. Her presence alone caused Psycho to lose count and lose focus on what he was doing.

"I swear that shit should be illegal." Psycho shook his head.

"What?" Pauleena asked looking at her naked body in the full length mirror. She placed her hair in a loose ponytail as she made her ass jiggle to the sound of Young Jeezy's voice flowing through the speakers.

"Having all that good pussy," Psycho said as he joined Pauleena in the full length mirror. He hugged her tightly from behind and placed soft kisses on the side of her neck. "I sent Prince and Trouble out to Virginia."

"We got problems out there?"

"Nah, nothing that Prince can't handle," Psycho said confidently. "Fuck all that! I want to know how we going to handle this Spades situation."

"That will be taken care of today," Pauleena said with a smile. "Instead of going after Wolf, I'm going to make Wolf and The Spades come to me."

"And how do you plan on doing this?" Psycho asked curiously. He knew his woman was a genius, but he just had to hear how she was going to do this.

"Simple," Pauleena smiled. "Men have such big egos... Poke at their egos a little bit and any man will respond,"

"I love you," Psycho said suddenly out of nowhere. He spun Pauleena around so that he was staring in her eyes. "You know that; right?"

Pauleena nodded... "Of course I know that... And I love you too."

"Losing you once was the biggest mistake of my life," Psycho said grabbing a hold of Pauleena's hand. "And I promise to not ever let you down again." Psycho reached down into his back pocket and removed a ring box. He slid down on one knee and looked up at Pauleena. "Baby will you marry me?" He asked snapping open the ring box revealing a five carat diamond ring.

"Oh my God," Pauleena said covering her mouth with her hands. She had a shocked and surprised look plastered on her face. "I can't believe this," she said at a loss for words. "Do you know what you are asking me?"

"I do," Psycho replied looking up from the one knee position. "So what do you say?"

Pauleena paused for a moment as her eyes began to water. No matter how tough she was at the end of the day she was still a woman first.

"Will you marry me?" Psycho asked again. Pauleena taking her time to give him an answer caused him to get a little nervous and worried.

"Yes... Yes I will marry you," Pauleena sang happily as Psycho slipped the five carrot ring on her ring finger.

"You just made me the happiest man in the world," Psycho beamed looking his new fiancé in the eyes.

"You really want to spend the rest of your life with me?" Pauleena asked.

Psycho pulled Pauleena's naked body into his and kissed her like he missed her. His hands made their way down to Pauleena's ass as their tongues did a long slow dance.

Psycho scooped Pauleena's naked body into his arms like she was a baby and carried her over towards the king sized bed. The two's lips stayed locked until Psycho gently laid Pauleena down on the bed. He stood back and admired her nakedness for a moment before handling his business.

Psycho buried his face in between his soon to be wife's legs and gave her the oral pleasure of a lifetime. Pauleena panted and jerked as Psycho moved his tongue up and down her narrow slit. He was determined to make her cum and determined to please every last one of her needs. He wanted to keep his soon to be wife happy.

"Yes... Yes... Yes...," Pauleena moaned loudly as her hands found the back of Psycho's head. She ripped the hair tie from his hair letting it all flow down freely. She pulled Psycho's hair as she continued to moan and move her hips matching Psycho's tongue thrust for thrust. Pauleena moved slow as she felt her body start to quiver. Her right leg began to shake uncontrollably. Pauleena moaned good and long, enjoying every second of her orgasm. Psycho then climbed in between Pauleena's legs and mounted her missionary style, tongue to tongue, face to face. He entered her walls slowly, wanting and needing to feel all of her. Psycho started off with slow strokes, but once Pauleena was used to his rhythm, he sped up his strokes. He fucked her long and hard. The headboard was beating against the wall like a steady drum. Pauleena's moans deepened as her nails dug deeper into Psycho's skin. She was clawing away at his back. She jerked and made sounds that told Psycho she was on fire; a fire that only he could put out. Pauleena frowned as Psycho slid in and out of her making the most beautiful/ugly faces ever.

Psycho stiffened up and let out a loud groan. Then he collapsed on top of Pauleena. Both of them were breathing like they just finished a two mile sprint.

"Damn baby," Psycho smiled with his eyes closed. Before he could say anything else, him and Pauleena heard a loud knock at their bedroom door. Pauleena hopped up off the bed and slipped on a blue silk robe. Then she made her way to the door. "What's up," she asked when she saw Malcolm standing on the other side of the door.

"One of the brothers just spotted eight black vans pull up a block away," Malcolm informed Pauleena. "We suspect it's The Spades... How would you like to handle this?"

"Strap up," Pauleena said with a smile. Then went back inside her bedroom and closed the door.

"Wolf and The Spades are here," Pauleena said. She entered her walk in closet and returned carrying a tailor made white suit and a pair of four inch white pumps with a red bottom.

"What's the plan?" Psycho asked as he quickly slipped back into his clothes and checked the magazine to his Glock.

"I'm going to lead Wolf and The Spades to a well known location that you're going to be waiting for them at," she said checking her appearance in the mirror.

"What location?"

"Manna's"

"The soul food restaurant on 125th street?" Psycho asked with a confused look on his face.

"Yes," Pauleena answered with a smile. "I'm going to lead The Spades straight to the restaurant," she paused. "You're going to already be waiting on the roof. If they follow me inside the restaurant, you can pick them off one by one. If they don't get out the vans hit whoever is in the front seats, but I'm a hundred percent sure that they'll get out the vans and follow me inside of the restaurant."

"What happens if they try to take you before you make it to the restaurant? Then what?"

"Don't worry, I'll make it to the restaurant," Pauleena assured him.

"I don't like this plan. What if something goes wrong?" Psycho asked with his face full of concern.

Pauleena walked over and kissed Psycho on the lips. "Stop worrying so much. I'll be fine. I promise... I'll meet you at the soul food spot."

Psycho grabbed his suitcase that held his sniper rifle inside and headed for the door. He stopped suddenly in the middle of his tracks. "You better make it to that restaurant," he said one last time then turned and left. Once Psycho was gone, Malcolm entered Pauleena's bedroom. "What's the word?"

"You feel like taking a ride with me?" Pauleena asked with a smirk on her face. Malcolm slowly walked over towards Pauleena's gun closet and removed an A.K. 47 along with several clips. "Sure, why not," Malcolm said while smiling and stuffing the extra clips down into the pocket of his all black suit. Fifteen minutes later Pauleena stepped foot out of her mansion along with Malcolm and ten other Muslim bodyguards. Malcolm held the back door to the Escalade open for Pauleena.

"Nah, I think I want to take the Benz today," Pauleena said surprising everyone. "Malcolm come ride with me. The rest of you stay close behind me."

Pauleena hopped in her cocaine white CLS-C218 Benz. Pauleena's Benz was outfitted with Rynohide Armored Technology which made the entire vehicle bullet proof. Malcolm climbed in the passenger seat resting his A.K. in between his legs. Pauleena popped Snow's mix tape in and then pulled off of her estate followed by four black Escalades filled with Muslims.

Pauleena bobbed her head to Snow's music. Prince had been telling her about his cousin who was nice on the mic, but this was her first time listening to Snow's mix tape and she had to admit she was impressed. Not only was Snow's lyrics hot, but the beats he picked were trunk rattlers. "I might have to invest in this young man," Pauleena said out loud as she noticed Malcolm bobbing his head to the beat as well.

Pauleena glanced through the rearview mirror and noticed the black vans following behind her bodyguard's Escalades.

****

Wolf sat behind the wheel of an all black Dodge Charger and in the passenger seat sat Dice. Eight vans full of Spades stood standing by waiting for Wolf to give them the word. After a forty-five minute wait Wolf and Dice spotted Pauleena stepping out of her mansion surrounded by several of her Muslim bodyguards.

"Where's Live Wire?" Dice asked watching Pauleena's every move closely.

"I called him a few times to check up on him, but got no answer," Wolf told Dice as he slid a ski-mask down over his face. On his lap sat a Tech-9. "You ready to do this?"

Dice nodded as he watched Pauleena's white Benz pull off of her property. He slid his ski-mask down over his face and held a tight grip on his Uzi. Once the Charger pulled out into the street and followed the Benz and fleet of Escalades, the black vans followed the Charger's lead. It was time to find out who was really running shit and who was just running their mouth.

****

Over in the cut sat a royal blue Crown Vic unnoticed. Agent Starks sat behind the wheel. He had been tailing Wolf and knew it wasn't a coincidence that Wolf led him straight to Pauleena's mansion. Agent Starks knew something big was getting ready to go down. He didn't know what, but he did know he would soon find out. Agent Starks kept a seven car distance between him and the last black van in hopes of not being noticed. He was determined to either get Wolf or Pauleena off of the streets today and honestly he didn't care which one it was.

****

Pauleena kept her eyes glued to the rearview mirror as the Benz smoothly glided down the highway. Her and Malcolm rode in complete silence after listening to Snow's music. They both were anticipating the drama that they knew was about to come. Pauleena cruised along, keeping up with the rest of the traffic. The sound of loud machine gunfire caught her attention. "Here we go," she said looking up into the rearview mirror. She saw her bodyguards holding the black vans off as the two crews exchanged gunfire right in the middle of the highway. Pauleena's eyes took turns moving quickly from the road back up to the rearview mirror as she saw two of the black vans lose control and crash into some other cars. Seconds later one of the Escalades loss control and crashed into the metal divider.

Pauleena glanced up at the rearview mirror and saw a black Charger pulling up to her driver side at a fast speed. The Charger pulled up side by side with the Benz while both vehicles were doing 90 mph. Pauleena glanced over and saw the window to the Charger roll down. A man wearing a ski-mask aimed an Uzi at Pauleena's face and squeezed the trigger. Pauleena ducked down out of reflexes as the bullets bounced off the bullet proof driver side window. She quickly swerved over two lanes and gunned the engine.

"These motherfuckers are too close on our ass!" Pauleena said weaving from lane to lane avoiding other cars on the highway. The Benz zoomed down the highway with the Charger close on its heels.

"I'll take care of this." Malcolm rolled his window down, grabbed his A.K., and hung halfway out the window and opened fire on the Charger.

"Shit!" Wolf cursed as he quickly weaved two lanes over when he saw a big Muslim brother open fire with an A.K. 47. Wolf drove the Charger like he was a Nascar driver. Wolf and Dice took cover as a few A.K. rounds shattered the Charger's front windshield. Dice returned fire and again the Uzi bullets bounced off of the body of the Benz.

"Fucking bullet proof car," Wolf huffed as he looked up in his rearview mirror and saw flashing lights. "We got company behind us," he announced.

Dice glanced backwards and saw flashing on the dashboard of a royal blue Crown Vic. He immediately hung half his body out the window and opened fire on the undercover cop car. The Uzi's bullets shattered the Crown Vic's windshield and shot out the headlights.

****

Agent Starks took cover as several bullets tore the front of his car up and decorated the front windshield with fresh bullet holes. He quickly called in for backup as he slowed his vehicle down, but made sure he remained close enough to the Charger to stay in eyesight. It was no way he was going to let that Charger out of his sight.

****

Psycho stood up on top of the roof of the soul food restaurant setting up his sniper rifle. He glanced down at his watch and anticipated Pauleena showing up within the next ten or fifteen minutes. He didn't like Pauleena's plan, but he trusted that she knew what she was doing. Psycho loved Pauleena and planned on protecting her by any means necessary. He just prayed that she make it to the soul food restaurant safe and sound.

****

The white Benz zoomed down the highway weaving from lane to lane. Pauleena tried to pass in between two eighteen wheelers that were in front of her, but the two big trucks denied her access and slowed her down in the process. Good Samaritans at their best.

Pauleena looked over at Malcolm and gave him a head nod. With that being said, Malcolm hung out the window again and shot out the tires on both of the eighteen wheelers. He reloaded and then sent shots flying inside both trucks until both of the eighteen wheelers opened up and parted like the red sea. Pauleena gunned the engine and zoomed pass the two big trucks. She peeked through the rearview mirror and saw the Charger still behind her. Pauleena quickly turned the steering wheel hard sending Malcolm into the door as she took the next exit. She then cut to the right, cutting hard without warning. This move sent Malcolm's body slamming into Pauleena. Up ahead Pauleena could see the soul food restaurant, but a bullet exploding into the back tire almost caused her to lose control over the vehicle. The Benz came to a dramatic stop in front of the Magic Johnson Movie Theater. Malcolm quickly hopped out the passenger seat of the Benz and opened fire on the Charger while Pauleena hopped out the driver's seat and ran in the movie theater with Malcolm close behind her. Once inside the movie theater Pauleena kicked off her heels, snatched one of her 9mm's out of the holster, and sent two shots up into the ceiling sending the entire place into a frenzy. While everyone scrambled for their lives Pauleena and Malcolm jogged up the escalator steps.

Wolf and Dice hopped out the Charger and ran inside the movie theater after Pauleena as they saw several cop cars pull up to the scene. Immediately Wolf spotted Pauleena and Malcolm making their way to the top of the escalator. He aimed his Tech-9 at the two and opened fire without thinking twice. Wolf and Dice pushed their way through all the people who were desperately scrambling for their lives. When they reached the top of the steps, Wolf saw the door to one of Tyler Perry's movies closing. Wolf and Dice quickly made their way over to the theater and entered with caution. It was dark inside the theater except for the tiny lights that went down the aisles. The sound of loud gunfire rang out followed by screams and another stampede. Wolf turned the corner and saw Pauleena run out the side exit door while Malcolm stood over in the corner holding an A.K. 47.

"I'll distract the big man while you go after Pauleena," Dice yelled over all the noise and then opened fire on Malcolm. Malcolm quickly returned fire not caring who he hit in the process.

While Dice and Malcolm tried to kill each other, Wolf slipped out the side exit and went after Pauleena. He made it out into the hallway and saw Pauleena run through the staircase door. Pauleena looked back and saw a masked man running after her. Immediately she knew the man behind the mask was Wolf. She fired two shots over her shoulder and let the staircase door slam. Pauleena ran down the steps skipping two at a time. When she heard the staircase door bust open above her, she blindly fired three shots up in that direction. When Pauleena reached the ground level, she busted out the exit door and found herself outside on the other side of the theater. Pauleena looked left and then right trying to find a good escape route or any kind of escape route period. Her eyes locked on the subway and without thinking twice she ran full speed towards the subway. Wolf came out the exit and saw Pauleena heading down the subway steps. He quickly took off behind her.

****

After a three minute shoot out with Malcolm, Dice tossed his Uzi down to the floor, snatched off his ski-mask, and blended in with the rest of the people who were trying to stay out of harm's way. As Dice ran down the carpeted hallway along with everyone else, he spotted Agent Starks jogging towards the action with a 9mm in his hand. Dice ran right pass Agent Starks and never looked back.

Agent Starks eyes scanned left and right trying to get a good look at as many faces as possible. He knew for sure that Wolf and Pauleena were definitely somewhere in the building and he didn't plan on stopping until he found one of them if not both. As Agent Starks walked towards the theater that was showing a Tyler Perry movie, he saw a big man wearing an all black suit hurry pass him. Agent Starks couldn't put his finger on it, but something about the big man didn't' sit well with him.

"Excuse me sir!" Agent Starks called after the big man. Malcolm ignored the agent's calls. If it was one thing that Malcolm hated the most, it was the police. If the agent wanted to arrest him, he'd better come correct because Malcolm wasn't going down quietly or without a physical altercation.

"Excuse me sir... Hold on for a second!" Agent Starks yelled again. Still he got no response from the big man. "I said hold on for a second!" Agent Starks said grabbing the big man's shoulder. Malcolm quickly spun around and landed a hard elbow in Agent Starks face. The two had a scuffle/fight right in the middle of the hallway. In the midst of the fight, Agent Starks pulled out his taser and pumped thousands of volts into Malcolm's body. Seconds later several officers joined in and forced Malcolm down to the floor and cuffed him.

****

Psycho stepped foot out the building with his hand down in his waistband. He stood on the wrong side of the roof expecting Pauleena to arrive from one direction, but heard loud gunshots coming from the opposite direction. When Psycho made it outside all he saw was Pauleena's white Benz surrounded by cops. It looked as if a million cops flooded the streets and the front of the movie theater. As Psycho stood on the opposite side of the street along with all the other nosey pedestrians, he saw several cops escort Malcolm out the movie theater in handcuffs. "Fuck!" Psycho cursed under his breath as he waited for the police to bring Pauleena out in cuffs next. As Psycho stood in the crowd he heard a door slam. He looked to his right and saw Pauleena running down the steps that led down to the subway with a man with a ski-mask close on her heels.

"Shit!" Psycho cursed as he quickly took off in the direction of the subway.

****

Pauleena descended the steps two at a time. Once she reached the ground level Pauleena spotted a cop standing ne to the toll booth making sure everyone paid their fare.

Pauleena paid the cop no mind as she jumped the turnstile right in front of him. Immediately the cop took off after Pauleena yelling and screaming causing a scene. Pauleena ignored the cop as she headed down the steps leading to the train platforms. When she made it to the platform she thought about jumping down onto the tracks and running across towards the other side of the station. Pauleena looked down at her bare feet and had a change of heart. The thought of the big New York City rats running across and by her feet didn't sit too well with her. Not having any other options, Pauleena tossed the 9mm she had in her hand down onto the tracks along with her second 9mm that rested in her holster.

"Ma'am, come with me!" The officer said roughly grabbing Pauleena by the arm. "You're under arrest!"

"No, wait!" Pauleena said resisting. "He's trying to kill me!"

"Who's trying to kill you?"

"Him!"

When the cop looked up, he saw a man wearing a ski-mask with a gun in his hand running down the stairs. The cop reached for his waistband, but two shots exploded into his chest before he could remove his gun from its holster. A train pulled into the station Justas the cops body violently crashed down into the concrete floor. Immediately Pauleena took off running down the platform and hopped on the train. She looked behind her and saw that Wolf had also boarded the train and only two carts separated the two.

Psycho hurried down the steps and hopped on the train just as the doors were closing. Four carts away he spotted the man in the ski-mask moving from cart to cart at an aggressive pace which only meant that Pauleena was in trouble.

****

Pauleena scrambled from one train cart to the next one. She pushed and shoved people out of her way. With no weapons in her possession, Pauleena was willing to do anything in order to stay alive. Pauleena pulled open the door that led to the next cart and peeked over her shoulder. All she saw was Wolf gaining chase on her.

"Shit! Shit! Shit!" Pauleena cursed as she heard loud gunshots echoing from behind her followed by the sound of glass shattering and people screaming. She pushed her way through men, women, and even kids. At this point Pauleena's main focus was to stay alive. She pushed and pushed until she reached the last cart. She was now trapped and stuck between a rock and a hard place with nowhere to run. She had reached a dead end. Pauleena did the only thing she could do at the moment. She grabbed an old lady who sat over in the corner all by herself and threw her in a choke hold using the older woman as a shield.

Wolf reached the last cart and saw Pauleena standing behind an old woman. The way Pauleena used the innocent old woman as a shield disgusted him and made him want to kill her even more.

"Get back!" Pauleena yelled. "Get back or I'll snap this bitch's neck!" She warned. From the tight grip Pauleena had on the old woman's neck Wolf believed she would indeed snap the old woman's neck if provoked.

Wolf took cautious steps in Pauleena's direction. He held a firm two handed grip on his weapon. All the running combined with the ski-mask had Wolf sweating.

"Don't come any further or else I'm going to snap this bitch's neck!" Pauleena yelled tightening her grip on the woman's neck.

Wolf stood there for a second trying to decide if he should try to take the shot or not. He wanted so badly to take the shot. The thought of accidently shooting the old woman was the only thing that stopped him from taking the shot. Before he could make a decision, Wolf heard a loud blast followed by a sharp stinging pain on the bottom of his right earlobe. He quickly spun around and saw a Spanish man holding a gun. Immediately Wolf returned fire. Each man was firing and dodging bullets all at the same time. When the train came to a stop at the next station, Pauleena quickly dashed off the train right into the awaiting arms of the police. Once Wolf and Psycho saw police everywhere they ran in between carts, tossed their weapons, and hopped over the chained divider down onto the tracks. Wolf ran across the train tracks to the other side while Psycho took off down the tracks and disappearing in the dark tunnel.

Wolf made it upstairs, snatched off his ski-mask and blended in with the rest of the New York City crowd. He was upset that Pauleena had gotten away, but happy that he had escaped all the madness not in handcuffs or in the back of a police car. Wolf reached the corner and quickly flagged down a yellow cab. Once the cab reached the highway, Wolf closed his eyes and let out a deep breath as he silently thanked God that he was still alive.

Chapter 23
"A Nervous Wreck"

Ivy sat on the couch a nervous wreck. All day she had been watching the news and all that was being reported was the big shootout that took place on the highway that led into the Magic Johnson movie theater on 125th street. Ivy prayed and prayed all day that her man hadn't been harmed or arrested. The news reporter reported that several members from a street gang called The Spades had been arrested along with several other Muslim brothers. Ivy cursed at the T.V. screen as if the reporter could hear her. "The Spades aren't a street gang you dumb bitch!" she yelled. Ivy hated how the media could take something that was so positive and turn it into something negative. With so many outlets it was easy for the media and news to brainwash its viewers and have them believing that The Spades were in fact nothing more than a "street gang." The more Ivy watched the news, the angrier she became. The news reporter said that several Spades members had been arrested, but they weren't revealing the names of the members. Not knowing what else to do, Ivy picked up her phone and dialed Wolf's number only to reach his voicemail. She ended the call and then tried Dice's number. He picked up on the fourth ring.

"Hello"

"Hey Dice, it's me Ivy. Sorry to bother you, but I haven't' heard from Wolf all day and was wondering if he was okay?" Ivy said hoping Dice could answer a few of her questions so her mind wouldn't have to continue to wonder.

"I can't really talk about it over the phone, but I haven't heard from him since we parted ways. I just hope he's alright," Dice said. From the tone of his voice Ivy could tell that he too had been worrying about Wolf.

"Well if you hear anything, please let me know."

"I got you. You already know," Dice said as the two ended the call.

Ivy tossed her phone down onto the couch and continued to watch the news. All she could do now was wait and hope for the best. Forty-five minutes later Ivy heard the sound of keys jingling and being inserted through the key hole. Then she saw Wolf walk through the door with a slight smile on his face. His facial expression said that he had, had a long day and was happy to be home. Ivy ran and jumped into Wolf's arms and hugged him tightly. The thought of never seeing him again made her want to hug him forever.

"Oh my God baby! I was so worried about you," Ivy sang happily. The first thing she noticed was that Wolf was bleeding. Blood was running down the side of his face. Ivy couldn't tell if the blood was coming from his head or his ear. "Baby you are bleeding," she said.

"Yeah I know," Wolf said as if it was nothing. "Shit got a little crazy out there."

"It's all over the news." Ivy nodded towards the T.V. then paused. "Is it all over with?'

Wolf shook his head no. He knew that the ongoing war between Pauleena and The Spades wouldn't stop until one of them was resting six feet underground. He knew Pauleena's pride wouldn't let her back down. He knew the only way this could end was with a bullet in Pauleena's head.

"So now what?" Ivy asked a question that she already knew the answer to. She knew Wolf wouldn't stop until his mission was accomplished and until he was satisfied with his work. Ivy already knew what time it was.

"We continue to clean up the streets one block at a time," Wolf said removing his clothes and heading into the bathroom. All the running around made him a sweaty mess and not to mention the ski-mask he had worn all day was hot as hell. Needless to say he was in a desperate need of a shower. Ivy quickly followed Wolf into the bathroom.

"Hold on a minute," she huffed removing a bottle of alcohol and a box of cotton balls from the medicine cabinet inside the bathroom's mirror. Wolf sat down butt naked on the toilet seat while Ivy tended to his wounds. "Oh my God! I know that shit has got to hurt," Ivy said looking at the remaining half of Wolf's ear. The bullet that Psycho fired had blown half of his ear off, but Wolf would rather get half of his ear blown off instead of half of his head any day.

"It ain't too bad," Wolf said trying to convince Ivy more than himself. Once Wolf was all patched up, he hopped in the shower and let the pressure from the shower head massage and run all over his body. Wolf had a lot on his mind. Not to mention he had a lot of tough decisions he would have to make in the near future. He had the whole city depending on him and it was no way he would let his people down. Wolf stood directly underneath the shower head until he felt a pair of hands wrap around his chest and some soft titties on his back. Wolf paid the pair of hands no mind as his mind continued to think about all the shit that lied ahead.

"I got your back one hundred percent, no matter what," Ivy whispered still holding Wolf tight. The thought of losing the only thing good she had going on in her life scared her. Just the thought of something bad happening to Wolf made Ivy cry. She knew being with a man like Wolf was a no, no, but she couldn't control who held her heart. She knew if it ever came down to it, Wolf would give his life in order to protect and save hers and a love like that in Ivy's eyes was priceless.

"I know you do baby," Wolf replied. He was starting to see that Ivy loved him more that she loved herself which was a good thing in his book. The only bad part about that was Wolf knew he shouldn't have gotten involved with Ivy in the first place. With all the shit that was on his plate the last thing he needed to be worrying about was a woman. He knew loving Ivy was his one and only flaw, but at the end of the day he couldn't stop loving who he loved.

Slowly Wolf felt Ivy's hands make her way down below his belt line as she began working him into a stiffness. Her wet hands were touching all the right places. She knew Wolf had, had a long stressful day and now Ivy planned on helping him unwind. To her surprise, Wolf swiftly spun around and scooped her up in the air. He held her up with his hands underneath her wet ass and she instantly wrapped her legs around his slim and toned waist. Ivy moaned as Wolf slid inside her. She bounced up and down hard and fast with both arms around his neck hanging on for dear life. The sound of wet skin slapping against wet skin along with loud moans drowned out all the other sounds in the bathroom. Ivy continued to bounce up and down hard and fast until her orgasm took over and erupted causing her body to jerk and lock even tighter around Wolf's waist. Her moans turned into a howl. After Ivy's orgasm, she knew she would belong to Wolf for the rest of her life; no matter what and no questions asked.

Chapter 24
"Mind Games"

Pauleena sat in the interrogation room with a frown on her face. She had been left all alone in the room all by herself going on ten hours now. Pauleena knew the detectives were playing mind games with her. They were trying to mind fuck her, but what the detectives didn't know was that Pauleena was the master when it came to mind fucking people. If there was a class on mind fucking, Pauleena would qualify to be the teacher. As Pauleena sat and continued to wait she looked down at her feet. Her once freshly pedicured toes were now dirty and bloody from the small pieces of glass Pauleena had accidently stepped on while fighting to stay alive. She lifted her feet to examine the bottom and couldn't believe how filthy they were. The more Pauleena looked down at her dirty feet, the more she wanted to kill Wolf. She didn't like Wolf, but she respected him. He had some big balls and wasn't afraid to let them hang if necessary. Pauleena's whole plan blew up in her face and she had no one to blame for it but herself. Now that The Spades had made their move, the streets would be waiting to see what Pauleena's response would be. Pauleena had no clue what her next move would be. This was nothing like going head up with Marvin and his crew the way she had done in the past. This was a whole different ballgame and The Spades weren't Marvin. The Spades now had well over twenty thousand members worldwide. Twenty thousand members also meant twenty thousand different type of guns, twenty thousand different type of problems, and twenty thousand different ways that Pauleena could be killed.

"Kill the head and the body will fall," Pauleena mumbled as he thought of different ways she would be able to get at Wolf. There was strength in numbers and twenty thousand was a pretty strong number anyway you looked at it. Pauleena's thoughts were interrupted when the door opened and in walked Agent Michael Starks. He held a thick manila folder in his hand as his expensive hard bottom shoes rang loudly on the tiled floor.

"Pauleena Diaz," Agent Starks read from her file. "You did two years in a woman's federal camp in Florida, recently beat two murders and a man slaughter charge, plead guilty to possession of a control substance and took five years probation, and it says here that you are now currently out on bail."

"Yeah... And?"

"Yeah and it seems to me that you are a trouble maker or trouble seems to always find you," Agent Starks said sitting down at the metal table. He looked across the table at Pauleena. "Care to tell me what happened today?"

"Go fuck yourself!"

Agent Starks ignored Pauleena's response. "You're in some deep shit and if you don't want to go to jail and be somebody's bitch then I suggest that you start talking," Agent Starks raised his voice. "A nice, pretty, sexy little thing like you will be a hot commodity in prison. I can see them passing you around like a joint now."

Jail didn't scare Pauleena. She had done time before and had no problem doing time again "IF" she had to. Thoughts of spitting in the cops face crossed her mind. Pauleena yawned loudly not even bothering to cover her mouth. "You done yet," Pauleena said. Her tone showed no respect.

Agent Starks wanted to slap the shit out of the ignorant bitch that sat across from him, but knew it would be best for him to control his anger. "Right now I'm the only person in this world that can help you." He smirked knowing he finally had something to stick on Pauleena. "Not even your big shot lawyer is going to be able to help you out on this one."

"Enough with this foolishness," Pauleena huffed. "I got shit I could be doing right now so if you're going to arrest me then arrest me. If not then shut the fuck up and let me up out of here," she demanded.

Agent Starks smirk turned into a smile. "Okay! Have it your way you stupid cunt," he said. Agent Starks reached down into the manila folder and removed a small disk. He stood to his feet and walked over to the T.V. that rested on the wall and popped in the disk.

Pauleena looked on with a bored look on her face as she watched the video with no sound. The video seemed to be recorded from a traffic light that rested right in front of the Magic Johnson movie theater. Pauleena continued to watch the video as he watched a white Benz enter into the picture followed by a black Charger. She watched silently as a man wearing a suit hopped out the Benz and opened fire in the middle of the street with an A.K. 47. She watched as innocent people ran for their lives, as a woman hopped out of the driver's seat of the car with a gun in her hand, and quickly ran inside the movie theater.

Agent Starks aimed the remote at the screen and rewinded the video back to the woman holding the gun in her hand and then zoomed in. He zoomed in so close that he could even see that all the adrenalin had Pauleena's nipples hard as she stood there frozen on the screen. A perfect shot of her face, the gun, and the rest of her body as well stood there on the screen as plain as day.

"Got anything you want to say now?" Agent Starks smiled.

At the moment only one word floated around in Pauleena's mind. She said "lawyer."

Chapter 25
"What's What"

Wolf and Dice sat in the basement of the church and amongst them sat several important Spades members. The Spades were becoming so large that Wolf had to assign two leaders for each borough and each leader was to report to Dice. If it was ever anything Dice couldn't handle, he brought it to Wolf's attention. Everything was set up perfectly and running smoothly just the way Wolf liked it. It had been five days since the shootout at the movie theater and so far Wolf hadn't heard anything from Pauleena or anyone down with her organization which was a good thing. The once rowdy and violent drug infested community was now a quiet peaceful neighborhood where kids could play outside, ride their bikes, and not have to worry about catching a stray bullet. That alone made Wolf proud. He was proud to be a part of something so positive and powerful all at the same time. "The Bronx and Queens is looking as good as new," Wolf said. "But I have been hearing Harlem and Brooklyn still out there slinging poison like it's the 80's."

"Me and a few Spades members will go out there and look into it," Dice said. "I already got a twenty man Spades team out in Jersey working on cleaning up the streets out there."

"Once we done with New York our next two spots are going to be Atlanta and then Miami," Wolf announced.

"Last night I got some disturbing news," Dice said looking at Wolf. "I thought it would be best to tell you about it face to face and not over the phone."

"I'm listening," Wolf said. Wolf and the rest of The Spades members gave Dice their undivided attention.

"I got word last night from a valid source that the spots we had already shut down in Harlem and Brooklyn have been re-opened and a lot of product is being moved," Dice announced.

Independent workers or are we dealing with an organization," Wolf asked.

"An organization if that's what you want to call it."
"What's the name of this organization?" Wolf asked.

"They call themselves, "The Real Spades."

Wolf chuckled. "You're joking right?"

"Afraid not," Dice said.

"Who's the leader of these so called Real Spades?" Wolf asked.

"Live Wire"

"Live Wire as in my Live Wire?" Wolf asked not believing his ears.

Dice nodded his head. Wolf knew Live Wire was up to something, but he just didn't know what. He was wondering why he couldn't get a hold of Live Wire recently, but he figured Live Wire may have just needed a little bit of time to cool off and get his head clear. Never in a million years would he have ever thought that Live Wire was setting up his own crew; a crew he chose to name "The Real Spades" and a crew that was out to destroy the community that Wolf and The Spades were trying so hard to build back up. That pissed Wolf off! It made him angry and it made him want to put his hands on someone and that someone was Live Wire. For Live Wire to do something like that was like a big slap to Wolf's face.

"How you want to handle this?" Dice asked. He knew this was a touchy situation due to the fact that Wolf and Live Wire were so close at one point in time. The two had come up with a plan, executed the plan, and started the biggest and most powerful movement since the Black Panther Party Movement. The two had made history together and now all of those memories would be erased and forgotten. A once partner and creator of The Spades was now an enemy; an enemy who didn't back down or play by The Spades rules. This type of person would surely end up with a bullet in his head just like the rest of the drug dealing scum that were still out on the streets slanging poison. Wolf had a bullet with all of their names on it.

"I'll take care of it," Wolf said. The look on his face was now the look of a man with a lot on his mind. "I called you all down here because I had a big announcement to make," Wolf said looking around. "I did my rounds out in the community and I have been getting a lot of complaints that when people call 911 that it takes the police forever to show up," he paused. "If there were a real emergency, the people who called 911 would be dead before the cops even thought about showing up... We can't have that. Our people can no longer have that. So..." Wolf looked around. "We're going to have to start policing our own communities... Besides I would rather have one of my people who I know I can trust handle that instead of a stranger from the NYPD who is probably only going to show up when he feels like it."

"So what are you saying?" Dice asked. He wanted to make sure he was hearing Wolf correctly.

"We are going to start to police our own neighborhoods," Wolf said handing Dice a business card. "I rented out a five bedroom apartment and I have put switchboards and phone lines all throughout the apartment. Someone calls and tells us their problem. The women we have working the switchboards call out to the nearest Spades van and have him show up and take care of the problem."

"That's going to be a lot of work," Dice said.

"We have way more than enough members to run and control this whole city," Wolf smiled. "We'll set it up in shifts. We'll have a morning shift, an evening shift, and a grave yard shift."

"When you plan on having this up and fully running?" Dice asked.

"Before the month is out," Wolf answered quickly. "We are going to start with one borough at a time. In no time The Spades will be running and controlling this whole city."

Dice smiled at the thought. Wolf was a genius. The thoughts he could come up with were the thoughts of a world leader. The way he put a plan together was like no other and

Dice had his back one hundred percent. With the amount of money The Spades were pulling in off the streets from all the drug dealers and drug crews, it was easy for Wolf to set up a movement like this. Especially since he knew the money would never stop. Once New York City was clean of drugs, The Spades would just move on to the next state and squeeze and milk their drug dealers dry. It was as simple operation. All that was needed to pull it off was heart, loyalty, money, and discipline and The Spades had all four.

Wolf looked over at Dice. "Now that Live Wire has officially jumped ship, I'm going to need you to step up and hold things down."

Dice smiled. "I got you!" He was happy, proud, and excited to be a part of something so powerful and so historic. Dice was proud to say that he was a member of The Spades. "So what you wanna do about Live Wire?" He asked. "Do you want me and a team to go down there and take care of that?"

"Nah, that something I have to take care of myself," Wolf replied. In his heart he didn't want to believe what he was hearing about Live Wire, but unfortunately he knew it was true. Live Wire had been acting strange lately, but Wolf paid Live Wire's actions no mind. Live Wire had his own greedy thoughts about how The Spades operation should have been ran, but Wolf wasn't having it. No one man was bigger than The Spades movement; not even Wolf himself.

"I gotta get up outta here," Dice said giving everyone in the basement a pound. Dice and his team had a few more drug dealers to run down on before it got too late.

Once everyone had left, Wolf stayed behind in the basement. He was alone; just him and his thoughts. He leaned back in his comfortable and expensive chair and let his mind drift. Wolf had to figure out how and when he was going to deal with this Live Wire issue. Spending so much time with and being around Live Wire so much left Wolf with yet another difficult decision that he would have to make soon. He didn't want to kill Live Wire, but deep down inside he knew Live Wire had a lot to prove and was out to put on a show. Live Wire wanted to let the people know that he and his crew were "The Real Spades" and it was a new gun in town. Knowing all of this just made Wolf's decision that much harder.

Chapter 26
"Fresh Out"

Pauleena stepped foot out of the jail and was immediately met by her team of security. One of her Muslim security guards draped an all black shiny mink coat over her shoulders and escorted her towards her Escalade. He treated her like she was The President of the United States; like she was royalty. The Muslim bodyguard opened the back door of the S.U. V. and Pauleena quickly slid inside. In the back seat of the truck sat Psycho. He was happy to see his fiancé, but by looking at his face one would never know.

"Hey baby! Thanks for coming to bail me out," Pauleena said leaning over with her lips poked out for a kiss.

Psycho ignored her gesture. "What you did was stupid and dumb and you could of gotten yourself killed!" He raved.

"I'm still breathing; ain't I," Pauleena said sarcastically.

"Yeah and because of your stupidity you're soon going to be breathing jail air because that's where you are headed especially if you keep up with this wild cowgirl shit you got going on!"

"Listen baby," Pauleena began. "Me being a woman who runs shit makes it hard for me to be low key. I have to put on the way I do to let motherfuckers know that just because I'm a woman doesn't mean that I'm soft. I have to let motherfuckers know that if you fuck with me, my gun will go off. I have to let motherfuckers know that if you try to violate me in anyway... My gun will go off!" She explained.

"Baby I understand all that," Psycho said. "And now that's what I'm here for... To let motherfuckers know that if they fuck with my fiancé that my gun is going off... If they try to violate you or anybody in our crew, my gun is going off!" He explained looking into Pauleena's eyes. He knew that Pauleena was so used to doing things on her own that it would be difficult to get her out of her ways. "I'm here to help you. We're on the same team."

"I know baby," Pauleena said looking at Psycho. "You mad at me?"

Psycho's face formed into a weak smile. "You know I can't stay mad at you; especially with a face like that," he said placing a soft kiss on her lips. Psycho really loved Pauleena and promised to do right by her this time around and protect her by any means necessary. "I got a plan that's going to keep you out of trouble and get rid of The Spades at the same time." Psycho noticed that he now had Pauleena's full undivided attention.

"I'm all ears."

"When you are a leader or a boss, your job is to sit back and let your soldiers handle things for you," Psycho said. "You're not supposed to be out in the fields putting in work with the rest of the soldiers, cause then if something happens to you then who's going to lead the rest of the troops?" He said. "This is chess; not checkers and in chess you are supposed to use your pawns."

"I know how to play chess so what's your point?" Pauleena snapped. She didn't have time for the small talk. She wanted to hear Psycho's plan.

"Start using your pawns and the game will become much easier," Psycho smiled. "Let's use Live Wire and his crew to take out Wolf and The Spades. Let's give Live Wire all the financial support he needs. We take care of him and in return he'll take care of us and all of our problems."

Pauleena smiled. "You are a genius!" She said excitedly. She could see the outcome of Psycho's plan playing out in her head as the two sat in the back seat of the Escalade.

"You can control people with money," Psycho told her. "Control the way people think and the way they see things."

"I love you," Pauleena said. "I love you!"

Chapter 27
"The Real Spades"

Live Wire sat in an expensive Japanese restaurant. He looked like a new man and he also had a lot of new money. Live Wire and The Real Spades took over Harlem and Brooklyn with the product that Pauleena had given him at a great wholesale price. Needless to say, The Real Spades were rolling in the dough thanks to the plan that Live Wire had put together. He went around the city and rounded up all the toughest and most dangerous niggas that were still on the streets and gave them a job. He gave them an opportunity to join a "real" movement. He gave them the opportunity to join a powerful movement that was all about the mighty dollar and who better to run this movement than Live Wire. Live Wire dreamed, ate, and spoke about money all day long. He was enjoying his new wealth as well as being the leader of his own organization, but that wasn't enough for him. He had big plans and big dreams; million dollar dreams and federal nightmares. Live Wire knew the only way he would get to the level he dreamed of was to start expanding and building his movement and in the process he knew his pockets would have no choice but to rise as well. Sitting at the table across from Live Wire was his newest recruitment. His newest recruitment was a white woman in her late twenties with blue eyes and blonde hair. She had the face of a model and the body of a stripper or a porn star. The woman who sat across from Live Wire was no other than Tori, better known to everyone else as The Madam.

The madam was born and raised in Texas and well known for all of the whore houses and brothels all around the country. The Madam had heard about a man out in New York who was starting up his own movement; a movement that involved making a lot of money. She got word that this man was also about to put some new fresh face prostitutes out on the streets that didn't mind doing something strange for some change and didn't mind making a man holla for a dollar. Tori and her team of security flew out to New York to meet the leader of this movement. When Tori met Live Wire, the two hit it off instantly. Both of them agreed that if they worked together instead of against one another it would be more profitable for both sides. Not to mention, Tori had been hearing about another dangerous gang that called themselves The Spades. The last thing she needed was The Spades sticking their noses in her business. Tori had several hit teams on standby, but her motto was if a situation could be talked out that's what would be her first option. Her second option would be gun play.

Tori sat across the table from Live Wire with a stank look on her face with a wine glass and a bottle of wine in front of her. Outside in front of the restaurant stood four big oversized men who were paid to protect The Madam with their lives. Beside the four big men stood about ten members of The Real Spades who were paid to do the same for Live Wire. Each set of men were out scanning the streets looking for any signs of trouble.

"Who do I have to kill to put a smile on your face?" Live Wire said raising his wine glass to his lips.

"For starters, you could have called me back like you promised you would," Tori huffed. She wasn't used to men saying they were going to do something and it didn't get done. After the two met to discuss business that first night, Tori had made the mistake of sleeping with Live Wire. The sex was good, but the end result was Tori sitting by her phone waiting for Live Wire to call. This was all new to Tori because in her part of town she was the queen and she had men throwing themselves at her each and every day. Every request she made, there was a line of men waiting and willing to fulfill each and every one of her needs.

"Sorry," Live Wire said. "I've been a little tied up lately," he said with a grin. "But I am happy to see you again."

"The only reason I came was because you said you had some business you wanted to talk to me about. If it wasn't for that, I would have never given you the time of day to be in my presence again," Tori said in a matter of fact tone.

Live Wire ignored the slick comment and grabbed a hold of Tori's hand. She tried to pull away, but Live Wire tightened his grip. "Stop acting like that."

"I'm not acting like anything. Say what you have to say so we can go on about our business."

Live Wire knew that The Madam didn't fly all the way out to New York just to talk business. She flew all the way to New York to talk business and to lay her eyes on him. He could tell by the look in Tori's eyes that she was upset with him, but he could also tell that she missed him and wanted to forgive him for not calling.

"I called you out here cause I see a beautiful future for the both of us," Live Wire said in a more serious tone. "I got a good connect now and I called you out here to see if you wanted to join my empire?"

"Why would I want to join your empire when I have my own?" The Madam replied and then took another sip of her wine.

Live Wire said, "Let me rephrase that. I called you out here to see if you would like to combine both of our empires and create a super mega empire!"

"I'm listening," The Madam said giving Live Wire her undivided attention. Whenever money was involved she was all ears.

"I was thinking maybe you could come into my drug enterprise as a silent partner. My cut would be sixty-five and yours thirty-five," Live Wire said throwing it out there.

"And what's in it for you?" Tori asked knowing it was a flipside to this.

"You let me in on your empire. You keep sixty-five and give me thirty-five and together we can take over shit on the drug tip and on the pussy tip one state at a time," Live Wire said. "Plus us working together would give me more time to spend around you."

Tori smiled. The deal didn't sound too bad. Besides she knew Live Wire had a large team behind him. Each and every day The Real Spades numbers were multiplying and getting stronger and stronger. "I'll think about it... Give me a few days to think it over."

"How long you going to be in town for?"

"Three or four days," Tori answered. "Thinking about staying at the London Hotel."

"London Hotel?" Live Wire echoed.

"What's wrong with that?" Tori asked knowing Live Wire would want her stay at his place while she was in New York.

"I can't have you staying in no hotel," Live Wire smiled. "You're a guest in my city so it's only right to offer that you spend the next three or four days with me." Live Wire knew Tori wanted to spend time with him. That was the whole point of her being in New York. She had come to discuss business, but she also came to discuss the issue she had with Live Wire and to let him know that she wasn't happy with him not calling her.

Tori had only been with two black guys her entire life, but neither of them were anything like Live Wire. He had swag and the way he walked, talked, and just didn't give a fuck about anything attracted her to him. Tori hated to admit it, but she was feeling Live Wire in the worse way.

"Why should I stay with you for these next three or four days?" Tori asked seductively putting her wine glass up to her lips.

Live Wire looked up and returned her stare. "I can show you better than I can tell you."

Chapter 28
"New Sheriff in Town"

Wolf, The Big Show, and two other Spades members went door to door handing out business cards to everyone. On the business card it was a number that the people could call whenever there was an emergency and a Spades member would be there as soon as possible to handle the problem the best way he saw fit. Wolf didn't allow any of the women Spades members to participate in the field work. It was too dangerous.

A woman in her late forties snatched her door open and gladly accepted the business card from Wolf. "It is such a pleasure to finally meet you," the woman said. "You've done a wonderful job out there in these streets, especially during these times when young kids don't have any respect for anyone." She shook her head.

"Thank you ma'am. The Spades and I are just out here trying to do our best," Wolf said politely.

"Well you keep up the good work and may God bless you," the woman said as an eruption of noise sounded off a few doors down. The sound of a woman screaming could be heard followed by the sound of a skull banging against the wall. "Teresa and that no good man of hers is at it again," the old lady said as if it was nothing. "He's always putting a foot in her ass. If it ain't one thing, it's another."

"Enjoy the rest of your day ma'am," Wolf said as him and his team quickly made their way down the hall to the apartment that the violence was coming from. When they reached the door, the sound of a man cursing at the top of his lungs could be heard outside the door. The Big Show raised his fist and banged on the door like the police. Immediately all the yelling and screaming came to an end. The Big Show knocked on the door again. Seconds later the door opened as far as the chain lock would allow it to. Then a small slim woman looked out through the crack and said, "yes."

"We heard a lot of yelling and screaming ma'am. Is everything alright?" Wolf asked trying to look inside the apartment. The woman didn't reply. She just simply nodded her head yes.

"Are you sure?" Wolf asked looking into the woman's eyes. "Me and these men you see with me are down with The Spades and we are here to help."

"I'm fine," the woman said in a tone just above a whisper.

"Mind if I have a word with the man of the house?" Wolf asked. "We just want to make sure everything is okay."

The woman disappeared from the door. Wolf could hear the sound of two people whispering, but he couldn't make out the conversation. He could only make out a few words. They want to talk to you and The Spades was the only part of the conversation that Wolf could make out before the sound of the chain lock being removed from the door was heard followed by a big man's presence at the door. The big man stood in the doorway with sweat covering his face, a dingy wife beater covering his top, and a pair of stained sweat pants covering his lower body. The man's hair was in a wild crinkly afro. It looked as if he had just taken out some corn rows.

"Yo, what's up?" The big man's voice boomed and echoed out in the hallway.

"Is there a problem over here?" Wolf asked.

"Does it look like it's a problem?" The big man shot back while staring at the men who stood in his hallway looking at him like they were crazy.

"We heard a lot of commotion and we just wanted to make sure that…"

"Yo my man; we good over here!" The big man said cutting Wolf off. "Nosey motherfuckers!"

"You mind if we come inside for a second just to make sure that the woman is okay?"

"Fuck outta here!" The big man growled as he went to slam the door in the stranger's faces. Before the door could close, The Big Show's leg was already coming forward. The door busted open and The Spades quickly entered the small apartment.

Wolf looked around and saw that the place was a mess. He looked over to the right and saw a little boy sitting on the couch with a scared look on his face. Wolf also noticed that the little boy had a black eye and a few bruises on his arm. Wolf then looked over at the slim chick and the scared look that was on her face told it all. With the quickness of a snake Wolf turned and swung on the big man. The slim chick screamed and cried as she watched The Spades beat the shit out of the big man like he was a little boy. Once The Spades were done, The Big Show grabbed the big man by the ankles and dragged his unconscious body out of the apartment.

"Here take this," Wolf said handing the slim chick a business card. "If he tries to come back again, all you have to do is call this number."

"Fuck you!" The woman yelled like she was possessed. "Who do you think you are? Huh? What makes you think you go the right to bust up in my house and put your hands on the father of my kids?" The woman screamed.

"Sorry! I was just trying to help." Wolf told her.

"I don't need you or your help!" The slim chick huffed. "Now get the fuck up out of my house before I call the real cops," she threatened.

"Have a nice day," Wolf said as he turned and left.

"Fuck you too!" The slim chick yelled before she slammed the door.

Wolf stepped outside and realized that he would only be able to help the people who wanted to be helped. Some people enjoyed being miserable, stuck in their ways, and didn't want to change and that was cool with Wolf. For the people who wanted the help, The Spades would be there for them. The rest of the people could just keep living the way they had been living.

When Wolf hopped back inside the van he noticed that The Big Show had a smile on his face. "What?" Wolf asked.

"I just got a call from Dice."

"Okay and?"

"He said him and his crew found out where Live Wire hangs out at," The Big Show told him.

"Right now?"

"Right now," The Big Show replied. "It's either now or never."

"Fuck it! Tell the rest of The Spades it's time to strap up," Wolf said. "It's time to pay this fucker a visit."

Chapter 29
"Killa Season"

Live Wire stood in the liquor store along with Bills and a few other new Real Spades members. All together it was around twelve of them. Also inside the liquor store were a pack of half naked females looking for attention. Live Wire laughed as he watched his young goons spit game to the chicks in the liquor store. He was happy to see his team out having a good time and enjoying life. Seeing his team enjoying themselves put a smile on his face. Live Wire grabbed a bottle of Henny off the shelf, twisted off the cap, and guzzled straight from the bottle.

"Excuse me!" The owner said in a stern tone. "Please pay before you drink."

"Calm down! I got you," Live Wire said reaching down into his pocket. He paid for everyone's drinks as they all exited the store.

"Damn!" Live Wire heard one of the chicks say. When he looked up he saw ten black vans lined up back to back. Leaning up against one of the vans he saw Wolf, Dice, The Big Show, and about forty other members of The Spades with serious looks plastered on their faces.

Live Wire looked up and smiled. "What's good?"

"You tell me," Wolf replied. This was his first time laying eyes on Live Wire in over a month and a half. He would have been happy to see his long time friend if he wasn't there to shut down what he had going on.

"Doing me," Live Wire said with a smile. "Getting this money."

"And how you going about getting this money?" Wolf asked.

"Best way I know how," Live Wire shrugged. "But fuck all this small talk. You here for a reason, so what's up?"

"You already know what's up," Wolf said. "Now we can either do this the easy way or the hard way. It's up to you."

Live Wire took a swig from his bottle as his crew stood behind him. They may have been out gunned, but they had more than enough bullets to go around. "You just can't stand to see me shine; can you?" Live Wire said. "You've always tried to shut down my ideas because you were always scared I would out shine you."

"That's bullshit and you know it!"

"Now that I got some momentum behind what I'm doing, you want to come shut it down; right?" Live Wire yelled. "Do what you feel, but you already know how I'm giving it up," he said patting his waist line.

"You've been warned," Wolf spoke in his usual calm voice. He knew that this was how things would play out. He knew there was no way that Live Wire would be able to turn down the opportunity to make fast money and a lot of it. He knew the outcome of this meeting would result in two former friends trying to kill each other.

"Fuck you!" Live Wire growled as him and his crew watched Wolf and The Spades hop in their vans and make their exit.

"Fuck them niggas think they are?" Bills said standing next to Live Wire. "That nigga Wolf think he can just tell niggas what they can and can't do."

"Nigga a control freak!" Live Wire raised his bottle up to his lips and took a deep swig. "If he think he is shutting us down, he got another thing coming. I worked too hard to finally get us on the map to let this clown come and shut my whole shit down!"

"You believe this nigga; talking about you've been warned," Bills said as him and the crew busted out laughing. "That nigga done watched one too many movies."

"It's all good though. We gone definitely put him in his place once and for all," Live Wire said. The way Wolf had just approached him had Live Wire pissed off. It felt like Wolf was trying to strong arm him and trying to muscle him into doing things the way he wanted him to do them and Live Wire wasn't feeling that. He didn't want to kill Wolf, but if it came down to it he definitely would. He would kill Wolf twice if he had to. Live Wire knew what Wolf and The Spades were capable of and him and The Real Spades were well prepared for anything that might come their way.

"Yo, tell all the shooters to strap up. It's about to go down," Live Wire said to Bills as he hopped in his new all black Bentley and pulled off.

Chapter 30
"No Time to Play"

Wolf sat in his living room watching the movie "Black Barbie." As the movie played Wolf's mind was elsewhere, mainly on Live Wire. Wolf had already put the word out to all The Spades that Live Wire was next on the list. He didn't want to send the word out, but it was too late to turn back now. Wolf had to get rid of Live Wire for the good of the community. The longer Live Wire stayed on the streets, the harder it would be to get him off the streets for good. Now that Live Wire had his weight up, Wolf figured it might be a little more difficult to bring him down. As Wolf sat on the couch, he felt a pair of hands began to caress his chest from behind.

"Hey baby," Ivy sang in her usual soft tone. "I know that look...What's wrong?"

"Don't be acting like you know me like that," Wolf joked. He hated that Ivy had grown to know him so well.

"It's my job to know you like that. Now tell me what's wrong." Ivy walked around the couch and slid down on Wolf's lap.

"I just put the word out to have Live Wire taken down," Wolf told her. The reality of the situation still hadn't set in all the way yet. It didn't feel real, but Wolf knew it didn't get any realer.

"I know that had to be hard for you," Ivy said as she rubbed his back.

Wolf went on to tell Ivy all about how him and The Spades had ran down on Live Wire at the liquor store. He told her how the two spoke and acted as if they didn't know the other from a hole in the wall. Ivy gave Wolf her undivided attention as she listened and paid attention to every word he spoke. Just from the sound of it she could tell that things were about to hit the fan in the worst way.

"What about Pauleena?" Ivy asked. "Y'all gonna go after both Live Wire and Pauleena at the same time?"

"Yep"

"That's crazy!" Ivy shook her head. "Can't we just leave town before things get too out of hand."

"Things are already out of hand. I'm about to have my best friend killed."

As Ivy continued to listen, she just couldn't understand how Wolf could continue to stay dead smack in the middle of the fire when there was an easier way out. He'd done all he could do for the community. What else was it left for him to do; besides get killed or locked up...

"Please Wolf," Ivy said sincerely. "Can you at least think about it?"

"Think about what?"

"Leaving with me."

"I can't leave my peoples," Wolf said sighing loudly. He knew all of this made no sense to Ivy. To Ivy this all sounded like foolishness. Why would a man wait and sit around to go to jail? Wolf rarely argued with Ivy because he knew no matter how many times he tried to explain things to Ivy she would never truly understand.

"So you expect me to just sit around and watch you kill yourself or get shipped off to jail?" Ivy yelled, not hiding her anger.

"Kill myself?" Wolf looked up with a confused look on his face. "What is you talking about now?"

"Fuck you Wolf! Fuck you!" Ivy huffed as she stormed upstairs towards their master bedroom. She loved Wolf more than she loved her own self and she could no longer sit around and wait for something bad to happen. If something bad did happen, she wanted to be as far away as possible and she didn't even want to hear about the situation. Ivy made it to the master bedroom, snatched open her closet, grabbed two suitcases, and began filling them up with her clothes. Tears ran down her cheeks as she heard Wolf enter the bedroom behind her.

"What the fuck you doing?" Wolf growled looking down at the two big suitcases that rested on the floor in front of Ivy's feet.

Ivy said nothing. She just continued to pack her things inside the suitcase as fast as she could.

"So that's how you do? Soon as shit start to get a little hard, you want out; huh?" Again Ivy didn't reply. She just continued to pack her things into her suitcases.

"You ain't going nowhere!" Wolf yelled snatching Ivy's suitcase from her hands and tossing it across the room against the wall. Designer clothes flew through the air and landed all over the place. Ivy growled like an animal as she attacked Wolf. She slapped him, hit him with a closed fist, scratched his face, ripped his shirt, tried to gouge his eyes out, and sent several kicks to the private place between his legs. All the rage that Ivy had been holding in finally erupted causing her to snap. Ivy screamed out profanity as she continued to assault Wolf.

Wolf finally grabbed a hold of Ivy's wrist and wrestled her down to the floor putting all of his weight down on her chest in order to restrain her.

"Get the fuck off of me!"

"Calm down!"

"Get the fuck off of me Wolf!" Ivy repeated through a pair of clenched teeth.

"Calm down, I said!"

Ivy bucked her midsection up wildly trying to get out of Wolf's grasp, but it was no use because he was too strong.

"Calm down and I will let you up," Wolf told her. He had never seen Ivy act crazy like this before and honestly he was a little scared to let her up off the floor.

After about five minutes of silence filled with hard breathing, Wolf finally allowed Ivy to get up off the floor.

"Baby please don't go," Wolf begged. "Please baby!"

Ivy ignored Wolf as she got dressed, left her suitcase and all of her belongings behind, and headed for the door not bothering to even look back at Wolf.

"Can we at least talk about it?" Wolf called out. "Please?"

Ivy reached the bedroom door, stopped and then slowly turned to face Wolf. "There's nothing to talk about. You are choosing The Spades over me; plain and simple."

"Baby please don't do this," Wolf pleaded. "Please don't make me choose. I told you what it was up front."

"If you don't want to choose, you don't have to, but don't expect me to sit around and wait for you to get killed," she said as tears streamed down her face. "Just know that I'll always love you... No matter what!" Ivy said as she exited the bedroom and headed downstairs.

Wolf followed Ivy all the way downstairs and stopped her just as she reached the door. "What are you going to do for money?"

The same thing I was doing when you met me," Ivy told him.

"What am I gonna do with all of this money I got?" Wolf asked.

"Rub it on your chest," Ivy said as she turned and left Wolf standing there looking stupid. If he wanted to sit around and wait until he was killed or either sent away to prison for life that was on him. She refused to sit around and watch the man she loved throw his life down the drain for the community. The same community that would go back to being a fucked up place to live and raise a child once Wolf was dead and gone. Ivy didn't see the purpose and wanted to be as far away as possible when something bad did eventually happen. At the moment all Ivy could do was pray about the situation and put it in God's hands. She had done just about all she could do. Whatever happened from here on out was up to the man upstairs.

Chapter 31
"A Brand New Leaf"

Slow music pumped through the radio at a reasonable volume as Tonya had her face buried inside of a pillow in one of Dice's favorite positions, face down and ass up. The pillow muffled Tonya's moans as Dice licked, sucked, and ate Tonya's pussy from the back. He hummed on her clit as he slowly guided his middle finger in and out of her wetness. Dice licked on Tonya's clit until she creamed in his mouth. Once Dice had Tonya wet enough, he moved his face up to her ass and began gently licking it. He felt Tonya's body shake and vibrate as he laid his tongue game down licking her entire backside clean. Once that was done, Dice slid up in Tonya's hot wet walls from behind. She was so wet that he slipped right inside. Tonya's moans that started off soft became desperate. Dice stayed behind her dipping to get a good angle as he kept his thrust deep and steady. Dice moved Tonya into different positions. He pleased her from different angles. The only thing that could be heard in the room was skin slapping against skin, followed by long drawn out moans and groans. Once the love session was done, both Dice and Tonya lay stretched across the bed breathing heavily. Their bedroom looked as if it had been hit by a tornado. The sheets and comforter were all over the floor along with most of the pillows and their clothes. Ever since Dice had given Tonya a second chance to be with him, she had been nothing less than impressive. It was as if the old Tonya had died and this new and improved Tonya had been created. Dice wasn't complaining because the new and improved Tonya was proving that she could be the woman he needed her to be. Tonya even kept her part-time job after Dice told her that she no longer needed to work. She was definitely proving to Dice that she appreciated him and was thankful that he had come to rescue her. If it wasn't for Dice, Tonya didn't know where she would be right now. With little Dice at Tonya's mother's house for the weekend, Tonya and Dice had plenty of alone time to enjoy one another.

"I love you," Tonya whispered with her eyes still closed exhausted from her hard orgasm.

"Where did that come from?" Dice asked getting up and slipping on his boxers and a wife beater.

"My heart," Tonya told him. "Why are you so good to me? Especially after all the shit I have put you through."

"Everybody makes mistakes."

"Not the kind of mistakes that I have made," Tonya said sitting up on the bed. "When I think back on it all, I can't believe I was so stupid," she said embarrassed. She was happy that she would never have to see the pit again.

"That's in the past baby. All that matters to me now is the future," Dice said.

"Thank you!"

"Don't mention it," Dice said as he heard the sound of glass being broken coming from downstairs. "Get dressed," he told Tonya as he grabbed his .38 from off the nightstand and headed downstairs to investigate.

Dice quietly and cautiously made his way downstairs. When he reached the middle step, he smelled a strong wift of smoke. Dice made it downstairs and saw a hooded man standing over by the window with a lighter in his hand setting the curtains on fire. Dice fired a shot from his .38 and watched the man's hood fly off his head as blood splattered all over the window while the curtains went up in flames. Dice quickly ran to the kitchen and grabbed a water pitcher from off the counter and filled it up with cold water. Dice ran back to the living room and was hit from the blind side by another hooded man. He hit Dice hard. He grabbed him and lifted him off his feet as both men hit the floor fighting and swinging. Dice and the hooded man both hopped up to their feet and exchanged blows. Both men were fighting as if their lives depended on it. Dice threw fist, elbows, and knees. The man who stood in front of him was giving just as much as he took. The hooded man caught Dice with a good punch that dazed him and put him on his back. Once he saw Dice on the floor, the hooded man quickly hopped on top of Dice and continued his attack like a UFC fighter.

Dice covered his face trying to block as many on coming blows as possible, but the hooded man's attack was on going. As Dice lay on the floor trying to fight off his attacker, smoke filled the house as the place went up in flames. The more punches that landed and connected with Dice's face, the more dazed he became and began to lose his vision. Right before Dice blacked out he saw Tonya standing behind his attacker with something shiny in her hand.

Tonya raised the knife she had in her hands over her head and brought it down into the hooded man's back. She yelled out a million curse words as she stabbed the hooded man repeatedly until his body finally collapsed. Tonya rolled the hooded man's dead body off the top of Dice and struggled to help him up to his feet as she broke out into a coughing fit from all of the thick black smoke. Tonya and Dice made it out the house just as part of the roof collapsed. When they made it out on the lawn, several of their neighbors ran to their rescue and helped them get as far away from the fire as possible. Tonya and Dice coughed loudly as they watched their home go up in flames. At the moment Dice didn't know who was responsible for the fire, but the first person that came to his mind was Live Wire.

Chapter 32
"Praise the Lord"

Ivy sat in the back row of the church as the choir sang and clapped their hands getting everyone excited about giving praise to the man upstairs. Ivy stood on her feet clapping her hands, but her mind wasn't on the Lord at the moment. Right now her mind was still on Wolf. Her intensions were to come to church and have the Pastor pray for her, but Wolf had her mind so scrabbled that it was hard for her to think straight. Ivy still couldn't believe that Wolf was willing to end their relationship and kick her to the curb for the community. In Ivy's eyes he was choosing the community over her and their relationship. Ivy was still madly in love with Wolf, but she refused to just sit there and watch Wolf destroy himself for the community. In a matter of forty-eight hours Ivy had over thirty missed calls on her phone from Wolf. She badly wanted to take his calls, but she knew that his mind was already made up and with him being stuck in his ways and all; it was useless to take his calls. As Ivy stood on her feet clapping along with everyone else, tears suddenly started to stream down her face. Ivy tried to wipe the tears away, but each time she wiped one away three more seemed to take that one's place.

"Excuse me," Ivy said as she squeezed her way down the aisle and headed straight for the bathroom. She needed a moment to clear her head and get her thoughts together. She knew it was going to be tough to get Wolf out of her system, but if she planned on moving on with her life then this was phase one. Ivy stepped inside the bathroom and stared at her reflection in the mirror. She looked a hot mess. "Get it together," Ivy said to herself as she splashed a handful of water on her face. She badly wanted to scream at the top of her lungs and pull her hair out, but she had to stay strong. Ivy cupped her hands and put them under the faucet and then her body jumped from the loud sound of gunfire. As eh water she was going to splash on her face flew all over the place. She quickly pulled out her cell phone and called Wolf.

****

Three all black bullet proof Escalades pulled up back to back in the front of the church. Pauleena and Psycho hopped out along with her eight man security team of Muslims and entered the church. After having a long talk with Live Wire the night before Pauleena found out that the Pastor of the church was not only a silent member of The Spades organization, but the one who let them use his establishment a their main headquarters. After Live Wire gave Pauleena that information, Pauleena just had to meet this man of God in person and what better day to do than on a Sunday Pauleena thought.

****

Everyone bow your heads and join me in prayer," Pastor Anderson said as he wiped the sweat from his head with a silk handkerchief and began prayer. "Father God I ask that you bless each and every one that's sitting before me in this church right now..." Pastor Anderson cut his prayer short when he heard the main door of the church come busting open. As soon as he recognized Pauleena he knew he was in deep trouble. Members of the church whispered and looked on with nervous and scared looks on their faces as Pauleena slowly walked down the aisle with her mob behind her. Two of the Muslim guards stood by the exit holding machine guns underneath their arm pits. Their job was to make sure that no one entered or exited the building.
Just as Pauleena was about to reach the pulpit one of the deacons of the church stepped in front of Pauleena blocking her path to the Pastor.

"Sorry, but you can't go any further," the deacon said bravely.

Pauleena reached for her gun and pulled it out with a quick snapping motion. She fired two shots in the man's thigh sending him crashing down to the floor. Pauleena stepped over the deacon like he was trash and stepped up to the pulpit. Before Pauleena got a chance to do anything Psycho quickly stepped in front of her and spoke.

"Let me have a word with him real quick," Psycho said with fire dancing in his eyes. He was tired of people trying to violate his fiancé. Now it was time for him to let the streets know who was in charge. "Do you know who I am?" He asked the Pastor looking him directly in his eyes.

"No," Pastor Anderson replied with a calm look on his face.

"Well let me introduce myself," Psycho said as he turned and stole on the Pastor sending him stumbling back into the keyboard causing a loud ruckus. Members of the church whispered and looked on in shock as they watched the Pastor take a beating. Psycho caught the Pastor with a sharp hook to the stomach causing him to double over in pain. He then grabbed the back of the Pastor's neck with two hands and pushed his head down as he came up with a strong knee that laid the Pastor out. From the way blood poured from his nose Psycho immediately knew the Pastor's nose was broken. Pauleena looked on with a smile on her face as she watched her man put in work.

Psycho stood over the Pastor, lifted the keyboard over his head and dropped it down on the Pastor's face. The keyboard hit a weird note as it crashed down over the Pastor's face.

"Please stop... That's enough!" Pastor Anderson's wife yelled as she could no longer stand to see her husband take anymore punishment.

Psycho quickly made his way over to the Pastor's wife and smacked the shit out of her. He then roughly grabbed a hand full of her hair and dragged her up to the pulpit so she could join her husband.

"No please don't hurt her..." Pastor Anderson managed to say with a mouth full of blood.

"Shut the fuck up!" Pauleena growled as she raised her foot and kicked the Pastor in the face causing his head to violently jerk back.

"Are you scared right now?" Psycho asked the Pastor's wife with a sick looking smile on his face.

"I don't fear no man but God," the Pastor's wife shot back.

"Well you should be scared right now!"

"The devil is a liar," she said standing firm.

"I see your husband has really got all you fools in there brain washed," Psycho laughed. "So since you believe in God, I take it you believe in miracles. Am I correct?"

The Pastor's wife nodded her head.

"You've got twenty seconds to say a prayer before I start shooting people," Psycho said pulling out his Tech-9. "If this God of yours is as real as you say he is then I guess a miracle will stop everyone from getting their heads blown off. If not oh motherfucking well," he shrugged.

"Please don't do this! I'm begging you!"

"Nineteen... Eighteen... Seventeen...," Psycho began to count down.

"I hope you burn in hell!" The Pastor's wife yelled as she lunged towards Psycho. Her body violently jerked and turned in mid-air as her body hit the floor hard. Psycho looked down and saw a bullet hole in the side of the Pastor's wife's head. He then looked up and saw Pauleena's 9mm smoking.

"Thanks baby," Psycho said with a wink as he turned and faced the congregation then squeezed the trigger on his machine gun. He waved it back and forth shooting and killing everyone in the line of fire. Pauleena smiled as she sat back and watched her man's handy work. When the smoke was all clear, the only people who were left alive were the ones who had entered the church with Pauleena.

As Pauleena exited the church she never once thought to check the restrooms on the way out. Just as

Pauleena's three Escalades pulled off, two minutes later six black vans pulled up and came to a screeching stop directly in front of the church.

****

Wolf hopped out the van and ran inside the church along with several other Spades members.

"Ivy!" Wolf yelled as he stepped inside the church and saw dead bodies all over the place. Immediately Wolf's heart dropped as he began searching all of the dead bodies that laid around the church looking for Ivy's body. He couldn't believe that he had allowed something like this to happen to Ivy. Murderous thoughts filled his mind as he began plotting for revenge. Whoever was responsible for this was a good as dead. Just as Wolf got ready to snap, he heard a familiar woman's voice calling his name from behind. When he turned around and saw Ivy, he breathed a sigh of relief.

"They killed everybody!" Ivy sang as she ran into Wolf's arms.

"The rest of the place is clear," one of The Spades members announced.

"Get these guns up out of here before the cops get here," Wolf ordered as he focused his attention on Ivy. "What happened? Are you okay?"

"Yeah I went to the bathroom... Then I heard gunshots and loud screaming," Ivy cried. "I can't do this anymore... I can't!"

Wolf didn't know what to say so instead of talking he just rubbed her back and tried to comfort her.

"I'm leaving Wolf," Ivy said pushing away from Wolf's grasp.

"Where are you going?"

"I don't know yet, but I'm leaving New York for good. I can't do this anymore... I just can't," she cried. "I'm not losing my life over this bullshit," she paused. "Look around! All these innocent people are dead because of you!"

"But I didn't even…"

"I don't want to hear it!" Ivy yelled. "This is what you wanted; right? You wanted to start a war and now you've got one. I hope you can explain to all of these people's family members why their love one's had to die."

"The cops will be here any second Wolf. What's the word?" A Spades member asked sticking his head in the door.

"Get up outta here," Wolf ordered. "I'm staying here with Ivy."

With that being said The Spades left the scene of the crime. Wolf slowly walked up to the pulpit and stood over Pastor Anderson and his wife's body as his eyes began to get misty. He knew it was because of him that the Pastor and his wife lay dead on the floor before their time, but what could he do? What was done couldn't be undone. All Wolf could do was get revenge for the Pastor and all of the people who lay dead in the church.

"How many more innocent people have to die before you realize what you are doing is wrong?" Ivy asked.

"All I'm trying to do is help."

"What you're doing is like a gift and a curse," Ivy told him. "You're trying to help people, but in return innocent people are dying. You have the power to stop this, but yet you won't," Ivy said. "A real leader keeps his people out of harm's way."

"Where are you moving to?"

"I don't know yet."

"Why don't you come back home until you decide on where you trying to go," Wolf said.

"I'm giving you to the end of the week to decide on whether you're leaving with me or not," Ivy said ignoring what Wolf had just said. "If you love me as much as you say you do, I'll expect you to leave with me at the end of the week. You told me…"

"I'm not going anywhere," Wolf cut her off. "This is what I do. Now you can either love me or leave me alone," he said as he quickly made his exit through the back door just as the cops were entering through the front door.

Ivy stood in the middle of a church full of dead bodies with a stupid look on her face. It was finally over. Her and Wolf's relationship was officially over. Ivy wanted to cry, but she did her best to remain strong as she heard the footsteps of over a dozen officers entering the church. "Seven days and this will all be over with," she told herself.

Chapter 33
"A Rock and a Hard Place"

Agent Starks stepped inside the church and frowned. He knew this was the work of Pauleena and The Spades. The more dead bodies he stepped over, the madder he became. From the looks of things a group of armed men ran up in the church and opened fire on everyone leaving no prisoners. As Agent Starks continued his investigation, he spotted Ivy sitting over in the corner crying while two uniform cops questioned her.

"I'll take it from here," Agent Starks said walking up and flashing his badge. As soon as Ivy recognized Agent Starks she sucked her teeth.

"It's nice to see you again too," Agent Starks said standing directly in front of her. "You can't seem to stay out of trouble I see. The more you continue to deal with Wolf, the more trouble you're going to find yourself in."
Ivy said nothing.

"Care to tell me what happened?"
Ivy said nothing.

"A room full of dead bodies and you're the only one still alive. You better start talking now if you know what's best for you," Agent Starks warned.

"I didn't see anything. I was in the restroom then I heard gunshots," Ivy said. "I didn't come out the restroom until I was sure the coast was clear."

"When I came out, this is what I saw," she nodded towards all the dead bodies that rested around them.

"Are you in any kind of trouble?"
"Not that I know of…"

"You think people are targeting you in order to get to your boyfriend?" Agent Starks asked.

"Me and Wolf are no longer together," she told him. "Now if it's okay with you, I would like to get going. I got things to do."

For a second Agent Starks thought about arresting Ivy, but after giving it some thought he figured it would be smarter to let her go free and just keep a close eye on her instead. "Yes you are free to go," he said holding out his card. "If you hear anything, give me a call."

Ivy ignored Agent Starks and left him standing there holding his card as she exited the church and went on about her business.

****

Wolf sat in the basement of his home along with about two hundred Spades members. Each man was dressed in all black holding assault riffles. Dice had informed Wolf of what had went down at his home. With so many different things going on at one time, it made it hard for Wolf to think straight. "Tonight we get rid of Live Wire and tomorrow we get rid of Pauleena," Wolf announced. He was tired of going back and forth with the two crews and it was time to put an end to this once and for all. It was time to let the streets know who was holding the throne. Once Wolf finished giving out the orders, The Spades rallied up the troops and headed out for battle. Wolf stayed behind and used this time alone to think. He had a lot on his mind and needed this time alone to get his thoughts together. Wolf badly wanted to call Ivy and check up on her, but he knew that she still wasn't taking any of his calls. Ivy's mind was already made up and Wolf knew there was no changing that. He figured if she loved him as much as she said she did then they would still be together right now, but that wasn't the case. Ivy had left Wolf at a time when he needed her most and for that reason alone he was beginning to look at Ivy differently. Wolf still loved Ivy with all his heart, but couldn't understand some of the decisions she had been making lately. As Wolf sat in his basement he couldn't take it anymore. He picked up his cell and dialed Ivy's number only to get her voicemail.

****

Tori closed her eyes and made ugly faces while greedy sounds escaped from her mouth. Live Wire had her turned over, knees planted down on the bed, face in a pillow with her ass high in the air as he moved in and out of her wetness at a steady pace. He pulled her ass back towards him and went deeper. He held her waist firmly making sure she didn't run. He made her take every inch of him as he began to speed up his pace. Tori made sexy sounds and then came violently. The Madam's three day visit wound up turning into a two week stay. As much as Tori hated to admit it, she had developed some strong feelings for Live Wire. She couldn't seem to keep her hands off of him when the two of them were together. Her two week vacation was nice, but Tori had business to take care of and she had to head back to Texas.

"Do you have to leave so soon?" Live Wire said laying it on thick while Tori got dressed. Honestly he could care less if Tori came or went, but he had to try and make her feel good.

"Yes baby, I got a few things I need to take care of," Tori told him. "Money never sleeps."

"That's a fact," Live Wire replied. In all reality he wanted her to leave and get back to work, especially now that the two had agreed to become partners. Live Wire had big plans and refused to be denied. If it wasn't a way he was going to make a way like he always did.

After Tori got dressed, she headed to the door to leave with Live Wire right behind her dressed in only a pair of boxers and some jeans.

"Yo listen, you make sure you call me as soon as you touch down." Live Wire kissed Tori on the lips and cuffed her ass in front of her security. They all gave Live Wire a nasty look.

"Will do," Tori said heading out the door. "You make sure you stay out of trouble."

"I'm gonna try," Live Wire said as he watched The Madam and her team of security walk out the door, get in the car, and pull off his property.

"What's good my nigga?" Bills said getting out of his car and walking up just before Live Wire closed the door. "Chilling... What's good with you?" Live Wire said giving Bills some dap. "When I head back to my other crib I already know Sparkle is going to kill me," he shook his head. "But, what's good with you?"

"We had a little problem down at one of our trap houses," Bills told him. "I had to clap one of them niggas you had running the spot. Nigga had sticky fingers."

Live Wire nodded. "Is everything all good with that now?" He asked. For the past two weeks he had been spending most of his time with Tori making sure he had her right where he wanted her. While he was taking care of that, he left Bills in charge of running the streets.

"The cops kicked down one of the doors to one of our stash houses," Bills said. "But they didn't find anything. This new cat I put in charge of running the spot named Smash had just moved everything out and into the next spot."

"Smash?" Live Wire repeated. "Who the fuck is this new nigga?"

"Some young hungry cat from Yonkers," Bills answered.

"You trust him around that kind of money?" Live Wire asked suspiciously. In his world trust was something that you had to earn and a thing like that couldn't be done over night.

"Yeah this young nigga is official," Bills vouched for the young man.

"I want to meet him," Live Wire said as he put on the rest of his clothes, shoes and slid his .45 down in his waistband. He walked out the door with Bills right behind him. Live slid behind the wheel of his Bentley, Bills hopped in the passenger seat, and they pulled out of his driveway followed by four cars full of his goons.

Chapter 34
"Saved by the Bell"

Smash stood leaning up against a parked car. Ever since the stash house had been raided the block had been super hot, especially since they didn't find anything when they raided the stash house. Smash spotted an undercover D.T. car sitting over in the cut watching his every move. Smash smiled as he watched the police watch him. Around him were seventeen Real Spades members loitering, sipping liquor, and loud talking. As Smash stood leaning up against the car, he noticed a police car cruise by mean mugging him and the rest of the men who stood on the block.

About two blocks away Smash also noticed four black vans lined up back to back. He noticed the vans had been sitting there for the last forty-five minutes, but he had paid them no mind. He figured they were just more undercover cops harassing him and his crew. Smash stayed on point especially since he had the hammer on him. Ten minutes later Smash saw a black Bentley pull up bumping Rick Ross. Live Wire hopped out the driver seat wearing all black, an icy watch on his wrist, and a matching bracelet on the other. He had a foam cup filled with liquor in his hand as he walked up to the curb and gave dap to all the goons he knew. Bills hopped out the passenger seat wearing all black as well. Live Wire made sure he kept his windows down so the loud music could be heard.

"Yo, Smash," Bills said giving the young man dap. "I want you to meet somebody," he said. "This here is my man Live Wire."

"What's good Live Wire? I heard a lot about you," Smash said extending his hand.

Live Wire lifted his cup to his mouth, nodded his head, and left the young man hanging. The last thing Live

Wire wanted Smash to be thinking was that they were cool because they weren't. Live Wire didn't know shit about this young punk that Bills had put in charge of running the stash house. Just by looking at Smash, Live Wire could tell that the kid would cross his own mother if the opportunity of a come up ever presented itself.

"Where you from?"

"Yonkers," Smash answered proudly.

"Who you know over there?" Live Wire pressed.

"I know everybody. I grew up over there," Smash told him.

"Word?" Live Wire smirked. "You know my man Big Toney?" He said just making up a name to see if the young kid who stood before him was full of shit or not.

"Yeah, yeah, I know Big Toney," Smash said excitedly. "You talking about that big nigga that always be in front of the laundromat; right?"

Live Wire turned and stole on Smash. His fist sounded off loudly as it connected with Smash's face. Bills and the rest of the crew watched as Smash's body hit the ground and flipped over placing him on his stomach. Once Smash's body hit the ground a few goons quickly tapped his pockets robbing him of his goods.

"You be wilding," Bills said as he looked down at Smash's unconscious body on the ground.

"Ya man was lying for no reason," Live Wire said as he noticed a police car come to a stop right in front of him. The driver was a male officer and his partner was a female officer.

The female officer hopped out and approached Live Wire and stopped directly in front of him. Her eyes went from the man who lay knocked out face down on the concrete back up to Live Wire.

"You have some identification on you sir?" She asked.

"Why?" Live Wire snapped. "What are we doing wrong?"

"Sir, your ID?" The female officer said in a much more aggressive this time with her hand out.

"Fuck outta here," Live Wire said waving the woman off as he began to walk off.

"Sir," the female officer yelled as she grabbed Live Wire by his arm spinning him back around so he could face her. "Put your hands behind your back!"

Live Wire quickly snatched his arm out of the woman's grip. "Fuck is you doing?"

The female officer quickly removed her night stick from her belt and jabbed Live Wire in the stomach with it. The blow caught Live Wire off guard and caused him to double over in pain. Live Wire came up and knocked the female officer out with a quick right hook to her temple. Once the male officer saw his partner get knocked out he quickly jumped out of the car and reached for his gun, but before he could get the pistol out of his holster he felt a blunt object strike him in the back of his head. The blow to his head caused him to drop down to his knees. Before he realized what was going on he felt fist and feet connecting with his face and head coming from all angles and he finally passed out. Live Wire and Bills quickly hopped back into the Bentley and burnt rubber leaving the scene. With everything that had just went down, Live Wire never noticed the black vans tailing him.

"That's what I'm fucking talking about!" Live Wire said excitedly. "That's what The Real Spades is all about," he continued to rant. "We pop on anybody; even the police," he laughed.

"That bitch is bugged out," Bills laughed. "I bet she will act like she got some sense when she wake up."

The two's conversation was interrupted when Live Wire's cell rang. He looked down at the caller ID and saw Psycho's name flashing across the screen. "Yo, what's good?" Live Wire answered.

"What you and your peoples getting into tonight?" Psycho asked.

"Nothing much... Probably some hoes; why what's up?"

"Pauleena want you and your team to come down to that new club they just opened up downtown. We down here partying hard letting the streets know who's still running shit," Psycho said.

"I'm on my way," Live Wire said and then ended the call. He was already headed downtown in the direction of the club. With nothing better to do Live Wire figured why not go to the club and let his face been seen. He planned on being the next king on the streets so the people needed to see and get used to his face; besides Live Wire wanted to see Pauleena again. In his eyes she was as sexy as they come and if Psycho turned his head for a split second Live Wire planned on scooping Pauleena right from under Psycho's nose. If Psycho wanted to get ignorant then so be it. The Real Spades were now running the streets and whoever didn't like it could kiss Live Wire's ass.

****

Dice sat in the back of the van as he watched Live Wire assault some young kid and then knock out a female officer. Dice and The Spades were just about to make their move until Live Wire hopped back in his Bentley and peeled off. Dice didn't know where Live Wire was headed, but wherever the Bentley stopped, that would be where Live Wire took his last breath. After thirty minutes of following the Bentley, it finally pulled into a parking lot in front of a big night club. As Dice sat back and watched the Bentley closely he noticed four Muslim brothers all wearing black suits walk up to the Bentley. Seconds later Live Wire and Bills emerged from the Bentley with smiles on their faces as the Muslim brothers escorted them inside the club.

Once Dice saw the Muslims, he immediately knew that Pauleena was also inside the club. He pulled out his cell phone and dialed Wolf's number. On the third ring Wolf picked up.

"What's up?"

"I think you might want to come down to that new club they just opened up downtown," Dice said.

"2400?" Wolf asked in codes. 2400 meant it was an emergency.

"2400," Dice repeated.

"Say no more. I'm on my way," Wolf said ending the call. After Dice said 2400, he knew he meant business and he was on his way.

Chapter 35
"If It Ain't Rough, It Ain't Right"

Live Wire, Bills, and a few other Real Spades members squeezed through the crowd. The club was packed to its capacity. Live Wire spotted a few chicks who caught his eye as the Muslim guards led them over towards the back of the club where they spotted Pauleena, Psycho, and dozens of Muslims all wearing black suits.

"Glad you could make it," Pauleena said smiling with a drink in her hand. She was glad that Live Wire and his crew had showed up. With all of them standing next to her, she looked even more powerful.

"Anything for you," Live Wire said as he hugged Pauleena and let his hand brush up against her firm but soft ass. Psycho was standing right there, but Live Wire paid him no mind. "I see you looking all good and all that," Live Wire said openly flirting with Pauleena.

"Good looking on that info you gave me about the church," Pauleena said changing the subject. She wasn't looking at Psycho, but she knew he was smoking mad and doing his best to control himself.

"Yeah I heard about that on the news," Live Wire said helping himself to a glass of Rosay.

"Any word on where Wolf is laying his head now a days?" Psycho asked cutting in. To him Live Wire was a clown and as soon as he served no purpose, Psycho planned on putting Live Wire's brains all over a wall somewhere.

"Depends on how much the info is worth," Live Wire said sitting down next to Pauleena. Bills and The Real

Spades members looked on as Psycho and Live Wire went back and forth.

"What we paid you for the information on Pastor Anderson should be enough to cover that info and the info on Wolf's where abouts," Psycho told him.

"Look business is business," Live Wire said. "Either you want the info or not."

"If you know what's best for you, you better watch your mouth," Psycho replied. The young street punk in front of him was really starting to get on his last nerve. It was bad enough that Live Wire was trying to flirt with his woman right before his eyes. "I'm not with all that tough guy talk."

"You not bout that life," Live Wire told him. "Stop fronting before you get yourself hurt," he said taking a sip from his drink.

"Get myself hurt," Psycho repeated. "In my world you wouldn't even last one…"

"Listen my nigga, fuck all this small talk. The bathroom is open." Live Wire hopped up and removed his .45 from his waistband and handed it to Bills as he headed to the bathroom. He was on his jail shit.

"You don't have anything to prove," Pauleena said placing a hand on Psycho's chest. She knew Live Wire was a hot head and didn't think it was necessary for the two to fight. Psycho ignored Pauleena as he removed his 9mm from his holster and sat it down on the small table and headed towards the bathroom behind Live Wire. Bills and a few of Live Wire's goons headed over towards the bathroom to make sure shit didn't get out of hand. Bills stepped foot inside the bathroom and pulled out his hammer and made everyone clear out the bathroom. Once Bills stepped out the bathroom and announced that it was empty, Live Wire and Psycho stepped inside to handle their business. Bills stood outside the bathroom door looking out towards the crowd making sure nobody entered the bathroom as Live Wire and Psycho got it on. As Bills stood posted up outside the bathroom door, he heard loud booming and banging noises coming from inside. He ignored all the noise as he focused on all the beautiful women who were walking around the club. Four minutes later Live Wire exited the bathroom alone with his shirt ripped at the collar.

"Light work," Live Wire said removing his ripped shirt and tossing it to the floor. He walked through the club wearing a black wife beater.

"Where's Psycho," Pauleena asked when Live Wire made it back over to the table.

"He sleep," Live Wire said as Bills and the rest of The Real Spades members busted out laughing. "I told you to leave those clowns alone and come fuck with the God."

Pauleena ignored Live Wire's comments as she hurried off to the bathroom to check up on her man. She didn't like how Live Wire and his crew had come up in the club and tried to style on her man. Her team of Muslim security entered the bathroom first to make sure it was safe for their boss to enter. When Pauleena entered the bathroom she saw Psycho standing in front of a mirror checking to see how much damage had been done to his face. Down inside the sink were specs of blood.

"Baby you alright?" Pauleena asked walking up behind him. She looked over his shoulder and into the mirror to see how bad his face had been injured. Psycho had a little knot right above his eye and a bloody nose; nothing too serious.

"I'mma kill that motherfucker," Psycho growled as he splashed a handful of water on his face. "He lucky I slipped," he lied just to save face in front of his woman.

"Whatever you wanna do, I'm with you," Pauleena told him. There wasn't anything she wouldn't do for her man.

"You got the hammer on you?" Psycho asked.

Pauleena opened her purse and handed Psycho a .380. As soon as the gun touched Psycho's hand, the sound of several gun shots sounded off inside the club.

****

Wolf, Dice, and about a hundred Spades showed up in front of the club. Each man was holding a killing instrument and the look on their faces said they weren't afraid to use them.

"Please don't come in here with all that," the bouncer who guarded the entrance pleaded with his hands up and palms out. "We don't want no trouble in here."

"Shut the fuck up!" One of The Spades members growled as he pressed the barrel of a shotgun to the side of the bouncers head while Wolf and the rest of The Spades entered the club.

The inside of the club was dark, hot, and loud. Thousands of people partying made it hard for Wolf to find his targets in the crowded night club. Wolf silently gave Dice the order to split up and for him and half of The Spades members to cover one side of the club while Wolf and the other half covered the other side of the club.

****

Live Wire sat in the back of the club sipping on a drink as thoughts of going back in the bathroom and beating Psycho up again crossed his mind. He didn't like Psycho since the first day he met him.

"Be on point just in case this clown can't take an ass whopping," Bills said. He didn't trust Pauleena or Psycho. In his mind he felt that The Real Spades didn't need them and they were slowing them down.

"I stay on point," Live Wire said nodding down towards his .45 that rested on his lap.

The crowd went crazy when a new song from Snow's mix tape came on bumping through the speakers. Bills sat on the side line talking to a thick light skin joint when he saw a man wearing all black holding something chrome in his hand making his way over to where him and Live Wire stood.

"Yo, Live watch out! It's a hit!" Bills yelled. He pushed the light skin chick out of his way, pulled out his .357 and opened fire on the man wearing all black. Once the two loud thunderous shots echoed throughout the club, all hell broke loose. The Spades and The Real Spades had an old fashion shoot out in the club. Live Wire hopped up, fired three reckless shots over his shoulder as he scrambled to get up and out of harm's way. He was pushing and shoving people out of his way in the process.

****

Wolf was on the other side of the club when he heard the loud blast from a big gun being fired. Immediately Wolf and The Spades members who was with him pushed through the club heading over towards the sound of gun shots. Wolf held and Uzi as he moved through the packs of party goers until he spotted Live Wire. At that very moment the two men made eye contact with one another. Out of reflexes both men aimed their guns at one another and opened fire. Each man was trying to send the other one to his maker.

The Uzi rattled in Wolf's hand as its bullets followed Live Wire leaving a trail of bullet holes all throughout the walls. Without nowhere else to run, Live Wire ran inside the man's bathroom.

"The Spades are here," Live Wire said out of breath. He looked at both Psycho and Pauleena and they both looked unmoved and unfazed. "It's about a hundred of them motherfuckers up in here..." Before Live Wire could finish what he was saying, he collapsed as two bullets exploded in both of his thighs. Another loud blast echoed throughout the bathroom as a bullet hit and broke Live Wire's collar bone. Another bullet followed up and grazed the side of Live Wire's head leaving him laid out bleeding on the bathroom floor unconscious.

Pauleena stood over Live Wire's body holding a smoking .380. Psycho opened the bathroom door first and opened fire not caring who was on the other side of the door or who he hit. While Psycho fired his weapon, Pauleena quickly ran out the bathroom firing her .380 at anything moving as she ran barefoot through the club. The Spades,

The Real Spades, and Pauleena's team of Muslim security continued to shoot it out until finally the cops showed up. The police ran up in the club shooting at any and everyone who they thought was involved.

Psycho and Pauleena escaped out the side door only to run into more Spades members. Thankful for them, there were several cops out scattered all around the parking lot. Pauleena and Psycho blended in with all the pandemonium and disappeared in the mist of all the chaos.

Wolf exited the club two minutes later out of the same side exit door and power walked through the parking lot until he reached one of the awaited black vans. As soon as Wolf got inside, the driver peeled off leaving the scene.

Bills wiped down his gun then tossed it. He then rushed inside the bathroom to grab Live Wire so they could make their escape. Bills froze as he held the bathroom door open and stood there in shock. Laying on the bathroom floor before him was Live Wire in a pool of his own blood.

"I need an ambulance over here!" Bills yelled with panic all in his voice. "I need an ambulance!" When the police finally showed up at the bathroom, they roughly tossed Bills down to the floor and handcuffed him.

"Fuck is y'all niggas doing?" Bills yelled from the floor as the officers roughly and forcefully escorted him out of the club and into the back of a police car. The cops arrested several men from each gang along with a few brothers who had nothing to do with the situation. As Bills sat in the back seat of the police car, all he could think about was Live Wire.

Chapter 36
"Nothing to Talk About"

Ivy stood behind the bar serving drinks. She didn't have much money, but regardless how much money she had she was still leaving at the end of the week. She still wished that Wolf would join her, but she had finally come to realize that he was just in too deep. To keep her mind off of Wolf and their problems, Ivy decided to go back to her old job. It wasn't for the money, but to give her something to do besides think about Wolf all day. Ivy served drinks with a smile on her face, but on the inside she felt like shit. The truth was she felt empty and incomplete without Wolf. She hated to admit it, but it was the truth.

"Can I get some service; please?" A big fat man asked with an attitude.

Ivy looked up snapping out of her thoughts and saw one of her best customers standing on the other side of the counter.

"Hey Bob! You scared me there for a second," Ivy chuckled. Bob was a fat sloppy man who had a crush on Ivy since the two were kids. He was a real nice guy, but he just wasn't Ivy's type.

"Where have you been?" Bob asked nosily. "I haven't seen you around here in a while."

"I was just living life you know. I had to escape my reality for a little while, but I'm back," Ivy told him forcing a fake smile on her face. At the moment she didn't really feel like talking, but just to be polite she continued to conversate with Bob.

"Well life must have been treating you real good," Bob nodded towards the ring that sparkled on her left ring finger. The engagement ring that Wolf had gave her less than two months ago was sparkling like ice on her finger.

"Life must not have been treating me too good," Ivy chuckled to keep from crying. "Me and him are no longer together."

"His lost," Bob said quickly. "He wasn't good enough for you anyway."

Ivy smiled. "Thanks Bob." Bob may have been a little fat, but he was a good man and had a good heart. Ivy knew whatever woman Bob ended up with would have a good man. As Ivy and Bob continued their conversation Ivy looked up and saw Wolf walking through the front door carrying a book bag in his hands.

"Oh boy…" Ivy huffed.

"What's the matter?" Bob asked with his voice full of concern.

"My old boyfriend just walked in," Ivy said. "I don't need no more problems right about now."

"Don't worry about nothing," Bob said confidently. "You don't have to worry about nobody upsetting you while I'm around."

Ivy was about to tell Bob that she didn't need his assistance, but before she got a chance to let Bob know what was up Wolf was already standing in front of her on the other side of the counter.

"Why the fuck you haven't been answering my calls?" Wolf snapped.

"Wolf please, I don't feel like being bothered right now," Ivy said.

"You don't feel like being bothered right now?" Wolf echoed with his voice rising. "Since when you start talking to me like this?"

"Excuse me brother, but the lady said she didn't want to be bothered right now so why don't you just step off," Bob said sticking his nose into business that didn't belong to him.

Wolf turned and looked at the fat nigga like he was crazy. "What!?"

"You heard me!" Bob said matching Wolf's tone. He rolled up his sleeves like he was ready to get busy. Wolf turned and hit Bob with a quick rabbit punch, a punch that stunned the big man. Wolf then slammed Bob's head down on the bar top and a knee to the big man's stomach came next. Then a hard forearm blow to the face sent Bob down for the count. Just as Wolf went to stomp the fat fuck into the floor, Ivy stopped him.

"What the hell is wrong with you?" Ivy screamed as she knelt down by Bob's side hoping he wasn't hurt too bad. "You're turning into an animal!" she said with a disgusted look on her face.

"Sir I'm sorry but we're going to have to ask you to leave," a big man said in a firm tone. He wore a black shirt with the word security written in white letters on the front. Wolf thought about telling the fake cop that stood in front of him to kiss his ass, but decided to just leave on his own. He didn't want to cause any more trouble and by the look on Ivy's face he could tell that she didn't want anything else to do with him. The look on her face hurt Wolf the most. Ivy had called Wolf an animal. When he looked down at the big man laid out on the floor with several people standing over him to make sure he was okay, it made Wolf feel like an animal. He had only come to the bar to have a word with Ivy and drop her off some money. Wolf exited the bar and looked up at the sky. At that very moment he didn't know what to do and he needed some answers. Without Ivy in his life, Wolf no longer cared about anything and by the look on Ivy's face the two of them were officially through.

Once Bob came back around, Ivy hurried outside so she could talk to Wolf, but when she made it outside Wolf was already long gone. A part of her felt like the way Wolf had reacted was her fault, but at the end of the day what was done couldn't be undone. When Ivy stepped foot back inside the bar she saw that Wolf had left the book bag he had brought in with him on the bar top. She picked up the book bag and peeked inside. The book bag was filled with money and a note. Ivy pulled the note out of the bag and began reading it.

"Hey baby if you are reading this note then things didn't turn out the way I planned so with that being said here's some money to help you out on your big move out of town. I sure wish I could come with you, but we both know and knew what we were getting into from the beginning... I will always love you baby and you never know, one day we might meet again. If not in this life, then definitely in the next... Love Wolf"

Ivy balled the note up as tears fell from her eyes like raindrops. That note was confirming what she had already knew; that her and Wolf were over and done with and they would never be a couple again.

"You alright?" The big man wearing the security shirt asked.

"Yes, I'm fine... I have to go," Ivy said. She grabbed the book bag from the bar top and made her exit. Ivy had a lot on her mind and had some serious thinking to do as well as some tough decisions to make.

Chapter 37
"Team Work"

Dice stood over by the window and peeked through the blinds every so often. This was a habit he had picked up since his last house had been set on fire. Now he had a few Spades members watching over his home twenty-four hours a day. It was his job to protect Tonya and his son by any means necessary.

"Hey baby, you alright?" Tonya asked stepping out of the bathroom wrapped in a towel.

"Yeah, I'm good," Dice replied with his eyes still focused on what was going on outside his window. He had a lot on his mind and was happy that Tonya was back in his life. He was happy that he finally had someone to talk to in his time of need.

"I have something I want to tell you, but I don't want you to get mad at me," Tonya said.

"I'm listening"

"I want to join."

"Join what?" Dice asked with a confused look on his face.

"The Spades," Tonya said with a smile.

"Why?"

"Because I want to do my part in giving back to the community."

Dice laughed. "Is that right?"

"Yup, what's so funny?" Tonya asked letting her towel drop down to the floor as she applied lotion to her soft skin. Tonya looked up and saw Dice staring at her. "What? Why you looking at me like that?"

"Cause I wanna eat that pussy?" Dice said walking up to Tonya. Tonya smiled as she laid down on her back on the king size bed.

"This pussy is all yours. Do to it as you please," Tonya said in a seductive tone as she took two fingers and massaged her clit with sex all in her eyes. Dice slapped Tonya's hand away and began kissing her other set of lips slowly. His soft kisses quickly turned into licks. With her hands on Dice's head, Tonya shifted her hips towards his face and released a slow long drawn out moan.

"YES… Yes eat this pussy baby," Tonya moaned loudly. Just as she was getting ready to cum a loud knock at the door disturbed them.

Dice quickly hopped up and grabbed his .357 that rested on the night stand and headed downstairs to see who was knocking on his door unannounced especially at this time of night.

Whoever it was, Dice wondered how they had gotten pass The Spades members that stood outside watching over his property, especially without him not hearing gunshots.

"Who is it?" Dice yelled a few feet away from the door.

"Wolf," the voice on the other side of the door replied. Once Dice recognized the voice, he quickly opened the door.

"What's good?"

"Ivy left me," Wolf said stepping pass Dice making his way inside the house. "She's not coming back this time."

"What happened?" Dice asked curiously.

"She wants me to leave town with her at the end of the week."

"What about The Spades?" Dice asked while pouring him and Wolf a drink.

"She wants me to just up and leave," Wolf fumed. "Fuck all the hard work we've put in! Fuck all the improvements we made in our community! Fuck it all! It means nothing to her!"

"Damn," Dice said. He knew it must have been bad if Wolf came to his house to talk about it in the middle of the night. Wolf wasn't an emotional type of guy, but love would do that to the toughest most ruthless killers. "It's not nothing y'all can do to work it out?"

"Nah, she's done with me," Wolf told him. Never in a million years did Wolf think a woman could or would have such a strong hold on his heart. The feelings he felt for Ivy he had never experienced with another woman so this was still all new to him. "Then to make matters even worse, earlier I went down to her job and beat one of her customers up."

All Dice could say was, "that's crazy."

"She's talking about she is leaving town next week... She is making me choose between her and The Spades," Wolf continued to vent. The more he spoke about the situation, the madder he became.

"When is your court date?"

"In two months," Wolf answered. "Motherfuckers shoot up my Range Rover and I have to go to court."

"How you plan on dealing with that?" Dice took a sip of his drink.

"I plan on dealing with it head on."

"Maybe leaving with Ivy might not be a bad idea after all," Dice said. "Mr. Goldberg already told you that your chances of beating the case are slim to none."

"So what you saying?"

"I'm saying maybe you should leave with Ivy," Dice told him. "I know you a soldier and all that, but why spend the rest of your life in jail especially when you have a chance to ride off in the sunset?"

"What about The Spades?"

"I can take over in your absence," Dice said. "I think I'm the best candidate for the job." He knew the only way to save Wolf's life was by stepping up to the plate and for Wolf; Dice would give him his left hand if he had to.

"You think you can handle a responsibility like that?" Wolf asked with a raised brow.

"I know I can," Dice said with a smile. It was time for the torch to be passed and he was next in line. "Go leave with Ivy and we will keep in contact so I can keep you up to date on everything."

Wolf sat there for a second in deep thought as he sipped on his alcoholic beverage. A lot was running through his mind and he had a few tough decisions to make in a short period of time. "Give me a few days to think about it and I'll get back to you," Wolf said as he finished off his drink, stood, and headed for the door.

"You sure you alright?" Dice asked looking at Wolf?

Wolf put on a fake smile. "Yeah I'm good," Wolf said and then left and hopped in his Range Rover and pulled away from the curb.

Dice stood in his doorway until the Range Rover's tail lights disappeared around the corner.

Chapter 38
"Hard to Kill"

Live Wire sat laid up in a hospital bed with his arm in a sling and his legs extended up in the air. His whole body was in pain, but he was happy to still be alive. A smirk danced on his lips as he replayed him being gunned down in the clubs bathroom. He had to give Pauleena her props; she was definitely an official chick who handled her business. Live Wire respected her, but for her actins Pauleena had to die and Live Wire was going to make sure of it. The more he thought about it, the more he wanted to rewind the hands of time and kill Psycho in that bathroom instead of just beating him up. Live Wire had been in the hospital for a week and several detectives had came in and questioned him and they all left with the same amount of information that they had come in with; nothing.

Live Wire's head snapped to the right when he heard the door to his room open. He breathed a sigh of relief when he saw Tori walk through the door with a scared and worried look on her face. By the look on Tori's face, Live Wire could tell that she had just got word about what had went down.

"Oh my God baby! Are you okay?" Tori asked stopping at the side of Live Wire's bed. Her face was the face of a concerned wife or a concerned parent.

"Yeah, I'm good," Live Wire smiled. He was in pain, but he was also happy to see Tori.

"I came as soon as I found out what happened to you," Tori told him. "Something told me I should have stayed in New York a little longer... What happened to you?"

"I got shot."

"I know you got shot, but by who?" Tori asked.

"By some chick named Pauleena."

"You got shot by a woman?" Tori asked with a surprised look on her face.

"Yup!"

"Oh hell no!" Tori snapped. "Ain't no bitch putting their hands on my man and getting away with it."

"Your man?'

"Yup, you heard me," Tori huffed. She was so upset that her entire face was as red as an apple. "You just get your rest and I'll take care of this Pauleena bitch for you."

Live Wire smiled. "Pauleena is a powerful woman so..."

"So am I," Tori said quickly. "And I'm going to show her just how powerful I am."

All Live Wire could do was smile. Hearing Tori talk tough turned him on. He wanted to take care of Pauleena on his own, but he wanted to see just what Tori was all about. "I don't want you getting involved in my bullshit."

"Can you let me be your woman; please... Damn," Tori huffed. "Some woman got my man laid up in a hospital and you expect me to do nothing about it? TUH... You must have lost your mind." This may have not been Tori's home town, but she was more than capable of turning it up in any city she set foot in. What really pissed her off was the fact that she had to find out about Live Wire being laid up in the hospital by someone else. "How much longer do you gotta be up in this hospital?"

"A few more days," Live Wire replied. The only thing on his mind was revenge. His street rep as well as his street credibility was on the line and the streets were soon going to be on fire.

Chapter 39
"Do Your Job"

Pauleena and Psycho sat in Pauleena's office with serious look on their faces. Across from them on the other side of the table sat Mr. Goldberg and in front of him were a bunch of legal documents. With reading glasses on his face, Mr. Goldberg focused on the papers that sat before him.

"Fuck all this suspense shit," Pauleena snapped. "What's going on?"

"Okay Pauleena, I'm going to give it to you straight up," Mr. Goldberg began finally looking up from the papers in front of him. "The lowest offer I could get for you was four years flat." He paused taking the time to take in Pauleena's and Psycho's facial expressions.

"Four years flat?" Psycho repeated with a frown. "You couldn't do no better than that?" It was no way that Psycho wanted to see his fiancé spend one day in jail let alone four years. All the money Mr. Goldberg was being paid Psycho was expecting a better offer than four years; a much better offer.

"I'm afraid not," Mr. Goldberg said bluntly. He turned and faced Pauleena. "They have you on camera firing a pistol in a public environment and with that being said, four years is a pretty good offer."

"Listen," Pauleena said in a calm and smooth tone. "You've been robbing me blind for the last two years." She paused as she removed a .380 from her desk drawer and gently sat it on the table. "You're gonna do better than four years."

"I don't know what you expect me to do," Mr. Goldberg said nervously. "Four years is the lowest offer I could get you... You're caught red handed on tape."

"I don't give a fuck!" Pauleena yelled. "In this last year I done gave your greasy ass well over a million dollars and now you going to finally earn all that money that you have received or else!"

"Or else what?" Mr. Goldberg asked looking from Pauleena then back to Psycho. "Are you threatening me? I hope not because just like you know people so do I, but the difference between me and you is I know real heavy hitters so I'm the wrong one to fuck with," he said in a matter of fact tone. "Don't let the suit and briefcase fool you."

Psycho slowly got up from his seat and walked over to the door and locked it. Pauleena looked up at Mr. Goldberg and shook her head. Right then and there Mr. Goldberg knew he had fucked up and let his big mouth get him into some shit that he wasn't ready or prepared for. Pauleena sat back and watched as Psycho beat the shit out of Mr. Goldberg. Mr. Goldberg yelled and screamed as Psycho pounded away at his exposed face and rib cage.

"I'm sorry! I'm sorry!" Mr. Goldberg yelled out in defeat. Once Psycho was done with the greasy lawyer, there was blood everywhere. Pauleena walked up and stood over Mr. Goldberg's bloody body. "Like I said, you better get me a lower offer or else," she said as she lifted up her leg and stomped Mr. Goldberg's head into the floor one last time for good measure. Psycho opened the door and two big Muslim guards came in and dragged Mr. Goldberg out of Pauleena's office by his ankles.

"You think he gone tell?" Psycho asked.

Pauleena shrugged nonchalantly. "Who cares... The bottom line is I'm going to have to do some time regardless. The question is how much?"

"No matter what they give you, you know I'm going to hold you down," Psycho told her. "Every visit, I'm up there."

Pauleena smiled. "You better be up there every visit and you better not give my dick away while I'm gone either, or else…"

"Or else what?" Psycho smiled. "Are you threatening me?" He said mocking Mr. Goldberg.

"Trust me, you don't want to find out," Pauleena replied. "I would hate to have to kill a bitch… again."

Chapter 40
"Love Is Pain"

For the past three nights Ivy wasn't able to sleep, eat, or think straight. Her mind was focused on one thing and one thing only. That one thing was Wolf. She missed his presence being around, missed talking to him, and she most definitely missed his touch. Ivy was still mad at Wolf for beating up her friend Bob, but what really bothered her was the fact that there was only two days left until she planned to leave New York for good and Wolf still hadn't reached out to her. No phone call, no text messages, no nothing and that bothered Ivy. Ivy sat on her bed looking at The Terminator on T.V. talking shit about his next upcoming opponent.

"Somebody is going to knock his ass out one of these days," Ivy huffed and cut the T.V. off. After living with Wolf for so long in that nice big house, Ivy's little apartment now felt like a cardboard box. After sitting up in that apartment for so long, Ivy felt like the walls were closing in on her.

"Fuck this, I'm going to go get my man," she said as she went in the bathroom and threw her hair in a loose ponytail, grabbed a light jacket and headed out the door. On the ride over to Wolf's house Ivy sang along with the Mary J. Blige CD that pumped through the speakers. Ivy was determined to get Wolf to leave with her. If he really ever loved her then it was no way he would not leave with her. Twenty minutes later Ivy pulled up in Wolf's driveway, parked, hopped out, and walked up to the front door and rang the doorbell. Forty seconds passed before Ivy rang the doorbell two more times and then finally she heard movement coming from behind the other side of the door.

Seconds later Wolf answered the door wearing a pair of basketball shorts and a black wife beater. "Wassup?" Wolf said dryly.

"We need to talk," Ivy said.

"We ain't got nothing else to talk about," Wolf told her as he went to shut the door, but Ivy stopped him.

"Why are you treating me like this?" Ivy asked as her eyes began go get watery. "After all the shit we been through, you just going to slam the door in my face?"

"Listen," Wolf began. "We done already spoke about this a hundred times already and I'm tired of talking about this shit. You knew what it was from day one and now you wanna come over here talking about how could I do this to you... Come on with all that dumb shit."

"Why are you talking to me like I'm trash?" Ivy asked as silent tears rolled down her cheeks. "Why are you getting mad at me because I don't want to see you throw your life down the drain?"

"Listen," Wolf said clearly aggravated. "Fuck all that fairy tale shit. This is my life and you been knew that so I don't understand..."

"Wolf is everything alright?" A woman's voice said. The voice came from inside the house behind Wolf. Ivy craned her neck to the side and looked over Wolf's shoulder. Behind Wolf stood a slim light skin top less woman with her face was full of concern.

"Yeah I'm good. Just go back upstairs," Wolf said quickly. He wanted to defuse the situation before it got out of hand, but from the look in Ivy's eyes Wolf knew that she was a ticking time bomb just waiting to explode.

"Who the fuck is that?" Ivy asked.

"Nobody," Wolf replied quickly. He tried to ease the door close behind him, but Ivy was quick on her feet. Before Wolf could stop her, Ivy had passed by him and was already inside the house and heading straight for the top less woman with a murderous look in her eyes. Wolf watched as Ivy tackled his top less friend down to the floor and began pounding away on her. By the time Wolf got control of the situation, blood was everywhere and Ivy held a hand full of hair in her hands.

"What the fuck is wrong with you?" Wolf barked. Ivy took a swing at Wolf as tears streamed down her face.

"Chill!" Wolf yelled as he did his best to restrain Ivy without hurting her in the process. Ivy bit Wolf and tried to scratch his eyes out as she went berserk.

"This what you out here doing?" Ivy yelled. I'm sitting up here stressing and worrying about you and this what you out here doing? Fucking with these groupie bitches?" She yelled.

"Baby I'm sorry…"

"You're sorry?" Ivy yelled looking like she was going to attack Wolf any second. "You right, you are sorry and I'm sorry I ever loved you!"

"You don't mean that," Wolf said. "I fucked up… I know I fucked up!"

"Fuck you Wolf," Ivy huffed. She then turned and made her exit. Wolf followed her over to the door. He thought about trying to stop her, but then decided to just let her go. He knew she was upset and needed time to cool off. As Wolf watched Ivy storm off in her car, he wished he could of told her that he loved her.

"Baby"

Wolf turned around and saw his top less friend standing there with a wet rag held up to her nose. He felt bad that she had to take a beating for being at the wrong place at the wrong time. If he could go back in time and change things, he definitely would. Wolf knew Ivy truly loved him and would more than likely do any and everything for him. As he stood in the doorway he started to wonder if being the leader of The Spades was actually a gift or a curse.

Chapter 41
"All Part of the Game"

P auleena stood in front of the full length mirror looking at her appearance. She wore an expensive woman's suit along with an expensive pair of shoes to match. The word on the streets was that some chick that called herself The Madam had put a $100,000.00 bounty on her head. Pauleena had so many enemies that she would drive herself crazy if she thought or worried about everyone who didn't like her. As far as she was concerned, The Madam could get in line and take a number like everybody else who had a problem with her.

"You spoke to that clown Mr. Goldberg?" Psycho asked sitting at the edge of the bed fully dressed with his face full of concern.

"Yeah I spoke to him."

"Is he going to show up in court today?"

"He doesn't have a choice," Pauleena said as she and Psycho headed downstairs. Immediately they were met by fifteen of Pauleena's Muslim security guards. Pauleena might have been taking her enemies lightly, but Psycho didn't play that shit. He made sure that he had all areas covered. His mind frame was it was better to be safe than sorry. He knew him and Pauleena wouldn't be able to bring guns inside the court room so he made sure him and Pauleena would be well protected on their way to and from court.

"What's all this?" Pauleena asked.

"There's a serious bounty on your head?" Psycho reminded her. He knew she accepted any and all comers who wanted a shot at her title, but sometimes it was better to play defense instead of offense. "Besides we hot right now."

"We been hot," Pauleena said with a shrug. She was tired of people trying her just because she was a woman.

Everywhere she turned it seemed like someone was out to kill her or take what she had worked so hard for. The bottom line was she was sick and tired of all of the drama.

Pauleena and Psycho hopped in the back seat of the bullet proof Escalade along with two bodyguards. Two Escalades full of more bodyguards pulled out of the driveway behind Pauleena's Escalade. Just because Psycho was paranoid didn't mean he didn't have a reason to be.

When Pauleena's Escalade pulled up in front of the courthouse, she spotted Mr. Goldberg standing out front posted up on his cell phone. Around him were several members of the press. The press and the media had been posted up outside the courthouse all morning waiting for the drug queen pin to show up.

Several of Pauleena's Muslim bodyguards did their best to fight and hold off the media as Pauleena and Psycho slid out the back seat. Several different cameras flashed all at the same time as each and every reporter did their best to get a comment from Pauleena. Pauleena smiled and winked for the cameras as she strutted towards the courthouse entrance.

"Come on," Psycho said grabbing Pauleena by her hand forcing her to pick up her pace. Just because there were plenty of people around, the fact still remained that both him and Pauleena were naked; neither one of them had a weapon on them and that worried Psycho. Just as Pauleena and Psycho reached the front door of the courthouse, a loud series of machine gun fire erupted from behind them. Psycho quickly grabbed Pauleena and roughly shoved her inside the courthouse. All the while bodyguards, reporters, and innocent people who happened to be at the wrong place at the wrong time dropped right where they stood. Glass rained down on top of Pauleena's head as she heard the sound of tires burning rubber as the truck full of gun men peeled off.

Psycho helped Pauleena off of the floor as several police officers surrounded them. Pauleena didn't have a clue who the shooters were, but whoever they were, they were looking to collect the $100,000.00 that was on her head.

"You alright?" Psycho asked dusting off Pauleena's clothes. He seen this coming a mile away and he only wished he could have stopped it before it reached this point.

"I'll live," Pauleena replied. She looked around and saw glass, blood, and dead bodies everywhere. She hated that she had to live like this, but this was her life.

Chapter 42
"Final Straw"

Wolf sat in the living room sipping on a strong drink watching Sports Center. He was trying to keep his mind off of Ivy, but that task was becoming way harder than he had expected. It seemed like the more he tried not to think of Ivy and their situation, the more it sat on is brain. The Big Show sat on the other end of the couch watching Wolf closely. He didn't know what was bothering Wolf or what was wrong, but just by looking at his boss he could tell that something was wrong.

"Wanna talk about it?" The Big Show asked.

"Nothing to talk about," Wolf replied dryly. He wanted the whole situation to be over and done with, but he knew a situation like this wouldn't be easy nor would it just go away. As Wolf and The Big Show sat in the living room talking somebody rang the doorbell. The Big Show quickly hopped up to his feet and headed to the front door to investigate. He looked through the peep hole."

"Yo, it's Ivy," The Big Show yelled over his shoulder waiting for a response.

"Let her in," Wolf said.

"Hey Big Show," Ivy said politely as she stepped inside the house.

"Is it ok if I have a word with you in private?" She asked.
Wolf took another sip from his drink, nodded his head, and then said, "Let's go upstairs."

Wolf and Ivy stepped inside the bedroom and Ivy closed the door behind her.

"What's up?" Wolf said leaning up against the dresser. His appearance looked as if he could care less about what Ivy had to say, but they both knew that was far from the truth.

"I came to apologize about the other night," Ivy said. "I was wrong to just bust through your front door and attack your friend."

"It's cool."

"I also came to apologize for being so selfish. You were right, I did know what you were about when I first met you," she began. "Sorry, but I just love you too much to just sit back and watch you throw your life away."

"I understand."

"You are the best man I ever had and the thought of losing you forever scares the shit out of me. I can't just sit around and watch you just throw your life down the drain so with that being said," Ivy walked over to where Wolf stood and planted a soft kiss on his lips. "I love you and I'm leaving tomorrow." She reached down in her purse and handed Wolf a plane ticket.

"I already told you…"

Ivy put her index finger up to Wolf's lips to hush him. "Shhhh"

"Don't say anything," Ivy said in a hushed tone. "If you change your mind, you know where to find me tomorrow," Ivy said as she turned and left leaving Wolf standing there deep in his own thoughts. Wolf stood there staring at the plane ticket that sat inside his hand. He could hear Ivy's car pulling out of his driveway as her scent still remained in his bedroom, taunting him and flirting with his nostrils. As Wolf stood there he realized that Ivy was dead serious about leaving New York for good with or without him. He took a deep breath, looked down at the plane ticket, then up at the ceiling. He thought about how much Ivy meant to him. A knock at the bedroom door snapped Wolf out of his thoughts. "Come in," he called out.

The Big Show peeked his head inside the bedroom. "You alright?"

"Yeah I'm good," Wolf lied.

I just got a call from Dice and he said we got a little problem downtown that needs our attention."

"Let's go," Wolf replied.

****

Wolf stepped out the Range Rover with The Big Show and two other Spades members in tow. Wolf entered the house that was owned by The Spades and quickly headed downstairs towards the basement.

The first person Wolf saw when he reached the basement was Dice and several other Spades dressed in all black. In the middle of The Spades was a man tied down to a chair. His face was bruised and swollen, dried up blood was splattered all over his white tee that had M.O.E. written across the front in black letters.

"Who is this?" Wolf asked. The face of the man that sat before him was so battered that he wasn't able to recognize or make out who he was.

"Some clown from Snow's entourage," Dice replied. "I just beat some valuable information out of him."

"I'm all ears," Wolf said.

"He just told me that Pauleena is supposed to be having a secret wedding tomorrow," Dice smiled. "And one of our female Spades members got the word on where Live Wire been resting his head. She said he been shacking up with that chick he grabbed from Champagne's house that night... I think she said her name was Sparkle." Dice handed Wolf the half dead man's cell phone. Wolf took the phone and read out the address to where the wedding ceremony would be held.

"We up in there," Wolf said as he removed his P89 from his waistband and blew the man who was tied down's brains all over the floor. "Play time is over!"

"Who we going after first?" Dice asked. "Live Wire or Pauleena?"

"Pauleena," was Wolf's response. At the moment he had a lot going on and if he did decide to leave with Ivy, he would feel pretty good with himself if Pauleena was dead. Wolf slid in the back seat of the Range Rover and looked down at the plane ticket one more time. The final destination was Los Angeles. Wolf had never been out of New York before and thought maybe a change of scenery wouldn't be a bad idea after all. At the end of the day, L.A. was known for drugs and gang violence and if Wolf did decide to leave with Ivy, he could get The Spades movement popping out there as well.

"Get up outta here," The Big Show said glancing in the rearview mirror at Wolf as their eyes met briefly. "I see you back there struggling to decide on whether or not you should leave with Ivy…"

"It's a tough decision," Wolf admitted. Yes he loved Ivy to death, but on the other hand Wolf had big responsibilities that he couldn't just up and leave and abandon like that.

"If that woman got your face looking like that, then it ain't nothing to think about," The Big Show said glancing back at Wolf again. "Just go! You've done enough for the community. Pass the torch on to Dice. He has proved himself enough already. Besides you need to stay low until after your court date."

"Round up all the troops and let them know that tomorrow we got a wedding to crash," Wolf ordered from the back seat. He knew shit was about to get ugly. He just hoped and prayed that him and his team would come out on top.

Chapter 43
"Los Angeles Bound"

Alicia Keys hummed softly out of the small radio in Ivy's small apartment. Ivy packed up all of her things while she sang along with Alicia Keys. She still wasn't sure what Wolf planned on doing or whether he would be joining her on the trip to L.A. All Ivy could do at the moment was pray and hope that Wolf would do the right thing. After Ivy got done packing, she opened up the book bag that Wolf had gave her and counted out $25,000.00. It was way more than she had to begin with so she was more than thankful for the money, but without Wolf the money meant nothing. Ivy grabbed the framed picture of her and Wolf hugged up on 42nd street and examined the picture for a second before packing it with the rest of her belongings. Ivy pulled out her cell phone and just as she was about to text Wolf she heard a loud knock at the door.

"Who is it?" Ivy called out.

"Wolf," the voice on the other side of the door replied. Ivy smiled as she hurried and snatched the door open. Once she laid eyes on Wolf she jumped in his arms and hugged him tightly. "I love you so, so, so, so, so, much!" She said trying to squeeze the life out of Wolf.

"I love you too baby," Wolf smiled.

"Please come with me to Los Angeles," Ivy begged. "I promise I will be anything you need me to be... Just please come with me baby; please..."

"Tell me how much you love me and I'll think about it," Wolf said jokingly.

"I love you to death! I swear to God I do!" Ivy pleaded her case. "Please come with me?"

"I'll come with you baby," Wolf replied as Ivy planted wet loud kisses all over his face. "Chill baby," Wolf said slowly pushing Ivy off of him. "I'll meet you at the airport tomorrow at 7:00p.m."

"You promise?"

"I promise baby," Wolf said and then gave Ivy a slow, long, wet, and sloppy kiss. "I love you Mami, but I got something I need to take care of before I head to the airport," he said handing Ivy the duffle bag. "That's a quarter-mil."

"$250,000.00?" Ivy echoed.

"Yeah and I will meet you at the airport at 7:00 p.m., okay?"

Ivy nodded her head.

"What time I'mma meet you there?"

"7:00p.m."

"I gotta go baby. I love you," Wolf kissed Ivy on the lips. "I'll see you at the airport tomorrow," he said as he turned and left.

"Be careful baby," Ivy said as she watched Wolf disappear into the staircase.

Chapter 44
"Strap Up"

Live Wire sat on the couch watching music videos while Sparkle's head bobbed up and down in his lap at a rapid pace. Greedy sounds escaped her mouth as she orally pleased her man. On the seventy inch screen Live Wire watched 2 Chainz spit his rhymes in a strip club. Three minutes later Live Wire blew his load and Sparkle greedily caught every drop being sure not to spill one drop. When Sparkle looked up, she saw Snow on the T.V. screen giving an interview. She quickly grabbed the remote and changed the channel. "I can't stand that whack ass nigga," Sparkle fumed.

"I'mma take care of that clown next time we bump heads," Live Wire assured her. Sparkle had told him all about how Snow and his entourage had tried to violate and disrespect her.

A pinging sound went off letting Live Wire know he had received a text message. Immediately Sparkle's eye went to Live Wire's phone as she sucked her teeth. "Mmm... hmm, tell your stupid ass bitches that it's too late to be disturbing us," she said looking to pick a fight. Live Wire ignored Sparkle's foolish comment and walked in the kitchen to check the text message. He was tired of slapping the shit out of Sparkle so instead he just ignored her whenever her jealous ways started to kick in. Live Wire looked down at the screen on his cell phone and saw that the text message was from his good old friend Wolf. "Fuck this clown want?" Live Wire said out loud as he read the text message.

"Me, you, and Pauleena have some unfinished business... Tomorrow we settle this shit once and for all... Below is the address where the chapter ends. Don't disappoint me by not showing up... I look forward to seeing you tomorrow. No more warnings... Your brother Wolf."

A smile danced on Live Wire's lips after he read that text message. Wolf and Pauleena at the same place at the same time was a miracle. What else could he ask for? Live Wire loved Wolf like a brother, but fuck all that. Wolf was standing in the way of his money and for that reason alone Wolf had to die. Pauleena was a totally different story. She had shot Live Wire and left him for dead on a dirty bathroom floor. Live Wire promised himself that the next time he ran into Pauleena he would blow her head clean off her shoulders; her and her punk ass boyfriend Psycho. Live Wire quickly dialed Bills number and told him to round up all the soldiers... They had a wedding to crash.

Chapter 45
"For Better or Worse"

"How do you feel?" Mrs. Diaz asked with a smile on her face as she helped zip Pauleena's dress up from the back.

"Come on Mommy, don't start getting all emotional on me," Pauleena said wiping a tear from her mother's cheek.

"These are tears of joy," Mrs. Diaz smiled. "I just wish your father was here to see this."

"I'm sure you are going to take a lot of pictures and send them to him."

"This new jail they moved him to be on some bullshit," Mrs. Diaz raved. "I hope they let him have them."

"You worry too much," Pauleena said peeking out of her dressing room out into the crowded church. Just from a quick glance Pauleena spotted Snow, Trouble, The Terminator, The Mayor, a few A-List actors, a few video vixens, and the rest of the people in the crowd were just a bunch of blank faces to her.

"I didn't think you would have had this many people at your wedding," Mrs. Diaz pointed out.

"Everybody loves me," Pauleena said looking in the mirror at how the expensive tailor made white wedding dress clung to her curves.

In the other dressing room Psycho sipped on a strong drink as he slipped his twin .45s down in his shoulder holster and then slipped into the jacket to his tuxedo. Inside the dressing room along with Psycho was Prince, Malcolm, and Bobby Dread. Each man wore an all white expensive tailor made Armani tuxedo; well everyone except Bobby Dread. He wore his usual black jeans, black shirt, black combat boots, and a long black trench coat to conceal his A.K. 47.

"Yo, how the fuck you gone be one of the grooms and you got on that dirty ass trench coat?" Psycho huffed as everyone busted out laughing. "What's up with this nigga?"

Bobby Dread's facial expression remained unfazed and unmoved. "Everything is a game to you brothers until somebody's head get blown off!"

"I should blow your head off for wearing that trench coat," Psycho countered laughing hysterically as he gave Prince a pound. Bobby Dread shook his head with a disgusted look on his face as Psycho and Prince laughed until tears filled their eyes.

"You know what your problem is?" Prince said looking at Bobby Dread as he slipped his Beretta in his shoulder holster and then slipped into his tuxedo jacket. "You not a smooth nigga like me." He looked at Bobby Dread's trench coat and then continued. "A bitch ain't giving you no pussy wearing a coat like that," Prince said as him and Psycho fell out laughing again. "When the last time you had some pussy?"

"Listen brother, that's my personal business and we ain't gone get into that," Bobby Dread said sternly.

Prince and Psycho laughed even harder at Bobby Dread's response. The Pastor knocked on the door and stuck his head inside the dressing room. "Ready whenever you guys are."

"We gone finish this conversation later too nigga," Prince said over his shoulder.

"Leave the brother alone," Malcolm said.

"Nah, fuck that! I'm tired of him wearing that stupid ass jacket," Prince huffed as each man exited the dressing room. The first two rows in the church were filled with Pauleena's Muslim bodyguards. Psycho smiled as he watched Pauleena's mother walk down the aisle. Five minutes later it was Pauleena's turn to walk down the aisle. Pauleena walked down towards the altar in a slow confident stride. She looked and felt like a princess. When Pauleena reached the altar the loud sound of machine gun fire erupted coming from the lobby of the church and when the doors sprung open a masked man wearing all black holding a machine gun stepped foot inside the church. Before he got a chance to do anything, A.K. 47 bullets ripped through the gun man's body killing him instantly. Pauleena turned and saw Bobby Dread standing there with smoke swirling out the A.K.'s barrel. Seconds later several men dressed in all black came running inside the church opening fire on any and everything moving. Malcolm quickly tackled Pauleena down to the floor and shielded her with his body. Prince, Psycho, Bobby Dread, Trouble, Snow, and the rest of Pauleena's Muslim bodyguards returned fire turning the church into a war zone.

"Where's my mother?" Pauleena yelled pushing Malcolm off of her. She looked up and saw several of her bodyguards escorting her mother towards the back. "Gun!" Pauleena yelled with her hand held out. Malcolm quickly sat a 9mm in the middle of her palm. No matter how many Spades Pauleena's crew killed it seemed like more and more continued to storm through the front door. Pauleena fired six shots into six different Spades. She kicked off her heels and picked up a Tech-9 that lay on the floor next to a dead Spades member. Pauleena aimed the Tech-9 at the door and held down on the trigger picking off Spades one by one as they entered the church.

****

Live Wire and The Real Spades pulled up at the back of the church. Live Wire stepped out the back seat of a raggedy looking Hooptie. He was dressed in all black and in his hand he held a black Mox-Berg pump shotgun.

He looked down the alley and saw Trouble, Snow, and The Terminator hopping in a limousine. Live Wire paid them pussies no mind as him and The Real Spades entered through the back door of the church. A Muslim brother came running around the corner and froze when he landed in front of Live Wire's shotgun. Live Wire smiled as he squeezed the trigger and sent the Muslim skidding backwards across the floor.

****

Wolf entered the church and the first person he locked eyes with was the man with the dreads who had kicked him and Dice's ass. Before Wolf could make a move, Dice placed a hand on Wolf's shoulder. "I'll take care of this clown with the dreads. You go after Pauleena."

Wolf nodded as Dice quickly opened fire on Bobby Dread. Bobby Dread quickly returned fire.

Wolf ran through the church hopping over dead bodies left and right as he headed towards the back of the church.

****

Pauleena held her mother's arm tightly with one hand and she held a 9mm in her other hand. Malcolm was escorting Pauleena and her mother out the back exit, but stopped short when a loud burst of gun fire erupted up ahead.

"No fucking way!" Pauleena cursed. "It can't be that many of them," she said in disbelief. At that very moment Psycho came around the corner holding Prince up. Pauleena looked down and saw blood gushing out of a bullet hole in Prince's thigh.

"You alright?" Pauleena nodded down towards Prince's thigh.

"Nothing but a flesh wound," Prince replied with a wink.

"I'm out of ammo," Psycho announced.

"Me too," Malcolm confirmed.

Pauleena looked over towards Prince. "What about you?"

Prince shook his head and held up and empty gun. Pauleena removed the clip from the base of her 9mm, counted two bullets plus the one in the chamber made three. "Three bullets left."

"Fuck that, we gotta get up outta here!" Prince yelled and then swung his empty gun at the glass window. Immediately Psycho helped Prince climb out the window.

"Come on Mrs. Diaz," Psycho said in a hurried fast pitched voice with his hand held out. Before Mrs. Diaz could grab Psycho's hand, Wolf sprung from around the corner and opened fire on the group. Immediately Malcolm shielded Pauleena with his body as two bullets ripped and pierced through his back.

Live Wire sprung from around the other corner, raised his shotgun and blew Mrs. Diaz head off. Warm blood splashed across Pauleena's face as she watched her mother crumble down to the floor. Psycho and Malcolm quickly rushed Pauleena into the office section of the church and closed the door behind them. Once the hallway was clear the only two people left out there were Wolf and Live Wire. Live Wire jacked a round in his shotgun and aimed it at Wolf. Wolf also had his Tech-9 trained on Live Wire.

"How you wanna do this?" Live Wire asked with an evil smirk on his face.

"Let's put our issues to the side for a second," Wolf suggested. "We take out Pauleena now and then settle our score with one another later."

"How I know you won't try to shoot me in the back?" Live Wire asked never taking his shotgun off of Wolf.

"You got my word," Wolf said as loud gun fire continued ringing out throughout the church. "What do you say?"

"Let's do it," Live Wire answered.

Wolf walked up to the office door and kicked it open. The first person he laid eyes on was Malcolm. Wolf opened fire and sent bullets into the big man's mid-section until he ran out of bullets. Right on que Live Wire entered the office and shot Malcolm in the chest. The impact from the shotgun took the big man off his feet. Live Wire trained his shotgun on Pauleena and Psycho quickly jumped in front of her. Live Wire pulled the trigger on the shotgun... CLICK!

Pauleena knelt down by Malcolm's side as tears fell from her eyes. "I'm sorry…"

Malcolm flashed a bloody smile. "No, I'm sorry… It's been a pleasure working for you."

"The pleasure was all mine," Pauleena said sincerely.

"Them faggots are out of bullets… Kick they ass for me," Malcolm said and then took his last breath.

"Listen," Psycho said. "Either we can do this now or we can save it for another day." The sound of police sirens were getting louder and louder.

"Ain't nothing to talk about," Wolf said stepping towards Psycho. Psycho quickly took a step back and threw his hands up. Pauleena stood to her feet as she heard Wolf and Psycho getting it on. She ripped off the bottom part of her wedding dress and put her hands in a fighting position.

Live Wire smiled as Pauleena charged him swinging. Live Wire laughed as he easily weaved and blocked all of Pauleena's punches. Pauleena faked like she was about to swing and landed a kick between Live Wire's legs. When Live Wire doubled over in pain, Pauleena kneed Live Wire twice in his face. Then she landed a solid right hook to his jaw. Live Wire touched his nose and looked down at his hand and saw blood. The site of his own blood caused him to snap. Live Wire yelled as he ran full speed towards Pauleena tackling her like a line backer. The two went violently crashing out the window making a loud shattering noise as glass flew all over the place.

Live Wire was up off the concrete first. He effortlessly landed punch after punch on Pauleena's exposed face. Pauleena fought back to the best of her ability, but Live Wire easily over powered her. Pauleena fired off an eight piece combination, but her punches had little to no effect on Live Wire. Live Wire lifted Pauleena up over his head and violently slammed her down to the concrete. Just as Live Wire went to stomp Pauleena out he heard a voice behind him say "Freeze!"

Live Wire turned around and saw Agent Starks holding a gun aimed at the center of his forehead. "Please give me a reason!" Agent Starks yelled.

"Fuck you gone do, shoot me?" Live Wire said looking Agent Starks in the eye. "Huh?" Before Agent Starks could reply, Pauleena hopped up off the ground and took off running. She hopped the fence and then disappeared in the woods. While Agent Starks was distracted looking at Pauleena, Live Wire lunged at him and grabbed his wrist. The gun discharged twice by accident while Live Wire and Agent Starks fought for possession of the hand gun.

****

When Wolf and Psycho heard two gunshots ring out, they quickly stopped fighting for a second to glance out the window. Psycho looked around and didn't see Pauleena nowhere in sight. Without thinking twice Psycho hopped out the window, hit the fence, and disappeared in the woods. Wolf looked down and grabbed Live Wire's empty shotgun off the floor and quickly hopped out the window as well.

Agent Starks was finally able to overpower Live Wire and gain control of the gun. He aimed the gun at Live Wire, but just as he got ready to pull the trigger he heard the paralyzing sound of a shotgun being cocked back.

"You got three seconds to drop that gun," Wolf barked. Immediately Agent Starks did as he was told.

"Lay down flat on your stomach," Wolf ordered and then quickly handcuffed Agent Starks hands behind his back with his own handcuffs. Once that was done, Live Wire gave Wolf a head nod that said thank you and then turned and ran towards the fence. Live Wire hopped the fence and disappeared into the woods.

"Wolf you are never going to get away with this," Agent Starks said looking up from the ground. Wolf dug down in Agent Starks pocket and removed his car keys. He quickly ran around the church, hopped in Agent Starks Crown Vic, and pulled out into the street. As Wolf drove off, he saw the police having a shoot out with The Spades, The Real Spades, and Pauleena's Muslim bodyguards. The Crown Vic eased away from the church unnoticed. Wolf drove a few blocks away from the church and then ditched the Crown Vic as he quickly flagged down a cab.

"The airport," Wolf said when he got in the cab and then sunk down in the back seat.

"Which one?" The cab driver asked.

Chapter 46
"Trust Me"

Ivy stood in the airport glued to the T.V. A big shootout involving The Spades and Pauleena was on every channel. What made it so bad was that the news reported that several police officers had been killed along with several Muslims, Spades, and innocent people who were just at the church to attend the wedding of the drug queen pin Pauleena Diaz. Ivy glanced down at the time on her phone that read "6:55p.m."

She had already called Wolf over a hundred times literally and each time she caught his voicemail. The more the reporter reported news about the massacre that took place at the church the more Ivy prayed that Wolf was still alive. At the moment hearing that Wolf was in police custody would have been good news, at least she would know that he was still alive. As Ivy continued to watch the news she heard over the loud speaker the flight attendant announce that the 7:00p.m. flight to Los Angeles was now boarding. Ivy pulled out her cell phone one more time and dialed Wolf's number only to get the same result. Ivy exhaled loudly and looked up at the ceiling as if to ask God why her. While Ivy looked up at the ceiling, she felt a pair of hands wrap around her waist and then she felt a pair of lips kiss her neck gently.

"Why you over here staring at the idiot box when we got a plane to catch?" Wolf whispered in Ivy's ear.
"Oh my God baby I thought you were dead!" Ivy squealed as she jumped up in Wolf's arms and hugged him tightly. "Thank God that you are still alive!"

"You acting like you love me or something," Wolf joked.

"I love you more than anything in this world," Ivy confessed.

"Why don't you show me how much you love me when we get to Los Angeles?" Wolf smiled as him and Ivy boarded the plane never looking back.

Chapter 47
"Judgement Day"

Pauleena stood in front of the judge with Mr. Goldberg by her side. The D.A. (District Attorney) was pissed that they were not able to get none of the murders from the wedding to stick on Pauleena. Somehow she seemed to always squeeze through the cracks. Pauleena looked the red faced judge in the eyes as he sentenced her to forty-eight months in a woman's federal prison.

"I'm sorry, but four years was the best I could do," Mr. Goldberg whispered in Pauleena's ear.

"It could be worse," Pauleena replied with a wink as the court officer escorted her off to the bull pins. Pauleena looked back and saw Prince, Bobby Dread, and Psycho all sitting in the court room there to support her.

"I love you Maim!" Psycho yelled out getting nasty looks from the judge and D. A.

"I love you too Papi! Us against the world!" Was the last words Pauleena was able to get out before she disappeared in the back.

As Psycho, Prince, and Bobby Dread exited the court room, they were met in the hallway by Agent Starks.

"One down and three more to go..." Agent Starks shook his head with a disgusted look on his face and then walked off.

"Burn it up nigga!" Prince yelled at Agent Starks' departing back. He then turned and faced Psycho. "What's next?"

"What you mean? What's next?" Psycho asked looking at Prince like he was crazy. "We gone keep this shit afloat until Pauleena comes home... Ain't nothing change," he said as he pulled out his cell phone and sent off a quick e-mail.

From: Psycho
Subject: This shit ain't over with
Date: January 17, 2013
To: Wolf

Listen here you bitch ass nigga, me and you will forever have beef so wherever the fuck you hiding at right now, your best bet is to stay there and keep on hiding... Cause wherever I catch you at, that's where you'll be buried you bitch ass, clown ass nigga! **P.S.** Suck My Dick!

From: Wolf
Subject: Nigga Please...
Date: January 17, 2013
To: Psycho

First off if you think that I'm hiding from you, you're crazy. I handle chumps like you without breaking a sweat... Right now I have little unwanted heat on me. One of you niggas probably snitched on me, but hey it's all a part of the game. Just please know you haven't heard the last of Wolf. Trust me, I'll be back real soon and when I do return I ain't taking no prisoners. The streets will feel my wrath and you my friend will feel my pain. I promise there will be blood... You've been warned!!!

Books by Good2Go Authors

New Releases

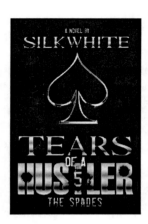

On Our Bookshelf

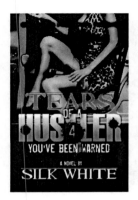

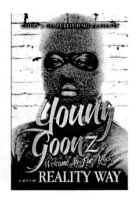

Silk White

Good2Go Films Presents

Tears of a Hustler 4 You've Been Warned

To order films please go to www.good2gofilms.com
To order books, please fill out the order form below:

Name:

Address:

City: _____ State: _____ Zip Code:

Phone:

Email:

Method Payment:
    Check   ☐VISA   ☐   MASTERCARD   ☐

Credit Card#:

Name as it appears on card:

Signature:

Item Name	Price	Qty	Amount
He Loves Me, He Loves You Not - Mychea	$13.95		
He Loves Me, He Loves You Not 2 - Mychea	$13.95		
Married To Da Streets – Silk White	$13.95		
Never Be The Same – Silk White	$13.95		
Tears of a Hustler - Silk White	$13.95		
Tears of a Hustler 2 - Silk White	$13.95		
Tears of a Hustler 3 - Silk White	$13.95		
Tears of a Hustler 4- Silk White	$13.95		
The Teflon Queen – Silk White	$13.95		
The Teflon Queen 2 – Silk White	$13.95		
Young Goonz – Reality Way	$13.95		
Subtotal:			
Tax:			
Shipping (Free) U.S. Media Mail:			

Silk White

Total:

Make Checks Payable To:
Good2Go Publishing
7311 W Glass Lane
Laveen, AZ 85339

CPSIA information can be obtained at www.ICGtesting.com
Printed in the USA
LVOW06s1439230715

447375LV00017B/712/P

9 780985 673475